I0760500

JAIME CASTLE

CJ VALIN

HARRIER

INVASION

aethonbooks.com

INVASION

Aethon Books
www.aethonbooks.com

Print and eBook formatting, and cover design by Steve Beaulieu.

Published by Aethon Books LLC.

ALSO IN SERIES

NOTE: RAPTORS and HARRIER stand alone with no need to read the other for enjoyment.

Raptors

Sidekick

Superteam

Scions

Baron Steele

Mega-Mech Apocalypse

Harrier

Justice

The Trench

Invasion

Always, for Robyn. You are my everything.
Could I BE any more in love with you?
—JC

To my brother Tim, gone too soon and the most interesting character I ever knew.
—CJ

PROLOGUE

EAGLESTAR

Invasion?

Not on my watch.

These Tuldarians—alien-lizard creatures from across the galaxy—have come here before, trying with all their puny might to enslave our world, and we defeated them soundly each time. We will do so again. It may take the combined fury of the Guild—back in action after a couple of years of sitting on the sidelines—but make no mistake: defeat them, we shall.

And soundly.

Again.

I may even try once more to recruit Baron Steele to the cause. He will not be happy about it. But, let's face it, the man is perpetually and eternally disgruntled and grave. For Pete's sake, he has destroyed more than one brasserie due to receiving the wrong beverage. Had I any other choice, I would no longer even consider him material worthy of the Guild.

But alas, Earth is at stake. Additionally, he will not soon forgive that I recently imprisoned him for breaking the anti-vigilante statutes.

But it had to be done, no question about it. Paul never did like playing by the rules, which was one of many reasons we have clashed like the Titans we are over the years. But I shall credit the man where credit is due: when something like this comes along, he possesses the self-awareness to put aside personal feelings and fight for the greater good.

I have already contacted the others—Bastet, Fastlane, Cupid, Omar the Defenestrator—and they're on their way to assist. A couple of others, namely Firefly and the Black Harrier, are a bit more complicated. The former, Marion "Mac" MacGregor, up until recently, had been leading a group of vigilantes known as the Resistors who refused to stand down. He is now in custody along with the rest of them, and I am unsure how he is going to react to finding out that I now need his assistance.

And the latter... Well, I contacted Franklin Douglas III, the original Black Harrier, to ask how he would like to be utilized in the effort to save humanity, but he has not replied thus far. Having known Frank since he was a mere pup, I took his involvement for granted. I failed, however, to take into account the latest changes in the man I once called a friend. Those facts notwithstanding, I believe he too will do what is right in the end.

Frank is nothing if not a servant of the world.

His son, Sawyer William Vincent, the current Black

Harrier, has been incarcerated in the Trench, so to the best of my vast knowledge, he would not even know of the threat looming above us. It is therefore safe to assume he will not be one to count upon.

Ah—it just occurred to me. That may also be why Frank is less than eager to rejoin the Guild. I suppose it could be considered my one weakness—not immediately grasping the concerns of ordinary humans after being, well, the way I am for so long.

As the most powerful being on Earth, I have pledged to protect this planet from all threats, great and small. Just last month I diverted a meteor the size of Rhode Island from pummeling the globe and initiating a new Ice Age or worse. Then, mere hours later, I rescued a kitten from a tree. The smile upon that little girl's face when she held little Raisin in her arms once more was precious beyond words.

However, I have not been truly free to wage war against the numerous villains that plague this planet for quite some time now. Not since the advent of the Anti-Vigilante Act and the creation of the Counter-Vigilante Taskforce. Indeed, the taskforce was partially my doing—and I believe it was a fine move—but my frustration has been on the brink of culmination. Now that I finally have a valid target and the permission of both the President of these United States of America and the General Secretary of the United Nations to take action, I will bring the full force of my limitless power against these invaders.

Not that there would be anyone left to punish me if they

hadn't offered said permissions or if I (somehow) didn't succeed.

It is rather ironic that I will be the one bearing the privilege to serve these invaders justice, for it was by their hand—their glowing alien relics—that I was suffused with my abilities, after all. Their technology, left on Earth thousands—perhaps millions—of years ago, was so advanced, it almost appeared like magic to the humans who'd discovered the artifacts a century ago.

The Second World War was an exciting time full of terror and bravery. During my service, an important SS officer called WeissWulf—the White Wolf—was transporting the artifacts he had collected from nearly every continent to Germany. The bastard himself, Adolf Hitler, had scientists aplenty, with machinations to weaponize these discoveries.

But the Allies had other plans.

Yes, we did.

My squadron of multinational pilots—the best of the best from the Allied nations, the Capital Guardians—had been combatting the Nazi menace all over Europe. But at that point, we now had a solitary mission: to send the German fighters escorting the Zeppelin containing the aforementioned artifacts to hell with all we had. It was a brutal air fight, since their pilots were undoubtedly the finest they had as well.

I, Jonathan Powers, was the last one standing. Indeed, I rose above them all, as I have done now for decades, finally managing to defeat Il Forza. Never heard of him? That's acceptable. Il Forza was an Italian aerialist whose wings gave him the ability to fly without a plane. This unique power allowed him to attack us in unconventional ways and made him nearly impossible to get a bead on with our Gatlings. The man was truly an acrobat, and the target of my ire in many a campaign.

When I ran out of fuel from the long, intense dogfight, the only option left to prevent Hitler and the Axis powers from obtaining the alien technology that could possibly assure him victory was to crash my plane into the Zeppelin.

So that was what I did.

A selfless sacrifice for the world I loved.

There was never any question in my mind as to whether I would go through with it. I had assumed it would be my last act as I mentally said goodbye to everyone I had known, and prepared myself for the end. I remember the calm peace of the moment, the joy I felt knowing I would be the greatest hero of all time.

Then, I felt a jolt as my plane met the dirigible. Glass shattered around me, cutting, digging, slashing. Bursting through the windscreen of my plane, a blinding light flashed. Intense heat like I'd never felt before rushed past and through me. The damnable blimp exploded.

But still, I was not dead.

It was, however, the last real pain I've ever experienced. And little did I know, it was the first time I would experience the exhilaration of true flight.

Through some bizarre combination of circumstances, the exploding artifacts, instead, infused me—as well as Weiss-

Wulf and a few others who survived the explosion—with unimaginable gifts. For that is what they truly are—gifts. I became exceedingly strong, incomprehensibly fast, and virtually invincible. My eyes now glow with intense energy that I can beckon forth from within my awesome being. These aliens inadvertently created me, and now I will use the very powers imbued upon me through their technology to bring about their end.

I have not donned my old red, white, and blue Eaglestar uniform in what feels like ages, but now that it embraces me once more, I feel every bit the savior I was created to be.

A gray, oblong vessel hovering three miles above New York City is the biggest aircraft I have ever witnessed. The wind sends my cape into a whipping fury behind me. Very few of the new heroes wear capes. I do not know why so many of those young punks look down upon them. Nothing embodies the word "hero" like a cape.

It just feels... right.

These youngsters think they're so swell and hip with their modern *costumes*. Too good for a cape. Too good for a form-fitting uniform. They all want the body armor and leather now for added protection. One might as well admit to the enemy that they live in constant fear of injury or death. We original heroes were unafraid to go into battle wearing nothing more than a thin layer of cloth. And we looked damn good doing it.

Speaking of fear, that is precisely the emotion these aliens will experience when they realize what a tremendous error in judgment they have made in coming here.

Invade this planet… Pffft.

My planet?

I will teach them a valuable lesson they will not soon forget.

Though, perhaps they will. Having never died, I am unaware of whether one retains regrets in whatever is to come after this life.

Nevertheless, there remains no reason to hold back against these creatures. They are not human. They are not even mammals. Oh, I will spare a few of them to limp back to their home planet and warn their species never to set foot in our solar system again.

But only a few.

Shrugging off the projectiles being fired from their ship's cannons, I tear a gaping hole in the side of their hull and soar through with a smile.

No less than ten of the vile beasts turn to greet me. They are even more hideous in appearance than I remember. Their scaly flesh, varying from shades of green to deep purples, well-nigh glistens with some form of excretion that stinks to high heaven, especially with my elevated olfactory sense. One of them roars something unintelligible and fires an energy weapon directly at me.

"This is America," I say, defiant to their attacks. "Here, we speak English."

I know from the last time they reared their ugly heads on

Earth that they have developed some sort of technology that translates their slithering sounds into human languages. Yet they continue to shield their words from me.

From me!

In response, more of the pests mutter their nonsense and take up armaments, unleashing bolts I would assume to be plasma of some form from fancy-looking handguns. Their efforts do not even warm my impenetrable skin. It appears I will be able to make short work of these "invaders." Perhaps I will not even require the assistance of my Guildmates.

Their technology will also translate my words back to them so they can understand.

"I believe a reckoning has come," I say before using my super-speed to zip around the chamber—some sort of hangar. Equipped with a dozen or so of the smaller ships they have been launching in attack around all parts of our world, I would estimate its size at around a dozen city blocks squared. Parts of the hull are somehow transparent from the inside, like some sort of two-way mirror, offering a view of the city below.

Their blasts momentarily stop, their beady eyes whipping around as they attempt to track me. Only when I stop behind one of the foul fiends and my fist bursts through its back and out its chest cavity does their salvo resume.

"Now, you have seen that which you stand against," I shout. "Tuck tail and run, aliens, or face my wrath at an increased rate!"

A sizable Tuldarian charges me like a rhinoceros, head

down and curved horns intent upon my chest. Before it clears half the distance to me, I slice it in half with my laser vision.

"I see you have made your choice," I say, almost to myself.

Taking to the air, I swoop and grasp one of the mongrels by a ridge on its armored head. It dangles helplessly for only a second before I toss it out of the ship through the perforation I created in its side. Yes, there are faster ways to go about it, but I intend to savor this. It feels good to be back in action.

And, as they say, I am not messing around.

I tear through another gaggle of them while they continue their feeble attempts to thwart me. When they realize their energy weapons have no effect on the godlike being before them, they test out melee combat. What a joke. Nothing they do manages to even tickle. The tips of their spearlike weapons merely snap off like dry twigs. Their pseudo-sword blades are reduced to dullness upon contact with my hardened skin. Even their teeth crack and bleed against my superior flesh.

Their squad leader—or whatever it is—finally attempts to communicate with me. I still hear the skittering vocalizations emanating from its throat, but a small device against its neck translates and amplifies its words into plain English.

"Stand down, Earther! You will be extinguished if you continue to circumvent the will of the Hatchmother."

"I am going to locate your Hatchmother, detach her tail, and shove it down her throat!"

It is difficult to tell with these dinosaur-things, but I am nearly certain its expression turns to one of horror. I know nothing about them or their planet, but I assume this "Hatch-mother" is the most important individual in their culture.

Good. Let them know how little I care for their kind.

Without any more wasted words, I bolt for and grab the squad leader, flying it into the center of the room. It is there, in front of everyone, that I display my designs for their Hatch-mother through demonstration. The creature's screams are quickly cut off by a gurgling sound as I feed it its own bloody tail.

Several turn and run—the smart ones.

This time, I do not use my speed as I approach the next group of alien scum. I stalk—like a lion its prey. I want them to experience every instant of dread in knowing what fate awaits them should they not immediately evacuate our airspace and return to whatever pit they crawled out of.

The others now scurry only to return a moment later, hefting an enormous energy cannon. With it aimed directly at me, one growls something that sounds more like a baby burping after a feeding than any sort of intelligible language. The weapon is a hulking monstrosity covered in scales, much like their own bodies. Transparent openings at its sides faintly glow with the blue of the artifacts that gave me my powers.

What are they planning on doing, making me even more powerful?

Bring it on, I think to myself. *I could handle a boost after all these decades.*

"Run, you weak fools, or you will not be making the trip back to your home planet with the rest of your kind."

I smile to let them know I am not the least bit afraid of their measly, pathetic weapon. I take a small step, ensuring the aliens manning the cannon continue to tremble before I dispatch them back to the hell that spawned them. Even without my super-hearing, the power-up process would have been loud. I spread my arms, preparing myself to be bathed in the radiation that made me a demigod.

Finally, the weapon discharges an energy blast, not even powerful enough to slow my forward momentum. My smile grows wider and my eyes glow brighter red as I press forward, poised to twist the thing into a metal pretzel.

I cannot even recall the last time I'd been able to let loose like this. It's invigorating! I feel like I could wad this entire ship into a steel ball and hurl it back across the galaxy.

Then I start to feel something... *different*.

And it is not good.

At first, I cannot place the feeling, for it is something I have not felt since before the accident.

Horror-stricken, I gaze down at my hands and see... wrinkles? Liver spots? My fingers wither before my very eyes. White hairs fall from my head. My legs no longer support the weight of my body. So weak. Something is wrong.

Something is very, very wr—

CHAPTER 1
SAWYER

Blammo!

It's not until a soldier literally explodes from an alien weapon that I really grasp the magnitude of our situation. We've just escaped from the supposedly inescapable underwater mega-prison known as the Trench, and before we can even taste the tiniest bit of freedom, it happens: the alien invasion begins.

In case you forgot, we—me, Sawyer William Vincent, Crosscircuit, Sinsation, Royal Rampage, and my maybe-half-brother Justice—were picked up by some sort of government agency spec-ops dudes in suits, flying an aircraft I thought was gigantic. Now, compared to seeing the Tuldarian eyesore, it looks like a Power Wheel parked next to the Gravedigger.

At our helm, so to speak, is none other than Luis Chen, Frank Douglas's right-hand man.

The exploding soldier is displayed on one of many monitor

feeds in a small room off the hangar where we'd been roughly manhandled by Chen's soldiers. On another, a huge shadow looms over... St. Louis? Maybe? Yeah. St. Louis. There's the Arch—aaaand it's gone. Ho-lee crap. A massive blast from one of the smaller ships pouring out of a monstrous vessel unloads an energy weapon and sends fragments of the once super-recognizable landmark raining down all around it.

This is nuts. I've seen a lot of destruction over the years, first as Red Kite—Red Raptor if I'd had my way—and then as Harrier. But really, I can't recall anything quite this... devastating. Nearly a decade ago, when Crosscircuit unleashed metal hell upon mankind in what has come to be known as Mega-Mech Apocalypse was the closest thing I've seen. And lo and behold, now I'm somehow working *with* the guy who'd been behind that.

The Tuldarians have decided not to be the least bit subtle about their attempt to take over the Earth, showing up in extreme force. The battles the Guild fought years ago against them were obviously just preludes—maybe testing us, maybe just scouting missions, who knows?

No matter what, this is the real thing.

"Sawyer," Chen says behind me, "as you can see, things are not looking good."

"I'll take obvious answers for $500, Alex," I say.

"It's not a joke."

At that, I spin around and stand from the folding chair I was so comfortably relaxing in. I'm about to respond with another snide comment when I see his grave expression.

"Right. Okay. I'm sorry. I just can't believe he was right..."

Crosscircuit has been spouting off nonsense about aliens practically since the moment I met him in the Trench. I figured he'd lost his mind, or never had it to begin with. It wasn't until he mentioned the mysterious disappearance of the Arch Angels—our overwatch stationed on the moon—that I even began to consider he might be telling the truth.

To think, I was concerned we were being arrested and sent back to the Trench. From the way it looks out there, we'd be better off. It might end up being the safest place left on Earth.

"Just be glad I found you," Chen said. "My guess is with everything going on, you'd have been stranded out there for weeks unless you died of hunger or exposure first."

"That's a pleasant thought."

"How did you find me?" I asked.

"That craft is equipped with a beacon designed to ensure against escape from the Trench. In this case, it led me straight to you. Had this been any other time, without the presence of aliens, you'd have been picked up by someone who would have sent you right back. What were you thinking?"

The question catches me off guard. "Thinking? Huh. I don't know, maybe that I didn't wanna spend the rest of my life caged underwater like an animal just for being a good guy?"

Chen places his hand on my shoulder, and I'm reminded again that it's made of metal when I feel how cold it is. "You're right. I just meant... teaming up with Sean Meyers? Risky, no?"

I shake my head. "What choice did I have? You all just left me there to rot."

I take sick satisfaction in the grimace that washes across Mr. Chen's features. "Our hands were tied, Sawyer. You have to believe that. Frank, me... even Ale—"

"Don't." Maybe I'll learn to forgive Alex for what he's done —arresting me as part of his stupid taskforce—but not today. Deciding to change the subject, I ask, "So, what are we gonna do?"

Mr. Chen clears his throat and takes his prosthetic hand off my shoulder. "We are ten minutes from San Francisco." He looks at his watch. "Eight." From the corner of the room, he lifts a medium-sized duffle bag and tosses it to me. "Time for a quick change."

I stare at it for a minute, wondering if it could be true.

"Is this..." I unzip the bag to reveal my graphite Red Raptor costume. A part of me sours at seeing it and not the Black Harrier armor.

"It was all I could get ahold of in time," Chen says as a form of apology. "But I've got something special for you when we return to New York. Now, come on. Once we arrive, I'll need you at your best. Hope you didn't get too soft down there or we might never make it back there."

As soon as he says it, I get the feeling he thought better of it. But I let the joke go. Things are awkward enough. He offers a slight wave, then exits the room.

Wasting no time, I immediately begin to slip into the suit.

It's a bit small since I haven't worn it in a few years and, as Mom likes to say, I've "grown like a weed."

The thought of my mom puts me into a short wave of panic. Is she okay? Is New York under attack, too?

Of course it is. It's not like the aliens would go after St. Louis and not the bigger, more important cities. Sorry if you're from St. Louis. I'm sure it's a cool town and all. I just... Well, you live there. You know.

Finally, I slip on my helmet and it boots up.

"Hey there," a voice says in my ear followed by a very sensual purr. "*I've missed you, handsome.*"

Before I can do anything about it, a holographic image of one of the most—no, *the* most—gorgeous woman I've ever seen pops up in my field of view. She's blonde and currently wearing army fatigues. The shirt is unbuttoned almost to her naval, and the shorts are almost too short to even still be called that. But it's okay; most of her legs are covered by thigh-high leather boots.

"I thought I'd dress for the occasion," she says.

"Okay, wow. Well, uh. Hi, Tiff. Soooo, you need to go away."

"That's rude," she says, affecting a heavy pout.

"Not away-away. Just... voice only, okay?"

Her shoulders slump. "*I guess women should be heard, not seen.*"

"You know that's not what I meant!" I argue, feeling my cheeks get hot.

It's amazing how lifelike Frank made these AI. I'd

forgotten just how easily I could get sucked into an argument with her, like she was real or something.

In a little digital glitch, she disappears. I won't lie, since the drone Crosscircuit gave me was too dumb to follow me onto the escape pod, and I was too stupid to notice until it was too late, having backup would be nice.

"It's good to see—er, hear—you," I tell her, hoping to win some ground back—again, like she's not a computer.

"Awww, I love you too," she says. Then I hear a kissing sound, which is odd considering she has no lips.

"How long until we reach the shore?" I ask.

"Oh, a sailor on shore leave... my fanta—"

"Tiffany, please!"

"One minute and twelve seconds."

As soon as she answers, the door bursts open and Chen re-enters, this time with three of his armored soldiers at his wings.

"Time to save the world," he says, clapping once. "You ready?"

I crack my knuckles and roll my neck. "Hell yeah."

I won't lie, it feels damn good to be back in the suit—even if it's my old one and the crotch is a bit tight and the legs a bit short.

I follow him into the hangar where Justice, Sinsation, Royal Rampage, and Crosscircuit are waiting. The big gorilla is clearly frightened, but if I know him, he'll be the first to start throwing punches when the time comes. I mean, it's sort of his thing.

Each of my fellow escapees has been outfitted with something close to their preferred gear as well. Though, Sinsation relies heavily upon her appearance combined with chemical pheromones to distract foes, and she's in what amounts to Stormtrooper armor.

The soldiers usher me to a spot between her and Justice. I give him a reassuring look as the same hatch we'd been raised into opens up and we are all led to the edge.

"This is messed up," Justice says.

I nod, but keep my focus on what's going on below us.

Chen said San Francisco, but I can see the Golden Gate Bridge in the distance, and the land mass under our ship is surrounded by water. Some kind of island between two mainlands.

Fire and smoke rise from everywhere I can see, and military tanks are rolling through the streets.

"The U.S. Army has reclaimed San Fran for now," one of the soldiers—a guy with a thick mustache—says. "We need you to handle Treasure Island. More than two thousand men, women, and children are stuck down there with no means of escape. You're their last hope."

In a matter of—I don't know, hours?—things have quickly become "us" (humans) versus "them" (aliens). It doesn't even matter that we are a bunch of convicted criminals in the court's eyes.

"You can't do this to me," Crosscircuit argues. "Do you have any idea who I am?"

If anyone's listening or cares, they don't show it.

The dinosaur-like ground troops roam the tight streets with trained efficiency, disintegrating everything in their path —including people—with weapons that would make Battlegear salivate. I'm not sure if disintegrating is the right word. It's not like stuff disappears into billions of molecules or turns to dust. The beams from the weapons seem to superheat the liquids inside a person and cause them to blow up like a snack left cooking for way too long. Picture the gross stuff you've had to clean off the inside of a microwave, and then imagine that it's the inside of a human being.

Yep. *Horrific,* right?

We don't even have time to think before we feel hands on our backs shoving us forward. They don't exactly force us to jump, but it's clear what they want us to do.

"It's time for you to go down," Tiffany says.

"Enough," I growl.

"What?" Justice asks.

"I said that's enough waiting," I lie. "Let's go!"

I leap from the grated metal floor, gripping the line tight, and slide down using my graphene gloves to take the friction. My stomach turns a million times, but I'm used to stuff like this. I've been a superhero since I was thirteen, after all.

When we land, we all spring into action. Well, "action" may not be the best term for every single one of us, since Crosscircuit immediately runs and hides behind a military VTOL vehicle to our left. He may be the most intelligent person on Earth, but, from what I've seen, his fighting capabilities are about equivalent to that of a small child.

I don't have a lot of time to process things, but up close, the Tuldarians are even more terrifying than I thought. I've watched a lot of movies. A lot. Growing up, the *Jurassic Park* franchise was one of my absolute favorites. I always thought it would be super cool if I found myself in a zoo full of dinosaurs, even if they were trying to kill me.

Turns out, I was wrong.

As expected, the first to jump into the fray is Royal Rampage—literally. He leaps forward onto the nearest lizard-being he sees. Usually, he sort of holds back—powerwise—considering he's a super-strong gorilla. But apparently, when he's fighting non-humans, he doesn't have any problem going all-out. Which also maybe explains why he nearly killed Bull-shark in the Trench, since he probably doesn't understand very well that Bullshark *is* a person.

Well, kind of.

Once he's on the dino's back, Rampage starts pounding on its reptilian head. What comes next almost makes me laugh. I saw a coffee mug once that had a T-Rex lying in bed, holding a paperback. Because its arms were so short, the book was obscured by a giant snout. The caption read "Rex wishes he bought the audiobook."

As in that hilarious depiction, the Tuldarian's arms are too short to reach Royal Rampage, so it can't do much except try to shake him off. Then Roy—that's what I've started calling him for short—snaps his arm forward, clutches the top dino-jaw and rips backward. The result is not pretty, essentially tearing the top off the alien's head. The body slumps to the asphalt, and Roy descends with it. When he rises, he's covered in lizard guts and brains. Definitely not screwing around. Then, planting a foot up onto the lizard corpse, he pounds his chest in triumph. As gruesome a sight as it is, I still admire the big guy's style.

Sinsation shows no hesitation either. She's never been one to shy away from a fight, and she hasn't been able to do it much while locked up in the Trench.

"Three gross salamanders at your six," Tiffany warns me.

Just as Roy isn't worried about killing the aliens, I wonder if my "no-gun rule" needs to go out the window for these things. I don't know how I'm supposed to fight them otherwise, and they're certainly not showing us any mercy. I drop and roll toward the downed, now-headless alien, and scoop up the blaster-thing it was carrying. As I rise back to my feet, turned 180 degrees toward my attackers, I realize I don't have time to figure it out. Their own guns are trained on me and ready to fire.

Instead, I whip out my grappling hook, and fire it at the nearest building. This isn't New York, and we're on an island, so we aren't talking skyscrapers here. I zip toward the rooftop of a three-story YMCA building. Hot phaser or plasma fire whips past me on both sides, and I'm immediately grateful these things aren't crack shots like Justice or Deadeye. My guess is having eyes on the sides of their heads isn't exactly the best position for forward depth perception.

I hit the side of the building and climb up and over, dropping to what I've heard Marines call their fourth point of contact so I can take a moment to figure out how the gun works. I don't know why it's the fourth point. I feel like it's fifth or sixth, but maybe I don't understand the phrase.

Now probably isn't the best time to get lost in a phrase developed by people who eat crayons, though.

At first, I have a lot of trouble with the gun. Since the aliens' hands or claws or whatever are so much different from ours, they don't have grips or traditional triggers. I'm also scared out of my mind I'm gonna press one of these buttons and blow myself up.

Then I realize I've seen one of these fired. Sure, it was on a tiny, grainy monitor, but my superpower is a sort-of-but-not-really supernatural recall. And, thinking back to the video, I perfectly remember everything about it in staunch detail. Problem is, the soldier who became tomato soup was positioned in front of the camera at the time the Tuldarian's weapon fired.

Sighing, I carefully roll over and peer over the lip of the building. It doesn't take long to find a dinosaur shooting, but it's pretty far away.

"Tiffany, enhance my vision," I say.

She does what I ask, but not without a little quip afterword. *"Your vision would be* greatly *enhanced by letting me out of this cage."*

I ignore her and focus on the creature's weapon, and more importantly, the trigger mechanism on the bottom near the back. Almost precisely where I have the gun resting on my knee. Geez. I quickly reposition. That could have been bad.

Dropping back into a seated position, I work to find the best hand placement. Once I'm satisfied, the only thing left to do is pop up and pop off.

I take aim and fire.

It's hard to explain the feeling of power emanating from the thing. It's both spectacular and petrifying all at once. The bolt hits one of the reptiles and the thing bubbles a bit before it explodes into mist.

"Whoa," I say to myself. Then, "Whoa!" again as I immediately take cover from bolts of energy flying my way in retaliation.

Ducking does me no good since, well, like I said, these things practically evaporate anything they hit. I move just in time as the wall I'm hiding behind erupts.

After catching my breath, I lean out through the brand-new hole and try to fire, but nothing happens. Looking down at the gun, there's no sign I've broken it, but there is a small light that goes from blinking yellow to solid blue after a few seconds.

Charging? Maybe. That's probably the only thing preventing the Tuldarians from vaporizing us all within two minutes. I take the chance, targeting the loser that was shooting at me, and *kaboom!* He's dead. A glance downward confirms that yellow must be like our red, and blue means good to go.

While I wait, I survey the post-apocalyptic world three stories below me, trying to find allies. Roy is still hopping and dodging and doing serious damage. Sinsation seems okay, though I'm sure she's wishing dinosaurs had the same propensity for horniness as humans. And Justice, of course, has no problem with the dinosaur weapons. He's actually got two of them, using them in tandem, back and forth, firing while the other charges, and vice versa. I guess if you're good with guns, it doesn't matter who made them.

He may not be someone I wanna be friends with, but in a situation like this, I can't ask for a better ally by my side. He learned to fight the same way I did, and he's almost as good, despite his lack of training by someone like Frank Douglas. The way he wades through the aliens, I'd almost think he'd be able to take them all on alone. He has a certain confidence I've never had. And not caring what kind of death and injury he causes probably helps, too.

Could I actually be a little envious of him?

Nah.

"Harrier, are you okay?" The voice piped in through my helmet belongs to Luis Chen.

"Yeah," I answer. Then a thought pops into my head. Maybe Justice could take all of these things on by himself, maybe not. But there's one person who absolutely could. "What the hell is going on here? Why isn't Eaglestar taking care of this?"

Chen hesitates a moment before answering, and he's a man who never hesitates. "Eaglestar is dead."

CHAPTER 2
SEAN

No.

This isn't how things were meant to be. I was supposed to be free from prison and in charge. In command of everything once they had assurance I was correct all these years! *I* was supposed to save the world. These people have no idea what they're doing! We are barely surviving this first battle and it could hardly even be called a skirmish.

At first glance, it appeared the island was overrun, but that's only because the Tuldarian weapons are so destructive. Now that the Super Harrier Brothers have gotten ahold of those same weapons, the aliens seem to be in a form of retreat. Yes, they are still terrorizing the greater San Francisco area, but they are doing so on the way back to their ships.

Thankfully, they are here in the much smaller vessels meant to travel planetside from their mothership—or mother-ships, since I have no idea how many of the larger vessels are currently here.

It's not over. Not by a long shot. They'll regroup, likely return to finish what they've started, but with the arrival of several more masked crimefighters, including many I've never seen before, it seems today could be called a victory—by the smallest of margins.

And *of course* I hid. What do you expect? I'm not a brawler. I have methods, and fisticuffs doesn't fit into the equation. Besides, getting swooped up by the Men in Black was an interference I sadly hadn't accounted for. And to make matters more grave, I am now the most important person on Earth. If I had been killed, it would have resulted in the end of the world as we know it.

And *furthermore*, if these yokels have a Vertical Takeoff and Landing shuttle—which they do because that's my current cover—why was I shoved out of a hole on a rope?

When I was aboard what I heard referred to as the Techtriguard, the large airship better suited for World War III than Interstellar Armageddon, I tried to educate the fools on my importance. They, however, arrogant as they are, thought they knew better. I tried to explain that I have to get to my control center within my main base in Egypt. It's the only way to direct all of my robots at once—the only way we're going to defeat the Tuldarians.

And now we've just received word that the so-called world's greatest hero is dead. It never rains...

"Eaglestar was useless against them anyway," I say into my comm device.

"Crosscircuit?" Harrier says.

"Guess this is one big party," Sinsation comments, clearly out of breath.

"It is indeed me," I respond.

"Glad you're alive," Justice says. "Now I can kill you myself."

"Can everyone shut up?" Harrier says. "Chen, Eaglestar is... dead?"

"Can confirm," Chen says.

"How could you not know that Eaglestar was the worst possible option to send against them?" I say, peeking out from behind the VTOL to a mostly clear street.

"He's always been effective against them before," Chen says.

"Yes, yes, of course. Against their *ordinary* weapons. But it was inevitable they'd figure out a way to remove the artifact energy from his body, and there's no way they would have invaded until they were able to do that. Don't you see? That's why they're finally able to stage this invasion!"

Chen doesn't respond. The air whips around me, and I look up to see a vehicle similar to the one behind which I've protected myself.

They have more than one!?

As it lands, a ramp unfolds. It barely touches the ground before Chen and a military-type exits. From the man's regalia, I know he's a colonel, though we haven't yet been introduced. Not that I care. They're so far behind the curve that it's incomprehensible to me. I'm always working from the assumption that everyone else is light-years behind me, but this is ridiculous.

Chen doesn't stop until he's on top of me. But it's not him who speaks. The colonel grabs me by the collar and gives me a shake.

"You were sent down here to fight!" he barked.

"I was sent down here to die!" I respond with the same level of intensity. "And you'll forgive me, but I did not manage the impossible just to be slaughtered in round one."

"You are only still breathing because I have deemed it neces—"

"I am the only one capable of stopping this threat, and if you weren't such a blowhard, full-of-yourself pile of garbage with breath like horse dung, you'd know that."

It looks as if the colonel is ready to swing at me, but Luis Chen steps in.

"This is my prisoner, Colonel," he says. "Please unhand him."

The colonel eyes him. But in the end, he gives me a little shove—which I'll admit, sends me reeling. My butt hits the ground, but I don't stay there. I refuse to be treated like an animal. He's going to regret that later, believe you me.

As I rise, I'm already speaking. "Don't you see? I've been truthful this whole time."

Harrier approaches from the right, squeezing between the colonel and me. "I hate to say it, Mr. Chen, but he's right."

"Thank you," I say, offering him the slightest head dip. "That's why I had to create the robots. Superpowers are only going to work until they manage to extricate them from every hero and villain they go up against."

"Wait... what do you mean? Like, suck them out of us?" Harrier asks.

"Yes. By all means, let's dumb it down for the masses. '*Suck them out.*' Over ninety percent of super-powered beings on this planet have their abilities because of the alien artifacts. And with this new technology they've developed, they can take it all away."

"Is this true?" Harrier asks Chen.

Chen nods grimly, apparently grasping the ramifications of what I'm saying for the first time.

But again, the colonel can't seem to keep his mouth shut. "The radiation from the artifacts has been altering the DNA of individuals who come into contact with them little by little over centuries. Some alterations were good, but like any mutations, most of them were not. They caused birth defects or other health problems."

Justice and Sinsation enter the small circle. The shooter is still doing what he does best, walking backward and firing his new alien toy at the ships as they vanish into the horizon. The guy has focus, I'll give him that.

"Hell yeah! That was amazing!" Justice shouts, totally oblivious to the idea of reading a room.

Chen glares at him, then picks up where the colonel left off. "Most of the changes caused by the Tuldarian artifacts didn't amount to much, even when they were good. They might make someone exceptionally strong, fast, or intelligent. Or give them incredible talents—musical, athletic, artistic."

"I knew LeBron wasn't human," Justice interjects, finally turning away from his targets.

We all just stare at him. I'd like to think he was making a clever joke, but somehow I don't think he was.

Chen sighs. "People with abilities are still *human.* And these abilities and talents were often passed on to later generations, sometimes combining with the positive genes of others by chance and producing someone with gifts we now refer to as superpowers. It wasn't until the Nazis collected so many artifacts together and exposed many more individuals to them in what amounted to a short-term Chernobyl-like release of radiation that superpowers began to become more commonplace."

"Like Eaglestar?" Harrier asks.

"Eaglestar was an extraordinary case," Chen says. "He was born with the genetic sequencing to have the potential for fantastic abilities, and that had already made him an exceptional pilot from the beginning. Then he crashed his plane into an airship full of artifacts that exploded, basically setting off an artifact bomb. It was a perfect storm as far as he was concerned. Most of those involved were killed, but the explosion unlocked Jonathan Powers's full genetic potential and turned him into the ultimate super-being."

"But that was just the beginning," I say. Chen and the

colonel turn to me. About time. "There was also a chain reaction affecting others."

"Yes," agrees Chen.

"The fallout from that explosion affected thousands of individuals for good or ill," I continue. "A lot of people died from cancer..." I pause there, the memory of my mother and her struggle momentarily overwhelming my thoughts.

Chen takes that as an opportunity to cut in. "Or radiation poisoning, as you'd expect from any radiation exposure. But for others, it was an incredible boon to their lives. For example, a young army private named Franklin Douglas, one of the American soldiers assigned to clean up the crash site following the explosion and recover what was left of the artifacts."

"Franklin Douglas?" Justice asks. "The dude running for mayor?"

"No. His grandfather," Chen says.

I look to Harrier, wondering if he's stupid enough to give away any information to those around us who are not *in the know*. To his credit, he remains silent. Though, with his helmet still on, I can't see his reaction, I know there must be one.

Chen nods slightly, as if confirming something unspoken. "He apparently cut himself while bagging a fragment of one of the artifacts—which he decided to take home as a souvenir, by the way. It infected his blood and altered his DNA, giving him an extraordinary memory, which he was able to use to great benefit in his business ventures. He passed this ability on to his son, Frankie Jr., who chose to use the ability—which was even stronger in function than his father's—to become a criminal mastermind."

"Wow," Harrier says.

"Extraordinary memory?" Justice says, with something akin to wonderment on his face. "Like, he could see something once and... sort of remember how it's done?"

"Precisely," Chen says, slowly shifting his gaze from Justice back to Harrier and back again.

"I knew about all of this after breaking into the Douglas Industries archives while working there," I say.

This garners me a sidelong glance from Luis Chen.

"Yes," says Chen. "Just one of the numerous crimes and security breaches you committed during the course of your employment with us before you were discovered."

"And just some of the crimes I've been paying the price for in the Trench," I remind him.

"Not long enough, as far as I'm concerned. But we need you now, regardless," says Chen.

"We?" asks Harrier. "We who?"

I chuckle. "He still doesn't know, does he, Luis?"

Harrier's eyes bounce around like he's watching a tennis match. "Know what?"

"That Mr. Chen here has been secretly working for the government this entire time."

"Seriously?" young Harrier says. I have to admit I enjoy seeing his brain explode at all of these revelations. Figuratively, of course, not like those soldiers on the California streets. "What are you, CIA? NSA?"

"Oh, my dear boy, Chen's agency can't be boiled down to three simple letters," I say. "And you won't find it on the books anywhere."

Harrier tears off his helmet and glares at Luis Chen. "So you've been—what?—spying on my family all these years? Frank trusted you! We've trusted you! With everything."

Ah, there it is. Emotion gets the best of the best of us.

"Your… family?" Justice says.

Sawyer William Vincent's face turns a shade that matches his garish costume.

I spare him responding by throwing a little more fuel on the fire. "Tsk, tsk. Spying. Keeping them in check. *Using* them."

"Keeping them safe," Chen insists. "The government could have had Frankie Jr. arrested and taken everything in a civil forfeiture. But instead, they decided to keep the company going and use its vast wealth and resources for research and development."

"For its own purposes," I say. Harrier needs to know it wasn't an act of kindness.

"For situations like the one we're involved in now!" Chen says. "The politicians are too slow to act, and too quick to let their differences get in the way of what has to be done. By the time they reacted to this invasion, we'd all be dead."

"We still very well may be," I say. "That is why I need access to my robots!"

"We're working on it," says Chen.

"Work faster!"

Sawyer shoves his helmet on and walks away.

"Sawyer!" Chen calls. "Come back. Let's talk."

The colonel puts a hand out to stop Chen from following the boy. "Let him go, Luis. He'll come around to our way of thinking."

"Apparently you don't know the Douglases," Chen says.

Everyone stands there in silence for a long moment. You can't spell families without "lies."

"Family?" Justice says again.

Ah, to possess the freedom of mind this idiot has.

CHAPTER 3
ERIC

Bro.

This is the most insane thing I've ever witnessed. Even crazier than the time I saw the Guild swept away into a parallel universe in Times Square during a ceremony. They were honoring their sidekicks or something stupid like that—like anyone would care. I almost thought maybe it was a trap for supervillains or whatever, since it was just way too irresistible not to show up. I was watching from a rooftop, trying to figure out the best way to cause chaos, and then, all of a sudden, a big, shiny portal opened up right on stage and they were gone.

Vanished.

Yeah, I know. Right? Pretty sure that Harrier kid even wrote about it in one of his books.

But that's nothing compared to what's going on now. This

is end-of-the-world stuff. A giant spaceship hovering right over New York with smaller ships flying out of it in droves.

The big one is ugly—just gray and like a misshapen egg. But the little ones? Damn, they're cool. All glowing lights and this weird tech I've never even thought of. Oh, and the weapons? If I could get ahold of those things, I could reverse-engineer them to make some super badass guns.

"I don't know how we're gonna survive this," E-Man says behind me.

His brother or clone or whatever shakes his head.

"Y'all gotta have some faith," Yamo argues.

"In what—God?" Logan Andrews scoffs.

He's an interesting kid. Used to work for me when I was a supervillain. I'd started this awesome group called the Neon Knights. He took the place of another kid who died. Can't remember his name.

"In something!" Yamo almost shouts.

We're all just at the police station, watching everything from the window on the top floor. It's not like there's much any of these idiots could do about it with Glocks and lightning sticks. Me, on the other hand, I've got some stuff I'd love to try out on these bastards. I'm just waiting for Eaglestar—the big man himself—to give the word. Then it's on!

I step away, and immediately, my spot near the window is cannibalized by some no-name uniform.

"About time," the guy says under his breath. But I hear it, and fight the urge to shove him back out of the way.

Instead, I take a seat in one of the rolling chairs at someone's desk—doesn't matter whose. Opening my social media apps on my phone, I see that it's happening all over the world. I know there have been aliens here before, but not like this. This is bat-crap crazy.

Another uniformed officer grabs me by the shoulder. I spin on him and he lets go.

"Uh, Mr. uh—Mr. uh—sir."

I have to admit, I love to see these guys stammering. No one knows what to call me. Some of them don't even know who I am. It's a sort of power I've never had before and I love it.

"What?" I say, barely looking away from my phone.

"You've got a call."

I raise my phone. "No I don't."

"It's in the captain's office. It's uh... well, you just need to take it."

Color me intrigued. I stand and head for the elevator, giving one final glance toward the window. From there, it looks like any other day outside with the ships above shielded from view.

"You should probably hurry," the officer says.

I sigh and speed up a little. Not much. I don't take orders from pipsqueaks like him. But it seems like this actually might be important. Maybe it's Eaglestar telling me to go bananas. That thought encourages me a little and I break into a slight jog.

It would make sense that he called the captain's number, I guess. She's the liaison between the Counter-Vigilante Taskforce and the NYPD. Sort of a boss-not-a-boss. She can't really order us around, but she controls the budget and the backup. So, yeah, we kind of have to listen to her.

I go to knock, but she opens the door before I can even make contact. Giving me a strange look, she vacates her own office without a word. I pick up the receiver on her landline phone and tap the blinking button for Line 1.

"Hello?"

"Mr. McCabe, I have the Vice President on the line. Please hold."

Shocked doesn't even begin to cover my emotional state.

"Of the United States?" I ask, but whoever it was is gone. Apparently transferring me to the vice-freaking-president.

"The vice president? For me? What the—"

I don't even get a little song—you know, like when you're on hold with the internet company or something. Sure, it's annoying, but at least it lets you know you haven't been hung up on or disconnected. It's a nice courtesy—one the US government, apparently, doesn't care about.

"Mr. McCabe?" a woman finally says. "This is Vice President Bashir."

"Uh, yeah. I got that."

"President Stanford wanted to call you himself, but with you being who you are and all... well, we were a bit worried about the optics. You know how it is."

"Optics?"

"Come on, Eric," she says pleadingly. "You've gotta imagine what people would think if he was making calls from the Oval Office to former supervillains... It just doesn't look good. Understand?"

"I know what *optics* are. That's... whatever. I just don't understand why he would want to call *me* in the first place."

A slight pause. "We have an offer for you. I'm sure you're aware of the news."

"Do you mean the giant spaceship above New York?"

"And everywhere else," Bashir says. "World leaders are trying to appear as in control as possible to reduce panic, but it's bad. Real bad."

"I've been on Reddit," I tell her. "But that's just a bunch of internet trolls, right? How bad?"

There's another, longer, pause on the other end.

"Ma'am? Are you there?"

"I'm just going to come out with it, Eric. The whole place has gone to heck in a handbasket. The Tuldarians are wiping out the world's militaries like toy soldiers. It won't be long before there's nobody left to defend us. It's all just a—"

"Excuse me. Did you say Tuldarians?"

"Yes. Yes, I did. You know, lizard-aliens that look like dinosaurs."

I shake my head even though I know she can't see me. "I know what they are. I've read the files. Just making sure I heard what I thought I heard. The ships are *a lot* bigger than before. Didn't the Guild kick their asses last time?"

"That was last time. But things are... different now."

I'm not an idiot. I can read between the lines, but the words are hazy. There's something she's keeping from me.

But before I can ask, she says, "Anyway, we're going to send some teams out to deal with this whole mess, and we'd like you to join them."

"Teams?" I ask. "What kind of *teams*?"

"Well... the kind of teams that wear masks and generally have special abilities."

"You're kidding me."

"I wouldn't kid about something like this. My understanding is that you've been a valuable asset to the CVT over the past couple of years—"

"Yeah, but it's not like I had a choice." I know it's stupid to interrupt the vice president, but what the actual hell? After everything the CVT went through to stop masked crimefighters, it was for nothing? I decide to voice my opinions. Why the hell not? What could it hurt at this point? "So after making us all quit and turning those who didn't into wanted criminals, you expect everyone to help you? Isn't that sort of hypocritical?"

"Frankly, Mr. McCabe, I voted against the idea. I told the president he should just drop some nukes from orbit and be done with it."

"Wait... what? Seriously?"

"Well, you people make me pretty nervous, to be honest. I don't like the way you operate, and you don't fit very well into my worldview. But it's not my call."

"Honesty from a politician is nice," I say. "Even if it is telling me I'm scum."

"That's not what I said—"

"Relax, Madam Vice President. I'm just trying to lighten the mood a little. So, what's the deal? I go save the world, and then rot in a prison somewhere for using my powers?"

"Oh, no, no, no. We wouldn't do that. The president would never turn his back on someone who helps him out. Never. We know you have a deal in place where you stay free as long as you're working with the CVT. If you do this, there won't even be the threat of prison, no matter what happens."

"Uh-huh."

"I understand you being skeptical," she says.

"Considering I just helped fill the Trench with people who have been celebrated as the world's greatest heroes? Yeah. Call me dubious."

She sighs. "That's understandable. But I assure you. Things have changed. Whether I like it or not. You'll be free to go home afterward, assuming you, uh... survive. And the world is still here."

"That's it?" I ask.

"Well, not quite. You'd have to sign a document admitting guilt for all your past actions and guaranteeing that you'll give up dressing up in a little costume and committing crimes for the rest of your life. If not, *then* you would be thrown in a dark cell at the bottom of the ocean and be left to rot. And I'll need an answer now. We don't have the luxury of time. We're already in the process of assembling the teams at a special location and assigning leaders."

I take a deep breath. This is all-hands-on-deck action. It's time for everyone to put aside their differences and work together to repel this invasion. Of course I'm going to do the right thing. But first...

"Any chance I could also get a raise?"

There's silence on the other end, probably because she's trying to process my bold move.

"I'm sorry... a raise?" she asks.

Check and mate, mother-effer. Wait. I don't know if I can call a woman that. Or anything for that matter. "For my current job with the CVT. Assuming the world doesn't end, I mean."

"I don't know anything about that, Mr. McCabe. That's not my department."

"I guess I'll just ask Eaglestar, then."

Bashir doesn't answer.

"Hello? Is it okay if I ask Eaglestar?"

"I... suppose you're going to find out soon enough anyway." Bashir clicks with her tongue—a sound I find frustratingly annoying. "Eaglestar is dead. Killed by the aliens."

I feel it like a gut-punch. Yeah, he was my arch-nemesis, but I also considered him a friend. Even if that was pretty delusional of me. All those years of fighting one another and then working together, and now...

"Dead? Are you sure?"

"I'm sorry, Eric," Bashir says, and I can actually feel the

genuine sympathy. "Apparently, they took away his powers, and then blasted him once he was vulnerable. I suppose you're probably happy about that."

It takes me a few seconds to speak, and when I do, it's choked up. "No, ma'am. You're wrong about that. Sign me up for your kamikaze mission, Veep. I'm gonna go kill those motherf—"

CHAPTER 4
ALEX

Madhouse.

That's what this city has been ever since the alien invasion began. I called in the rest of my CVT team—the Counter-Vigilante Taskforce—to help with everything, but so far we haven't been able to even leave the station because of the chaos happening all over New York.

"Garner!" I hear my name being called by my boss, Captain Fernanda, over the cacophony of the station. That woman has a set of lungs on her.

"Yes, Cap?" I shout back, not even reaching half her volume.

"My office! Now!"

Really? We're doing this old routine at a time like this?

"Yes, ma'am!" I yell back. Because I know what's good for me. I've fought supervillains, superheroes, monsters, aliens, and would-be world conquerors. None of them ever scared me as much as Captain Fernanda.

I double-time it to her office and she indicates that I should shut the door.

"What's going on?" And then I add, "Ma'am."

"Last time I checked, the end of the world," she says. "But I'm being contacted from the highest levels and you're not going to like it."

"The mayor?"

"I said the *highest* levels, Garner. I'm talking about the White House."

"What about?"

"We're being *advised* to release Baron Steele."

I tilt my head like an idiot. "What? After what we went through to arrest him?"

She shuffles some papers I know she isn't reading. "Apparently they need him to help save the world or some-such. We're letting him go."

I lean back, crossing my leg in the best indignant pose I can think of under the circumstances. "Well, I don't want to be there when—"

"You don't understand, Garner. *You're* letting him go."

Leg uncrossed. Cue the rapid heart rate and sweat. "Me? I'll be lucky if he doesn't punch me straight up to that giant spaceship as soon as the power dampeners are off."

"Not my monkey, not my circus. This is CVT business, and last time I checked, you're the leader of your team. And it has to be immediate."

"Immediate?"

"As in right-freaking-now, Garner! Just do it!"

The look on her face sends me out of her office faster than if Fastlane had grabbed me by the collar and dragged me out full speed.

"Yes, ma'am," I say as I go.

In case you forgot, Paul "The Baron Steele" is about the only human being to ever match up to Eaglestar—unless you count Battlegear. And please don't count Battlegear.

He's got skin like, well, steel. And he's immensely strong.

While I'm heading down to the basement of the station, I get a notification on my secure comm device that tells me I have a priority email. After using the decryption app, I read up on my actual orders from the White House.

I approach the special maximum security cell that was installed in the lowest level of the station when the CVT was headquartered here. It has extra-heavy-duty power dampeners in place just for a prisoner like the person currently occupying it: Baron Paul Steele, former member of the Guild of Masked Crimefighters, former superhero trainer, and current CEO of Lord Steele Consulting, LLC, a special advisor to the President of the United States on matters related to super-powered vigilantes.

And my latest arrest.

"Howdy, Detective Garner," Opus, the guard, says. And yes, that's his real name. Turns out, his last name is Holland, and his parents really liked the movie *Mr. Holland's Opus*. So, yeah. You get it.

"Hey, Opus. Here to do something really stupid."

"No," he says.

I nod slowly. "I need to see the Baron."

"He's gonna kill you."

Still nodding, I say, "Yep. Just let me in and let me get this over with."

"It was nice knowing you," Opus says as he buzzes me in.

I walk into the block. The walls are lined with three cells on each side, all filled with those who broke the CVT laws and are awaiting trial to likely be sent to the Trench. At the end of the corridor, the most secure of all cells faces me. From behind the super-hardened plexiglass or whatever it is, Paul glares at me.

As you can imagine, he's not happy. He sits on the metal cot at the back of his cell, his eyes looking like they're going to jump out of his bald head and rip my throat out as soon as I get near enough.

"Well, well, well... if it ain't the man of the hour 'imself. You must be right proud just now, landing such a big catch. I'm sure it'll make quite the fish story once you're done embellishing your limited role in the whole affair. You come here to gloat?"

"Don't make this harder, Paul," I say, resting a forearm against the glass.

Faster than you'd think someone his size can move, the Baron bolts from his seat and slams both fists on the glass on either side of my head.

I leap backward, feeling like my throat just swallowed another throat.

He laughs. “Oh, poor boy can’t handle a little ribbing? What do you want, Garner?” He turns his back and slowly returns to his seat.

“Actually, I’m here to release you,” I say.

“What’s this rubbish?” He doesn’t stand, but he looks like he wants to.

I run my ID card through the card reader, opening the compartment that allows me to enter my nine-digit security code into the keypad, which in turn, opens an iris to reveal a lens. I place my eye against it, and the retinal scan begins.

“Confirmed, Detective Alexander Garner,” a computerized voice says.

It’s not the Trench, but they’re not messing around here, either.

The automatic locks on the cell door disengage and the bright lights dim as the power dampeners shut down.

“This some sort of joke, Garner? You takin’ a piss?” he asks.

“I wish. No, your buddy the president has ordered you to be released and sent to... Colorado, I think they said. They’re suspending the Anti-Vigilante Acts.”

“And why would they do that? It have something to do with all the commotion outside nobody will tell me about?”

“You could say that,” I confirm, opening the door.

Paul stays seated. “You know what, I kinda like it in here.” He leans back, getting more comfortable.

"Not an option," I say.

"Must be pretty bad. How 'bout the rest of them?" he asks, nodding toward the other cells.

I turn to see a bunch of nobodies poking their heads against the glass, watching us.

"Just you," I say which rouses the other prisoners to pounding on the glass and shouting.

He slaps his thighs, stands, and walks toward the open door. "You gonna be the one to clue me in?"

"It's not that big of a deal, Baron. Just the end of the world, that's all."

CHAPTER 5
SAWYER

Whoa.

The next thing I know, I'm on one of Frank's planes, bound for who-knows-where. I'm all alone, too, except for the pilots and the rest of my crew of escapees from the Trench, which makes me think maybe everyone else is already there and we're some kind of afterthought.

Or maybe Frank told them they couldn't use his planes unless they allowed me to be part of this. I haven't heard from him since I was taken to jail, and my calls since being out just go to voicemail. I assumed he must be part of this even before I saw the plane. *Daddy's* too busy trying to save the world to pay attention to me.

The story of my life.

Truth time? This whole situation is giving me PTSD. Last time I found myself alone in a moving vehicle, I was on my way to the Trench. And let me tell you: that crap sucked. Not recommended. 1 out of 5 stars.

I don't even know what I'm supposed to be doing. Are they just gonna stick me on a team with other heroes and toss us into battle against these aliens? They don't expect me to keep working with these people, do they? Especially Crosscircuit after the way he lied about having my mom killed by the Rifleman just to make sure I played along with his escape plan?

Without making it too obvious, I glance around at the others. Crosscircuit's eyes are locked on a tablet, engrossed in whatever it is genius, egomaniacal supervillains are interested in. Or maybe he's just checking like thirty years of email. I bet he still has an AOL account.

Sinsation is somehow sitting upside down with her legs folded over the back of her seat, snoring away. I don't think Justice has stopped goggling at her since they met. I can't really blame him—I mean, she's smoking hot. But she's also a psychopath—the kind of girl who would wear her partner's blood in a vial around her neck or something. Then again, Justice isn't exactly stable either.

Huh. Maybe they'd make the next golden Hollywood power couple.

He must sense my eyes on him, because he quickly averts his attention to the seat-back in front of him. Now I'm intrigued—and pretty bored. I continue watching while he stares at nothing. I wonder if he's one of those people with no inner monologue. Even without one of Frank's crazy AIs in my helmet, I can't turn off the voice inside my head. But I read that some people just don't have that at all. They just... stop thinking about stuff, I guess. Like a computer in standby mode.

Or maybe he's having deep thoughts, contemplating the meaning of life, the universe, and everything. What do I know?

Nah. He's probably just waiting for me to look away so he can go back to lusting after Sinsation. I give him what he wants.

It doesn't take long to locate Royal Rampage all the way in the back, taking up an entire row of seats with the armrests up. Sometimes I have to remind myself he's not a cute pet. I smile a bit as he watches out the window in fascination. It may be his first time on a plane.

Back to Justice, still absently staring. Weird guy.

I can't believe I let it slip that I'm related to Frank. I'm still trying to figure out how to handle the whole question of whether he's my half-brother. I just don't see any other way he could have the same abilities Frank and I do. He didn't know who his father was, which is another clue. Even if I bring it up to Frank, there's a chance he doesn't even know. In fact, if I had to bet, I'd say he doesn't. He didn't know about me until one of my mom's ex-boyfriends—a sleazebag lawyer—tried to blackmail him over having an illegitimate kid. How would Frank react if I *did* tell him? Would he take him on and train him the way he did me? Even knowing that Justice is a murderer?

I mean, he only killed criminals, but that doesn't make it okay. I don't know what kind of research he did before offing any of those people, but I'm guessing it wasn't all that extensive. In fact, I know some of those he shot down in cold blood were probably just guilty of robbing a bunch of rich people at a fundraiser. At least that's their only crime I know about.

Although, Frank has killed a couple of times himself, so maybe he'd be somewhat forgiving. Sometimes he surprises me, even after knowing him all these years.

"Hey," someone says, snapping me out of my thoughts, and making me jump in my seat.

Apparently I'd been staring into space just like Justice had been—enough so that he'd gotten up and slid into the seat beside me without my noticing.

"Uh, hey," I say.

"Didn't mean to scare you, bro."

Bro. I wonder if he has any idea how weird that is for him to say.

"You didn't scare me. I was just—"

"Yeah, pretty boring up here. Not even one of those TVs in the headrest. At least Sinsation is fun to watch."

I snicker awkwardly. I've never been one of those guys who can easily talk about women, especially like this.

"Yeah." Not an elegant response, but I'm not sure what else to say.

"So, I wanted to talk to you about something," Justice says, lowering his voice.

Crap. Here we go.

"That stuff Chen was saying—you know, about Frank Douglas having the ability to like... memorize stuff?"

I nod slowly.

"And you said he's your family..."

It's not a question. It's not even a complete sentence, I don't think. But it gets the message across loud and clear.

"My dad."

"Your... dad?" Justice repeats softly. Then he says a word reserved for M-rating shows on Netflix. "That's insane. Okay, listen. Hear me out, okay? This might be crazy."

Now I'm just waiting for him to get to the part where he catches up.

"So, I don't know who my dad is, right? What if like... what if we're... cousins or, you know, whatever. Like where we have the same dad but with different moms?"

I almost laugh. "That would make us half-brothers."

"Half-brothers? Wait, for real? Like actual brothers?"

"*Half*... Half-brothers."

"Wow... brothers," he whispers.

This guy is thicker than a Kardashian.

"But still. That would be amazing." He looks away, and I follow his gaze to see Sinsation getting up, and apparently, Justice can't resist the urge to watch, even in the middle of such an important conversation.

"It's possible," I say, redrawing his attention.

"You think so? Man... I never had family." He pats me on the leg, then stands. "We'll talk more about this later, okay?"

Without another word, he goes and slides in beside Sinsation, crosses his leg, puts an arm behind her, and they start talking. Or more Justice talks *at* her.

I watch him for a couple of seconds before staring down at my hands folded in my lap.

Family. Yikes. I'm honestly not sure how I feel about the idea of him being family.

Then again, none of this may matter anyway. We're in the middle of an alien invasion, and if the Tuldarians can take out Eaglestar, they can take out anyone. No wonder they're scrapping the Anti-Vigilante Acts and gathering all of us together. Masked crimefighters are probably the only ones on Earth who have even the slightest chance of holding these creatures at bay.

Chen didn't wanna tell me where we were headed, so I had to practically drag it out of him. Apparently, there's a special bunker buried deep in the highest Rocky Mountains in Colorado, where they hide the president and other important people in these end-of-the-world kinda scenarios. They're taking us there despite the fact that all of us escapees from the Trench—myself included—are considered highly dangerous criminals. That tells me that, number one, they must be really worried, and number two, they don't think the Guild can handle the situation on their own.

And that scares the hell out of me.

CHAPTER 6
SEAN

All-righty, then.

Our plane arrives at its destination shortly after daybreak without any further explanation as to our whereabouts. I know I am the one who assembled this little motley crew, but I hadn't intended for it to be a long-term thing. Now, I'm stuck with a couple of barely-out-of-their-teens boneheads, a giant primate, and an—albeit gorgeous—mental case.

So, where are we?

I deduce that it has to be North America since we didn't cross a large body of water. Coupled with the sun having set on the left side of the aircraft—I'm confident it isn't South America. Taking average airspeed of a jet such as this and the number of hours traveled, I'm certain we haven't crossed borders.

And, since it wasn't the Canadian prime minister who sent someone to pick us up, I figure it has to be the good old US of

A. Large mountains I presume to be the Rockies loom in the near distance as we touch down on a snow-covered runway that's barely long enough to entertain a stop. The scenery is certainly beautiful at any rate, if a bit unforgiving.

As a kid—I was never a typical kid, mind you—my parents let me fly to Colorado for a few days. I was about nine. My father had to work, and my mother had a violent aversion to the cold. I'm sure I was the only nine-year-old in history to be allowed to travel across the country and hike the Colorado mountains. Those were the days when I was quite a bit more physically active.

That trip taught me a valuable lesson—one I would never forget. Always know your surroundings. It could mean the difference between life and death. Furthermore, that sentiment continues to encompass those you find yourself in the company of.

To that point, I've been thinking about whom I might be meeting with. I'm sure they're not just sending supervillains here if it's such an urgent crisis, so undoubtedly the Guild of Masked Crimefighters will be in attendance as well. I'm not sure about their sidekicks, but I calculate the chances at being more likely than not. We'll probably need all the help we can muster, and these men and women are more like gods and goddesses. They've saved the world more times than most could count. One thousand, two hundred, twenty-seven times.

I said *most*—I am not most people.

I want to be honest and transparent about everything so the record firmly plants me on the side of those who once again saved the world. And this time, from the greatest threat it has ever known.

After all these years, it's finally time to execute my plan. So, as much as I hate to admit it, I'm somewhat nervous.

Who wouldn't be?

"All right, everyone," Luis Chen says, rising from the co-pilot's chair and taking off his over-ear headphones. "We're here."

"And where *exactly* is here?" I ask.

"You'll find out soon enough."

"I'd prefer to find out now."

Chen acts as if I've said nothing at all as he cracks open the cabin door and debarks the plane. It appears there are other individuals already present, and they've already rolled a staircase into place. I know this not because I can see, but because I didn't hear him scream as he fell and splattered on the ground. I'm the first to follow, noticing two soldiers standing on either side of the rolling staircase, eyes forward and locked on one another instead of us. In their hands... you guessed it. Automatic rifles.

One step outside and I'm hit with a wall of frigid air that I haven't prepared myself for. I—like my mother—never liked the cold, which is why I hiked these mountains in the summer. I certainly don't envy the soldiers.

Chen doesn't even spare a look behind him as he's met by a posse of suited men. I'm certain they're bureaucrats from the upper echelons of the United States government—probably mostly Department of Defense and State Department—

and perhaps a few representatives from various allied nations.

I feel a brush against my shoulder, turning in time to see young Harrier rushing to catch up. Fool. Doesn't know when he's unwanted. You'd have thought years of being ignored by one's father would clue one in to such details. I know it had that effect on me.

I descend the steps at a nominal pace, showing that I feel neither rushed nor excited to be here. *They* need *me*, after all. I realize I still require some sort of transportation and support to make it to Egypt alive, but once there, I'll most certainly be flying solo, so to speak. If only I can convince them that all of these other preparations are going to be meaningless once my plans reach fruition.

This entire planning session should consist only of figuring out the most expedient way to safely get me to where I need to go. The rest is merely a colossal waste of time and energy, of which we have no extra at this juncture.

I follow a small cavalcade to the base's hidden entrance and suddenly find myself panicked at the thought that maybe this is all some elaborate ruse. Perhaps this is actually a high-security fortress to hold super-powered beings, something even more secure than the Trench, and I'm being willingly led back to my own imprisonment. Considering it's a supposed meeting of super-powered crimefighters, there is certainly a dearth of such people around. Armed guards crawl around like little ants, protecting whatever queen awaits us inside.

Their rifles seem to be fairly normal—nothing that could

stop someone like Eaglestar or even Harrier. I don't believe I've ever seen a single member of the Guild thwarted by any such weapon. That, if nothing else, gives me the confidence I need to place one foot before the next and fall in line.

I can't help but wonder, though: is my further incarceration more important to them than my assistance? They need my robots—and thus, me—to fight off this invasion. Surely they realize that by now.

That triggers a new fear. What if the president is afraid I am going to discover—or have discovered—something he had done or was planning to do, and is rounding up all the superheroes to prevent us from taking action against him? I haven't been vocal about my politics, such as they are—and the idea of debasing myself by participating in such nonsense as "social media" makes me want to vomit. But I haven't exactly hidden my opinions, either.

Many years ago, when I was known as nothing more than a boy genius, I was invited to participate in the television show *Jeopardy*. A live special! A raise-money-for-charity type airing where normal people were invited to compete against me in hopes of... I don't know what any of them hoped for. There was no chance they'd win.

During one of the supposed commercial breaks, I was shown a pretty famous picture of the president at the time, kissing that baby on the Oprah show—you know the one that was four months old and could already count to six... By the way, I was speaking sentences by my fourth month... Anyway, the president was kissing the baby, but it looked more like he was whispering in its ear. I was asked to "caption this photo" as a way of entertaining the crowd during the break.

I said, "Get out of here, you're making me look stupid."

Turns out, they decided to air that part of the show in syndication. Groups of what I could only call "loyalists" picketed in front of our apartment, while others approached me on the streets to thank me.

I wonder if President Stanford is afraid of something like that.

I decide it's unlikely. I've been allowing my thoughts to go off the rails, so I decide to stop worrying until I know if there's something to fret about.

Paranoia. Not a fun trait to have. But it would be ludicrous to believe that my past wouldn't result in a well-founded skepticism about whose side I'm on. And I know I have to be careful not to be put back into a cage.

I give the place a once-over as we approach a massive steel door inset into the side of the mountain face. Luis Chen does what his type does best and gains us access through a series of protocols. When the door opens upward into the rock, warmth comes rushing out, enveloping me like a cozy blanket. Feeling returns to my extremities, and I begin to calm down, absorbing it like a junkie.

The others catch up, followed closely by the soldiers who'd stood by as we exited the plane. Even more armored men approach us from within.

"What is this place?" Justice asks no one in particular.

"Ms. O'Hare," one of the soldiers says through some sort of filtered helmet as he approaches Sinsation.

She looks at him with contempt. "I don't know who you're talking to, but my name is Sinsation."

"The time for all that is past," the soldier says. "Please come with me."

Two more soldiers flank her, both wearing the same sort of headgear. Looks as if they've done their homework and have no intention of being seduced by the lovely Ms. Jessica O'Hare.

Sure, I knew her name. I know all their names. But just because one has power, doesn't mean one must always flaunt it.

Without much choice, Sinsation allows them to guide her toward an open door on the left.

"Hey! Where are you taking her?" Justice shouts.

"Mr. Garner," another of the men says, addressing Justice. This should be fun.

"Garner?" Harrier asks.

"Yeah, that's my last—"

"Please follow us," the soldier says. "I assure you, we mean you no harm."

"Yeah, I always wave guns around at people I mean no harm to," Justice argues. "Fine. Fine. I'll follow. Not like I've got anywhere else to be."

"Mr. Chen..." Harrier says, just the right amount of concern in his eyes.

Giving Harrier a look that says "we'll talk soon," Chen

says, “Sawyer, why don’t you come with me. I had that special surprise I’d mentioned delivered.”

They leave together, and I’m left in a room with a bunch of armored soldiers who I can only imagine would love to open fire.

“I’ll just wait here,” I call after them, sparing no amount of sarcasm.

Finally, the soldiers part and a man wearing a dark blue suit with an American flag pinned on the lapel strolls down the middle.

“Boss,” he says.

I wait for whoever his boss is to speak up, but the entire room remains silent. After a moment, I look around to see who could be causing the delay.

“Jharmel Frederick, U.S. Agent, reporting for duty.”

I finish looking around and realize he’s talking to me.

Boss.

That is a good sign. Or is it just part of the ruse?

He stops about a yard away and salutes like I’m some general.

“At ease?” It comes out like a question. I’ve always wanted to tell someone that, though. “Boss?”

“Those are my orders,” Agent Frederick says.

“Orders? From whom?”

Agent Frederick answers a question I didn’t ask. “Sir, I’m your military liaison for this mission. Each of the mission leaders has one. And I’ve read your file. You’re brilliant, sir. I’m glad I got assigned to you.”

"Assigned to me by whom?" I ask, rephrasing the question.

"I think it would be best if I show you. Just this way."

He leads me down a hall to another thick metal door.

Boss? Mission leader? If there's a game being played, I can't figure out what it is. But I still have no idea what mission he's talking about. I'm going to stop the aliens with my robots, and I don't need any help doing it.

The unnecessary suspense is bothersome at least, and annoying at best. I'm ready to jump in and save the day, and my robots are in Egypt, not Denver, or wherever we are. The world is having one of its greatest crises in history, and I'm going to be in charge of the very serious business of enacting the only plan which makes sense to stop it.

He opens the reinforced door, and we enter into a cavernous chamber. Several high-ranking officials mill about, and everyone turns toward us.

Here we go, I think. This must be the situation room where they're planning how to save the Earth.

While my eyes adjust to the bright lighting, my ears immediately perk up. Is that... live music I'm hearing? Country music?

I despise Country music.

I follow Agent Frederick in and I'm both shocked and dismayed by what I see. Heroes, military officers, and government officials standing around with drinks in their hands next to fully decked-out tables with formal dinner settings. What I assume to be a famous Country music star is performing with his band on stage—don't ask me who... I wouldn't be able to tell you if you put a gun to my head. If I'm not mistaken, I also see the former super-villain they call Battlegear standing nearby.

And the President of the United States of America is finishing up a conversation with Baron Steele.

"This is going to be great," he says, hands flying around like he's swatting flies. "The greatest planning session you've ever witnessed. It'll be fantastic. Believe me!"

Then the president sees me, and without even so much as taking a breath, he's jogging up to me with his arms outstretched.

"There he is. The man of the hour! My boy!"

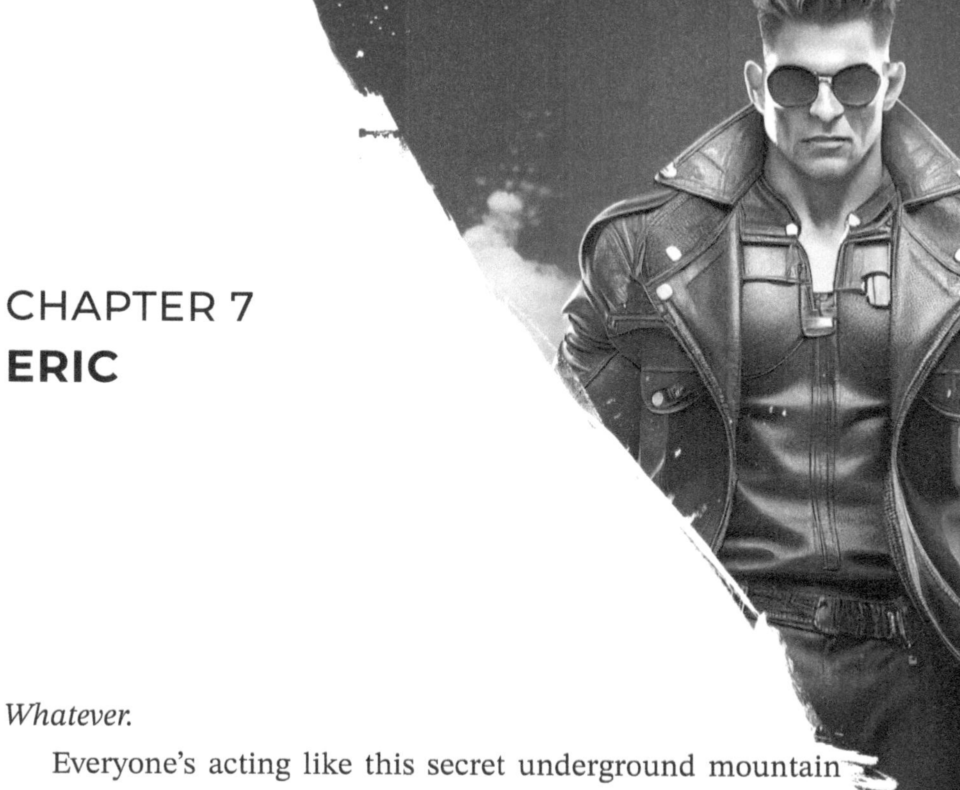

CHAPTER 7
ERIC

Whatever.

Everyone's acting like this secret underground mountain base is some big deal. Funded by the richest, most powerful government in the world with all the resources it wants at its disposal.

Pfffft.

After Eaglestar destroyed my house and my satellite base, I had a secret underground mountain base myself not so long ago, and I had to do it the hard way—fund it all on my own, draw up all the plans, and hire contractors who not only knew what they were doing, but also knew how to keep their mouths shut after they were done. I got the idea from some drug lord in New Mexico who'd built an underground meth lab that way. But that was small potatoes compared to mine.

Oh, and I think he had all the contractors killed after. Not me. I might've been a supervillain, but I've said it before, I'm not a murderer. Not me.

So, check this out...

Mine was a shining, high-tech fortress set into the side of a snow-capped mountain in Alaska, antennae and giant laser cannons jutting forth from its gleaming walls.

Don't worry. Lasers don't kill the person I'd intended all that for: Eaglestar.

Apparently, stupid lizard aliens do. Sad face.

Sigh. Back to the digs.

The light snow that fell most of the year would have given the scene the feeling of a Christmas card if it wasn't for the jarring angles of the metallic structure. But then my beautiful creation, the apex of my supervillain career, was destroyed.

By a woman.

But not just any woman. Anyway, I'll spill that tea later. Let me finish dishing on my pad.

Like my satellite, the control room was straight Gucci, filled with futuristic technology in sparkling chrome and vantablack. Haven't heard of it? Oh, man. It's what they call super-black, with total hemispherical reflectances below 1% in the visible spectrum...

I mean, it's dope, and I know chicks dig that look, so I always decorate that way. I heard Frank Douglas decorates that way, too, and his bodycount must be up there with the number of stars in the galaxy. Blinking lights lit the panels, some with purpose and others for show. I mean, most of the tech is touchscreen nowadays, but it doesn't look as dank.

There I was, my muscles bulging through my awesome black motorcycle leathers after working out in my personal gym. Quick shower, some Axe body spray, a little hair gel, a little more Axe, and this supervillain was down for anything.

I swiped through the controls as I monitored several giant video screens scanning for Eaglestar so I could continue to make his life miserable. It's the way I used to spend most of my days. He pretended to hate it, but I knew he'd have been bored without me to annoy him.

A metallic banging echoed throughout the fortress. I looked up at one of the monitors, then calmly stood and walked to the back of the room. I pushed my favorite button on a control panel and a section of the wall slid open to reveal a compartment full of weapons and special equipment. Pretty sure I chubbed. Usually do. Moving my goggles up onto my forehead, I peered into the compartment to find the perfect tool.

I started to grab one of the weapons, then pulled my hand back and stroked my chin, reconsidering. Classic supervillain pose. Should've taken a selfie. Bro, I could have the slappingest IG if I had the time. I moved a couple of steps to the right and snagged up a different weapon—bigger and more powerful-looking than my previous choice. Yeah, that one felt right.

The dissonant booms continued for another sec, followed by the sound of twisting, wrenching metal—then silence.

I pulled a lever and a small, transparent canister rose from a recess in one of the consoles. Once the steam faded—always gotta have steam—I saw the glowing, effervescent liquid inside. I opened the side chamber of my weapon, then carefully inserted the canister, closed it up, and pumped it like a shotgun. Second Amendment, bitches.

The weapon glowed and emanated a low hum. I love that part. I could easily make it quieter, but why? Just like the ladies, I make my weapons scream, yo.

I grabbed the black cloth from a nearby workstation and yanked it down over my head—the mask that covered most of my face, even though it didn't matter—then replaced my goggles. I waved my hand over a control panel next to the door and popped through when it opened.

In the center of the next room was a huge, round conference table with several high-backed chairs positioned around it. A different sinister logo adorned each one, some containing stylized letters, others with animals or symbols. I prefer the pointiest fonts I can find. TBF, I got the idea from the Guild. Look, they're losers at the end of the day, but that doesn't mean they don't have some fine ideas. Even a broken clock is right twice a day, you know?

These were the places where my *compadres* were gonna sit once I invited them to my new crib, to make up for the satellite base that had been destroyed due to a... minor miscalculation on my part. I'd given Eaglestar a little too much intel while monologuing, and they all ended up in the hospital, and then prison. But I already had a plan to bust them out before their trials so they wouldn't end up in the Trench.

I approached a chair emblazoned with a large, stylized "B"

—the one with the highest back and pointiest font, of course —and scooted it over so it directly faced the enormous steel door at the other end of the room. The perfect spot. I sat and attempted a menacing pose. After a second, I tried another, and then a third. This had to be just right.

Just as I settled into my best James Hetfield meets Rob Zombie pose, the door to the meeting room slammed to the ground with a tremendous crash and slid along the floor. Ouch. That was gonna cost a nest egg to replace.

In the doorway stood the drippiest, most gorgeous dark-haired woman in maroon spandex. She strolled in with confidence, her cape billowing behind her. After all, she was the most powerful supervillain in the world. And my on-again-off-again girlfriend.

"Battlegear." Her voice was silk. And British. Or Australian. I can never remember. Either way, it made me feel a certain kind of way. IYKYK.

I waited a beat for effect. And to show I wasn't fronting, despite the fact that she was basically a scaled down, gender-swapped version of Eaglestar. And don't read anything into that...

"Annihilatrix. How nice of you to stop by."

She approached the table nonchalantly. "I was in the neighborhood. Surely you heard me knocking."

She picked up one of the chairs with one hand and hurled it at my head without an ounce of effort. One step ahead of her, I tapped a button on the arm of my chair. The spring-loaded seat cushion sent me soaring high enough to execute a flip before making a perfect landing in the center of the table. I really wish I had it on video. It would have *killed* on TikTok.

"Yes, I apologize for making you wait," I said. "I was a *little* distracted."

I pulled the trigger on my super-weapon, which had been designed to fight Eaglestar himself, and it fired a blast of energy at my old bae. She sidestepped the sizzling stream of light almost faster than my eyes could follow her.

"I hope you don't mind that I let myself in." She leaped at me with blinding speed, but was rebuffed by an invisible force-field that caused her to ricochet across the room. She stood up, slightly dazed. "Huh. That's new."

With a flick of my thumb, I changed the settings on my weapon. "You know me. I always like to have a surprise planned when you drop by for some Netflix and chill." I shot again, this time with a wider beam that almost zapped her. She barely managed to avoid the blast.

Annihilatrix scoffed. "You always did need a bigger weapon to take care of me."

I tried to hide the fact that the comment stung a little. "That's funny. I seem to remember leaving you out of commission on more than one occasion."

Annihilatrix chuckled. "Sorry, I faked it so you didn't feel bad. You obviously put a lot of effort into it."

This time I found it harder to hide my feelings, but knew I had to keep up the banter to save face. "Then you must be a hell of an actress."

"I deserve a bloody Oscar!" Annihilatrix shot beams of red

energy from her eyes. They were less than half the power of Eaglestar's but definitely packed a punch. My forcefield absorbed the impact, but it was quickly starting to fade. "How could you think I wouldn't find out about you and my sidekick?"

I adjusted some controls on my utility belt, but my personal energy shield continued to weaken. "I didn't think you'd mind. You seemed to be tired of sparring with me yourself."

Annihilatrix's eye beams increased in intensity as pinkish smoke started to appear along with the smell of ozone. "And that makes it okay for you to go at it with her?"

"Well, she was certainly willing to give it a shot." I started to feel better as I felt the conversation begin to tilt in my direction. "And let me just say, willing to do *a lot* more than you were."

Anni—that's what I call her—didn't try to hide her anger anymore. "She had no idea what she was getting herself into. She felt humiliated when she came back to the lair."

"Well, maybe if you were up for it more often, it never would have happened."

Burn. Am I right?

My forcefield finally fizzled out, and a blast from her eyes threw me hard into the wall behind me. My gun went flying from my grip, and my mask came partially off my face. It's fine. She's seen my face plenty.

Plenty.

"Oh, don't worry, *Eric*. It's never going to happen again. With either of us."

Anni picked up my weapon and bent it with her bare hands until sparks flew and the hum died. Ugh. That was even more expensive than the security door.

I couldn't help myself despite the danger. "So I guess a three-way tangle is out of the question?"

Her fist flew toward my face.

I woke up in the hospital, wondering how long I'd been out. When I tried to move, I realized I was in a full-body cast.

Oh, well, I remember thinking: *This should give me plenty of time to plan my next scheme for winning her back.*

I never did, though. She ended up falling in love with her sidekick herself and quitting the game altogether. Wasn't meant to be, I guess. At least I know it wasn't me.

I never did get to rebuild my fortress, though.

CHAPTER 8
SAWYER

Awkward.

It couldn't have been more uncomfortable for me had I been standing naked on the stage in front of the leader of the free world, the joint chiefs of staff, and practically every masked crimefighter who was still alive and able-bodied. Black Harrier operates in the shadows. That's just how it's always been. Sure, when I was younger, I didn't mind going out in my costume in public so much during the day, but I still haven't gotten used to the fact that I'm the big cheese now—the man himself, and not just some sidekick.

With Eaglestar dead—something I can hardly fathom—Black Harrier is *the* world's most famous hero. The way everyone stared at me when I walked in—probably since they knew I had been arrested not so long ago—made me feel like a kid in a Halloween costume pretending to be someone much bigger and badder than I really was.

My time with Mr. Chen had been short. He pulled me into another small room and handed me a brand-spanking-new Harrier suit.

I know there's a lot going on, but I am floored by this uniform. And yeah, this is a uniform, not a costume. Finally, someone really took the time to *get* the motif. The new helmet is all black and shaped like a bird beak. Okay, it sounds a little dumb when you say it like that, but, trust me, it's menacing.

You ever see the masks those old plague doctors wore? It looks a bit like that. Sure to strike fear into the hearts of bad guys—or aliens. In this case, it works extra well, since birds and lizards are natural enemies. And guess who's the predator?

The eyes glowed orange, just two little beads instead of that awkward motorcycle-style helmet. And somehow, I can still see my whole HUD without it impairing my vision.

Before Chen left, all he said was, "We'll talk. Not now, though."

"Does Frank know?" was all I could get out before the door slammed shut behind him.

I never got an answer.

How does someone act so nonchalantly about the information I'd just been given? Justice is... what, Alex's brother? Actual-actual brother? And that makes...

Is Alex my half-brother, too?

No, I don't think that makes sense.

So many thoughts are still blazing through my brain as I amble aimlessly through a room filled with super-important people. Just what I need—to be wandering around in a daze with the fate of the world at stake.

The guy who was responsible for me escaping the Trench, Crosscircuit, stares me down. Who the heck is he to look at me that way? I did what he asked and helped him get out. If anything, I should be the one staring *him* down after he threatened to have my mom killed if I didn't go along with his plan. Just because it turned out to be a ruse doesn't mean I should all of a sudden be okay with it.

I glare back at him, though with my helmet on, he wouldn't know. I have half a mind to stick my tongue out at him, but I'm not a kid anymore. Besides, the beak would cover it... Maybe I should just go punch him.

Then I realize he isn't even looking at me as the President of the United States walks right past me on a beeline to Crosscircuit.

They have a brief conversation where the president seems way too excited to be talking to Crosscircuit, then they walk off together. That's when I spot Frank standing in the corner with a drink in his hand, as usual. He takes a big gulp of his Scotch as soon as he sees me approach, removing my helmet and tucking it under my arm.

"I see you got the invitation." He stops a waiter and places his empty tumbler on the guy's tray, then motions for another drink. The waiter looks at me and I shake my head and wave him off.

"You could say that. Go risk your life to save the world, or we'll disappear you back to the Trench, for good. Not much of a choice there."

"Well, look at it as a chance to put on the suit one last time and go out with a bang. Speaking of putting the suit on, that's snazzy."

I guess we're just gonna make believe everything is fine between us and he didn't just stand by while I got thrown to the sharks. Memories of my actual fights with Bullshark pop into my head, making me shudder.

"Yeah, Chen made it for me."

I consider telling him Mr. Chen has been a sellout spy this whole time, but I'm not sure I'm ready for that long a conversation just yet.

The silence carries on, and I don't handle awkward silences very well.

"How's Mom doing?" I ask with the tact and speed of a machine gun. I clear my throat and try again. "Is Mom doing okay?"

Frank sighs. "As well as can be expected. She's still confused about the whole situation and what part you played in it. Which is by design, of course. Also..."

Suddenly things get even more awkward and I'm not sure why.

"Also what?"

"After my run for mayor fell apart, I sort of went off the rails."

"Fell apart? What did I miss? I was... sort of otherwise detained."

He offers a very small smile, then shakes his head. "I guess after what happened to you, I just didn't have the heart anymore."

"So this is my fault?" I blurt out.

He presses two hands to the air like he's trying to calm me down. "I didn't say that, Sawyer. It was my fault. Me. I'm the only person alive who could have stopped it and... I didn't."

He didn't exactly say "I'm sorry," but that could be the best apology I've ever heard from Fra—

"And for that, I'm sorry."

I stand there stunned. Mouth open.

"You don't have to say anything. I'll be happy if you ever find it within you to accept my apology."

I didn't think my jaw could unhinge more, but it does. I'm glad I took off my helmet. I didn't know there was enough room in there for my mouth to open this wide.

"I did some soul-searching after that," he continues. "And I decided to make some changes."

I look at the drink in his hand, and assume that's not what he's referring to.

I try to talk, but it comes out hoarse. "What kind of changes?"

"I had a long talk with your mom." He looks down at his shoes. "We're... back together. In fact, I gave her a big, fat ring and asked her to marry me."

WHAT?

"I'm sorry." *Two* apologies! "I probably should have talked to you before—"

I grab his hand and shake it. Then I decide it deserves a hug, so I pull him in. I feel tears well up in my eyes. "Sorry? That's the best news I've heard in a long time. Mom's been miserable since you broke up, and you didn't seem to be at your best either."

"That's an understatement. We belong together."

"I assume she said yes?"

"She did." He nods and can't quite contain the smile he's trying to hide.

"Well, congratulations! I couldn't be happier. What'd you tell her about this whole thing?"

He waits to respond as the waiter appears again with a brand-new Scotch on his tray. "I told her the truth..." My eyes go wide as I try to process what he said until he clarifies it. He smiles. "... that the government had an emergency situation and they needed my expertise, so they brought me in as a consultant."

"Is that what they're calling you?"

He holds up his cane. "It's not like I can put on the suit. Plus, it looks damn good on you, son."

At the word "son," my eyes water up again. But I do my best Frank impression and make believe I have no feelings. "I thought that was pretty much for show these days."

It does seem like he's gotten worse again, however. I suppose the heavy drinking and lack of exercise for someone his age would do that.

"Mostly, I suppose. Besides, you're the Harrier they need. I have my place."

I shake my head, just overwhelmed by the number of *nice* things Frank is saying. It's so out of character. "So the deal they're offering me is real? If I hang up the cape after this is all over, then I don't have to go back to the Trench?"

He nods once, takes a small sip of his drink, and says, "Trust me, my attorneys made it ironclad."

"That's more of a relief than you can imagine. That place was awful."

"Again, I'm so—"

"It's fine, Frank. I'm fine." I dismiss his *third* apology with a wave. "Besides, there's something else I need to talk to you about—actually a lot of somethings—but I think they should wait until this crisis is over."

I'm sure it wouldn't be a good idea to bring up the fact that I think Justice is his son. He needs to be thinking as clearly as possible to coordinate this huge task. Not that the Scotch is helping with that.

"We can't talk about it now?" he asks.

"I don't think that would be a good idea."

"Later, then," he says, looking at me curiously.

I just look down and nod, not sure what else to say. "What about Alex? Where's he?"

Frank turns away, and his eyes narrow as he stares off at nothing in particular. "He won't be joining us."

"What? Why not? Isn't the fate of the world at stake here?"

"Alex is working with the CVT to do what they can in New York. He's not interested in being Redhawk anymore. Or Black Harrier. And certainly not Red Kite."

More than a little anger rises in me. "That doesn't matter. It sounds to me like we're gonna need anyone we can get for this—"

"Sawyer, why do you care? The guy threw you in jail."

I shrug. "He was just doing his job."

Did I really just say that? I guess I'm feeling pretty forgiving, all things considered.

He's suddenly exasperated. "Just—? Really, you're going to give him a pass that easily? If this mission hadn't come up, you could have been in prison for the rest of your life."

"And I forgave you, right?"

"I didn't throw the book at you!" I've rarely seen Frank this angry. I don't know how much of it is feeling protective of me and how much is his bruised ego over being betrayed by someone he used to treat like a son.

"Actually, I don't know if you heard, but thanks to Crosscircuit, I escaped just before the invasion happened."

"You *escaped* from the Trench?" he asks. There's something in his eyes that screams proud papa, but he quickly goes stoic again. "That's supposed to be impossible."

I shrug. "Turns out, not so much."

"Somehow they 'neglected' to inform me of that. Not a smart move, Sawyer. Do you want to be a wanted fugitive for the rest of your life?"

"I wasn't really given a choice," I spat.

"What's that supposed to mean?"

"That's one of the things we're gonna have to talk about later."

"Agreed. Although, I think there are some others you should have a talk with now." He gestures in the direction of a table where my old team, the Resistors, sits. They're all looking at me until I look back, then they pretend they're not.

"I have a feeling they don't have any interest in talking to me."

Frank finishes off his drink. "Choice isn't a luxury here either. They'll have to once they find out you'll be leading them on this mission."

"Wait—what? I thought I'd be going on a mission with the people I escaped from the Trench with."

He flinches back like someone shot him. "Why the hell would you think that?"

"I don't know. After everything, it sort of made sense for some reason."

He pokes me in the chest. "It's you. There's no reason to give the job to anyone else. Not only are you the Black Harrier now, but you turned the Resistors into a team in the first place, and you led them already. It makes sense for you to lead them again."

"Wasn't Mac leading them, though?" I ask, looking around for Firefly.

"He's back with the Guild. For the moment, anyway. We're also concerned about a head injury he sustained recently—in more ways than one."

I look over at my old team again. "What if they don't want me back?"

"It's not up to them. The decision has been made."

"What am I supposed to do?" I ask. There's a tone in my voice that I hope he picks up on. I'm asking for something only he could provide: fatherly advice.

He puts a hand on my shoulder, leans in and looks me directly in the eye. "You're their leader." He pauses and takes another drink for dramatic effect. "Go lead."

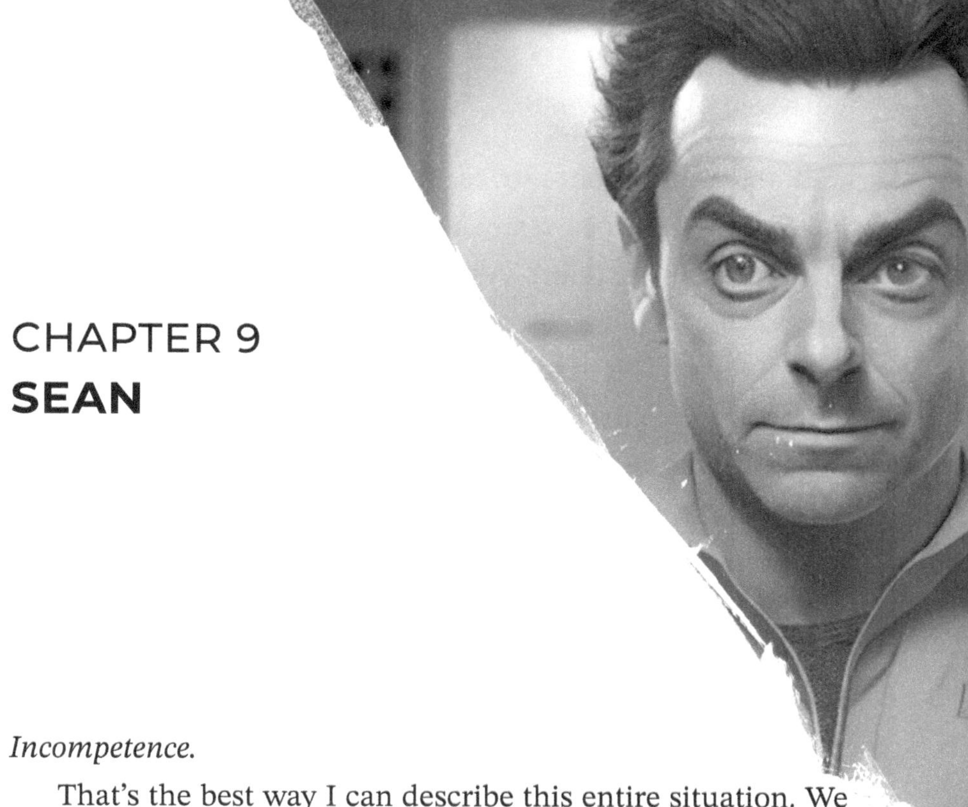

CHAPTER 9
SEAN

Incompetence.

That's the best way I can describe this entire situation. We should be planning our attack *now*, not tomorrow. And here's the most powerful person in the world telling me how much he loves the fact that I created all those robots.

"My people, they said I shouldn't trust you, you know. They said you were too evil, blah, blah, blah. But I knew I needed to bring you here as soon as I heard about you in the briefing. We need those robots of yours. I hear you've got the best robots."

"That I do, Mr. President. But I can't really control them without access to my main lab in Egypt."

"We know all about that. We have a plan—a good plan. Everything is set for you to go there as soon as your team is ready."

"My team?"

"Oh, yeah. Your strike force. We've got a team of international heroes ready to go. You're gonna love them. They're the best. South Africa, Puerto Rico, Sudan... everywhere. Global!"

He throws his hands out wide, and I'm not sure if he's gesturing or wants a hug. One hug is enough for me today, thank you, Mr. President.

"Will I, though?" My incredulity drips like sweat. "I don't love many people I meet."

"They won't be here until tomorrow, because—like I said—flying in from all over the world. And those aren't exactly friendly skies out there right now, if you know what I mean. Those dinos are shooting down anything they see in the air. We've all got some lucky stars somewhere that we made it here safely."

I can't even begin to figure out what that sentence means. But time is of the essence. "Do you think perhaps we should be preparing our plan now? I'm concerned about the irreparable damage that can be done in the time we spend..." I look around at all these world leaders and sycophants with their fluted glasses. "... waiting to begin."

"Plan? What plan? Our plan is ready to go. We're just waiting for everyone to get here, and we wanna make sure everyone gets a good night's sleep. We'll be fresh and ready to roll tomorrow, bright and early."

How does one argue with the president? I'll show you.

"This is foolishness. While the world burns, we are all imbibing alcoholic beverages and listening to loud country and western music. If sleep is what's needed, then get everyone into bed."

"Ah, I was told you were a bit of a fireball. I like it. I like it a lot. Like me when I was your age." He puts his hand on my shoulder. "The thing you've gotta realize, Sean—can I call you Sean? Of course I can. I'm the leader of the free world. See, Sean, most of these people are probably gonna die in the next couple of days fighting these aliens. I hate to be a neggy-nancy, but that's just the way it is. I've seen all the intel. We've got the best intel. You should see the PowerPoint. The bullet points. It's good stuff. Smart people made them."

I want to remind him that I am the smartest person in this room, but he won't shut up.

"What I'm trying to say is these aliens mean business and they're not pulling any punches. The least we can do is make these fine folk's last night enjoyable before sending them off."

This is one of those moments where I wish I understood sympathy the way some people do. But since I don't...

"Mr. President, this isn't World War II with slow troop movements and deployments via trucks and ships. You're giving these people the Bob Hope special while we're talking about enemies who can be anywhere on the planet within hours—minutes in most cases. *Any* delay is going to be followed by massive casualties."

President Stanford let out a long sigh. "Wow, I thought I was gonna like you. Boy, was I wrong. Hey, good luck working with your team. If you'll excuse me, I think I'm gonna go get a selfie with Bastet." He makes an "okay" gesture, and nods. "She's a smoke-show. Amirite?"

On that eloquent note, the most powerful man in the world walks away with his entourage in tow, leaving me to figure out how we are possibly going to stop an alien invasion with people like that in charge.

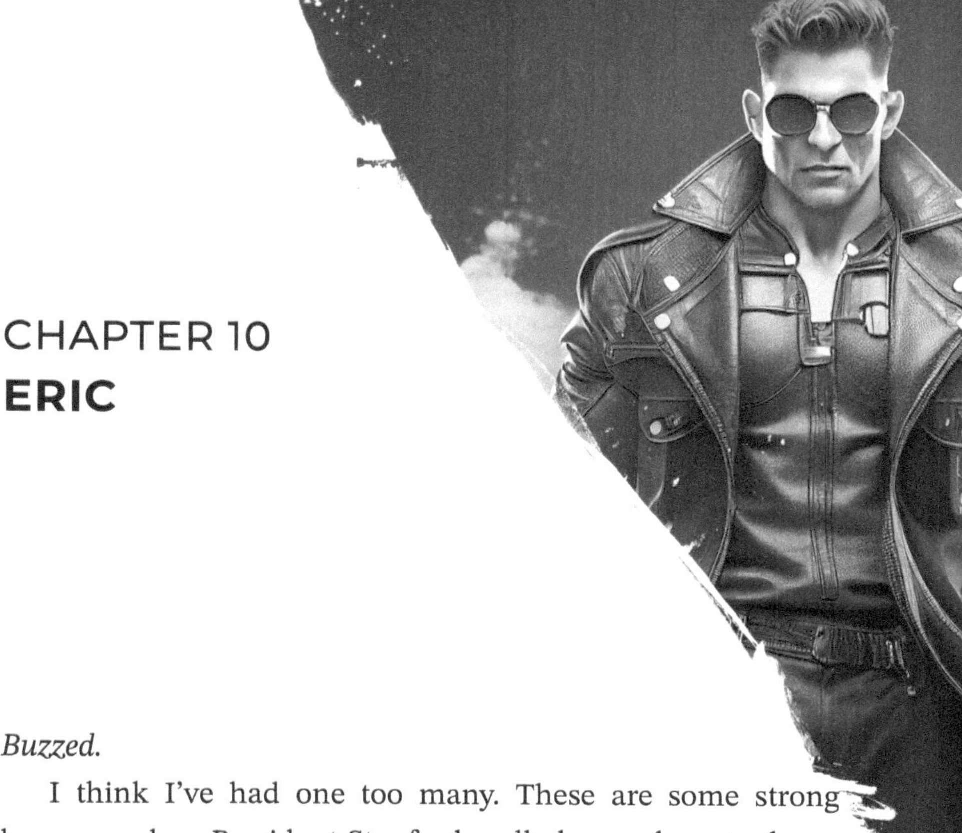

CHAPTER 10
ERIC

Buzzed.

I think I've had one too many. These are some strong beverages, bro. President Stanford really knows how to throw a party. Plus, I drank on the plane over. And did those shots every time a waiter walked by with a tray. I'm almost to that "out-of-body experience" phase at this point. Why shouldn't I be? I volunteered for a suicide mission. I'm gonna live it up tonight. If Tomorrow Me doesn't like it, he can suck it.

Standing in the corner, I scope out the scene. Could be my last night on Earth if we leave tomorrow to go fight these things. Is this how I wanna be spending it?

Who am I kidding? Like I really have a choice, right? If I was back home, I'd be scrolling through all my streaming services trying to figure out which show to start binging next. I haven't had a date in... I don't even wanna figure it out. And nobody wants to hang out with me.

God, I'm pathetic.

I thought maybe Alex Garner and I were starting to hit it off—as friends, you know?—but it was probably mostly in my head, just like my relationship with Eaglestar.

Oof. Just thinking his name feels like a gut punch. What am I gonna be without him? First he was my nemesis, then my boss. Was he ever *actually* my friend?

Don't fool yourself, Eric.

So are they even gonna have a funeral? I guess it depends on whether or not there's a world left when this is over with.

If they do, I'm gonna talk. When the priest dude or chick or whatever they have running the thing asks, "Does anyone have anything they'd like to say?" I'm getting up. First person. I've got a lot to say. Some of it, they won't like, but I don't care. That guy was the reason I got into the villainy game. He was also the reason I got my act together and became something legit.

While everybody here is partying it up, I'm standing here wondering how these people can be so ungrateful. Eaglestar was the reason *they* were who they were too. Now, none of us is anyone. Our names don't matter. Our powers are just a weapon to be trained against enemies we have no chance of defeating.

They killed Eaglestar. *Eaglestar!*

Who knows, maybe they're thinking the same thing I am: better enjoy it while we can, because soon we could all be dead.

Wow, that's depressing. Maybe I can hook up with one of these hotties tonight in a "last day on Earth" scenario.

I raise my glass. "*Moritūrī tē salūtant!*"

Everyone just gives me a look like I'm crazy. Oops, I'm letting my smarts show. That happens when I'm drunk. Can't let anyone know I had three semesters of Latin in college now, can I? Wait, what do I care?

"*Those who are about to die salute you*!" I shout. "That's... what it means."

Still nothing. Probably nobody heard me. It's loud in here with that honky-tonk garbage blasting from the speakers. Who listens to this redneck crap? Who *likes* this redneck crap? I guess highfalutin government officials and military bigwigs aren't metalheads. This band has to know something decent, though.

"Freeeee Biiirrrrrd!" I yell at the top of my lungs, holding up my beer. Nope. No response other than a few annoyed stares. How dare they be annoyed at me? I'm Battlegear, dammit! Eaglestar's arch-neme-meme-seme-sis.

Is that word always so hard to say?

I burp.

"Excuse me," I say to the waiter who just stares at me and keeps going.

Eaglestar. Every time I think about him being dead, I'm shocked all over again. Not gonna cry. Not gonna cry. I need to distract myself.

I should take a stroll around the room. Who knows?

Maybe some of these shorties are desperate. But the ratio in here is *not* promising. The hero biz is a real sausage fest. Or maybe women are just too smart to constantly risk their lives.

Then, I see her from across the room—my ex, Annihilatrix. Looking as hot as ever. Better, actually. Or maybe it's the beer goggles. I thought she retired. I guess that doesn't really matter when it could be the end of the world.

I wonder why her girlfriend, Torturess, isn't with her. Maybe they broke up. Bummer for her.

Hey, wait... *maybe they broke up*. That means she could be on the rebound.

I look around for a mirror to make sure I look good. Not a single mirror in sight. But there's a spoon on the table next to me. I reach over some woman wearing what looks like peacock feathers in her hat and steal her spoon.

"I'll give it back," I slur.

"Please don't," she says, but I'm already focused on smoothing down my hair. What am I worried about? I always look good.

I toss the spoon down, then take a deep breath.

Play it cool, Eric.

While walking casually in her direction, I pretend not to see her. As I get closer, I watch out of the corner of my eye. I'm about to run into her, and then, suddenly, she's not there.

I feel a tap on my shoulder, and spin. There she is. More accurately, there's her fist.

Pow!

She socks me in the kisser and I go down to the floor. Everyone around us is staring, but with the loud music, most people in the room didn't notice.

"I told you to stay away from me," she says, hand on her hip. God, she's sexy when she's pissed.

"Wait—what?" I say, rising. "I didn't even see you th—"

"Shut up, idiot. You were so bloody obvious. You might be good at a lot of things, Eric, but acting isn't one of them."

"You think I'm good at stuff?" I rub at my jaw, still struggling to stand fully.

"I saw you coming from a mile away and knew immediately what you were up to."

The room is spinning. One piece of advice: getting sucker-punched while drunk isn't fun.

"Okay, okay. It's been a while, so I thought I'd pretend to run into you. You know? See how you're doing."

She can definitely still pack a wallop. Not too many people around who can put me down that way.

She crosses her arms. "I don't want to talk to you. I didn't then, I don't now, and I won't at any point in the future."

"Got it. Loud and clear. I just figured since Torturess wasn't with you, then maybe—"

She punches me again. This time, I topple against the wall.

"Hey! Stop that!" I shout. "It hurts!"

"It's supposed to hurt, moron."

"I was just asking about your—"

Her glare shuts me down faster than one of those new

Mac desktops. Especially how brightly her eyes are glowing. I don't need to get a blistering sunburn right before going off into battle.

"She isn't with me because she's been captured by the Tuldarians. That's the *only* reason I'm here."

"Captured? Whoa... that sucks. Sorry to hear that. Any idea why they'd want her?"

"Like you care," she snaps.

I go to reach for her hand, then think better of it. "Hey! I do care. C'mon. I'm not trying anything. Just... why her?"

Anni sighs. "Your government people think it's because of her mind control powers. They've captured a few others with telepathic and telekinetic abilities as well, like Mezmer and GreyWulfe."

"Mezmer? They can have him. That dude's a joke."

"He might be a joke, but if they can amplify his abilities exponentially more than that device he already uses, it could make things very difficult for us."

I swear and rub the back of my neck. "Yeah. I guess you're right. That could be bad news."

Mezmer isn't nearly as smart as I am, but while I focus mainly on destructive tech, he's got all kinds of dangerous stuff as well. He wears this helmet that looks like a colander. Sounds stupid, but it allows him to alter people's thoughts. However, it's restricted to people close by. Like, in the same small room.

But amplified mind powers? Yeah, difficult could be an understatement.

"I'll help you—"

"Do yourself a favor and stay far away from me," Anni cuts me off, then turns to walk away.

Gotta admit, I like to see her leave.

CHAPTER 11
SAWYER

Man up.

None of the countless times I've charged into battle against supervillains can compare to the long walk across the room to talk to my former teammates. My stomach starts to flop around and my chest tightens as I approach their table. You know, pretty much how I spend most of my life.

There they are—Osprey, Bash, Pace, and my ex, Neith. All eyes are on me, and it feels like they all have Eaglestar's laser vision.

All right, Sawyer. Be smooth. Be eloquent. You are the Black Harrier.

"Uh... hi." Brilliant start there. Just brilliant. If there's an award for "best greeting of old friends who haven't seen one another in a couple of years," I just nailed it.

Pace is the first to respond. He usually is. "Well, well, look who it is! The Black Harrier himself. What are you doing over here in the cheap seats, Mr. Harrier, signing autographs? Hey, Osprey, maybe he can sign your boobs."

"Don't be crude," Osprey says.

Bash laughs. "He said 'boobs.'"

The rest of the team remains silent.

"Look, I know I haven't contacted you guys since…" I trail off, trying to figure out where I'm going with this.

It doesn't matter, though, because Osprey chimes in to finish for me. "Since you abandoned the team you started and went off on your own?"

Gut punch.

"I just didn't want anyone else to get into trouble. After the incident. After the law. After… everything."

Neith finally looks at me just long enough to roll her eyes. Then, with her gaze back on the empty plate in front of her, she says, "Perhaps you should have given us the chance to decide that for ourselves."

I rummage through my brain for excuses. Defenses. Anything. But come up with exactly *nada*.

"Yeah, you're right. I should have." As the one member of the team I've had any real contact with in recent years, I look to Osprey for some help. She doesn't give me any. "Well, if it's any consolation, it landed me in the Trench."

They all look shocked. Other than Osprey, anyway. I'm sure she heard about it from her dad, Luis Chen.

"Wait," Bash says. "You mean the secret underwater prison where they stash supervillains?"

"Yeah, maybe not so secret, since everyone seems to know about it."

"I'd heard you'd been arrested," Neith says. "But I would never have thought they would put you in such a place."

She was actually there when the CVT came after me, but the Resistors disappeared when Justice and I got captured, and I never did get the chance to talk to her.

"I guess they let you out to help with all of this, huh?" Pace asks.

"Uh… sort of. I actually escaped." Part of me wants to puff out my chest, but the other part is sort of ashamed at the fact that I worked with evil supervillains in the act.

Bash spits out the gulp of soda he just took. "Bullsh—"

"You're joking," Osprey says, cutting him off. "Nobody escapes from the Trench. That's the whole point of it."

"Yeah, well, try telling it to that guy," I say, nodding in Crosscircuit's direction.

"Whoa, whoa. What's he doing here?" Pace asks. "Isn't he an old school supervillain? We fought his robots back when we were kids."

"You were there?" I ask, then realize that's totally beside the point. "But yeah. That's him. Crosscircuit. He was the only one who saw this invasion coming. Claims that was the whole reason for the robots and everything, to get everyone ready for it."

"Better ways to do that than destroying entire city blocks and gettin people killed, I bet," Pace remarks.

"Yeah." I nod. "But I still think we're gonna be happy to have him on our side, even if it's just this once."

"You think we can trust him?" Osprey asks.

"Oh, no way. No way," I say, shaking my head. "We shouldn't trust that guy as far as we could throw him."

"I could probably hurl him to New Jersey," Bash says, cracking his knuckles.

"Okay, fine. I wouldn't trust him as far as *I* could throw him," I amend.

"Yeah, that wouldn't be very far," Bash agrees.

"I suppose we'll find out soon enough," Neith says.

"How far he could throw him?" Bash asks.

Neith rolls her eyes again. "If we can trust him."

"Oh, right. I was confused. Sorry." Bash leans back and sips on what looks like a Sprite with a cherry in it.

Pace stands and walks around me in a circle, checking out my Harrier uniform. "That new costume's cool, but it don't look right on you, man. Red's more your color."

"To be honest, it doesn't feel right, either. I still haven't gotten used to it, even after all this time. It's almost like I'm a kid trying on my dad's suit."

Osprey smiles, but I'm not sure if she's warming up to the idea of me or just getting ready to land a verbal jab. "Well, that's pretty much what you *are* doing, isn't it?"

Ouch. I decide not to respond, because I'm not gonna win no matter what I say.

Bash joins us standing, and it's a reminder of just how big he is. The table wobbles a bit, knocking over an empty champagne flute. He flicks my helmet's beak. "But I bet you can really mess some punks up with that tech."

"It's definitely an upgrade. The, uh..." I turn back to make sure Frank can't hear me. "... bank account that comes along with it isn't too bad, either."

Neith shoves her seat out and stands. "If you are trying to impress us, it is not working." She storms off.

"Shoot. It's working on me," Pace says.

I must look really distraught, because Osprey seems like she actually feels sorry for me when she speaks up. "She just needs some time. She'll come around."

"Yeah, well, I wouldn't blame her if she didn't. What I did was pretty crappy."

Pace wraps his arm around my shoulders. "You ghosted her, dude. You ghosted her."

"He ghosted all of us." Bash crosses his arms to show he still hasn't completely forgiven me.

Pace laughs at him. "Get a grip, loser. It ain't the same thing, and you know it."

Bash shrugs and looks away. "It still hurts."

Pace creases his brow and mouths a silent "WTF?" to me.

I gently push Pace aside and make my way to Bash. I squeeze his massive freaking neck muscles in a bit of a massage. My hands look like action figure appendages next to him. "I'm sorry, guys. I really am. I thought I was protecting you all, but I should've given you a choice on whether to continue to be part of the team."

Bash spins around faster than you'd think someone his

size could. Scares the hell out of me, to be honest. I'm not sure if he's about to send me soaring through a wall or what. Instead, he grabs me in a bear hug, lifting me completely off the ground and somewhat smothering me. "That's all I needed to hear, bro."

My head starts to spin a little due to lack of oxygen until he finally puts me down.

A couple of other young costumed heroes approach the table. I recognize them right away as Black Frost and White Hot, a couple who have been partners since they were teenagers. I met them just before I was arrested. Behind them is a giant costumeless bespectacled man with hair like a lion's mane who I've met as well.

"Looks like with Mac off working with the Guild again they're combining the Resistors teams into one," BlaKat says.

"Is he still stuck in his giant form?" Osprey asks.

"Yes," White Hot says. "Apparently, he sustained a pretty serious head injury when that CVT goon slammed him to the ground. Now, he can't shrink back down. They're still trying to figure it out."

"Let me guess," I say. "Logan Andrews?"

"I have no idea," she responds. "But he's almost as big as Bash, and probably just as strong."

"Bull crap," Bash says.

"Yeah, sounds like Logan," I say.

I guess there's no need to bring up the fact that Logan was the bully who tormented me throughout high school and eventually became a supervillain. I found out he joined the

Marines and was used as a test subject by Battlegear in some kind of super soldier program before being assigned to Alex's taskforce. He's also the one who actually wound up arresting me, even though it was credited to Alex.

Black Frost speaks up. "Looks like the CVT is busy fighting aliens in New York now that we're legal for the time being."

"I don't know how this is gonna end," I say, shaking my head. "But I promise you all, I will do my best to lead in a way you can be proud of." I look at each of them in turn, wishing Neith was still there. "Resistors?"

Each of them looks around at one another now. Then, Osprey is the first to say, "Resistors."

Soon, they all echo the word.

I've got my work cut out for me. But then again, we all do.

CHAPTER 12
ALEX

Summer.

No, not the season between spring and fall. My kind-of-sort-of-ex girlfriend who almost got killed when I decided to save Amy from a collapsing building instead of her. I mean, I knew BlackFrost was saving her, but I still feel like I messed up, at least in her eyes. I think I did a pretty good job of explaining my way out of it, but she still broke up with me.

Sort of. Like I said.

Anyway, we left it up in the air while she thought about giving me another chance. And just when I was about to contact her to see what she's thinking and how she's feeling, the alien apocalypse happens. Maybe I should take it as a sign that it's not meant to be?

I know I'm supposed to be doing the cop thing right now with New York City in state of emergency along with the rest of the world, but I have to know if she's okay.

I guess I'm a little sentimental right now. I recently found out that Luis Chen knows where my brother is. We were separated in the foster system when we were young. Our parents had been caught in the crossfire of a mob hit, and that was the last I'd ever seen of him. Of course Chen couldn't be bothered to tell me *where* my brother was. Bastard.

The sky is filled with the alien mothership and a bunch of smaller ships zipping around shooting stuff. And the streets are crowded with dino-troops marching around and killing everyone they can. The very superheroes I've fought to lock up for the past year are doing what they're best at—further destroying the city.

No, that's not fair. They're all trying to save as many people as they can.

Luckily, those people are smart enough to stay hidden for the most part and I haven't seen too many fatalities. But I know it's only going to be so long before they start blowing up more buildings and causing mass destruction.

I'd been watching Summer on the news since. She's a damn good reporter. Last I saw, they had her on-location near the Statue of Liberty. That wasn't long ago. She was up in the torch because the network thought it would be a cool shot with the alien ships behind her. The torch is supposed to be off-limits to everyone except the National Parks Service Staff, but leave it to Summer to talk her way up there for a story. She'd barely started talking when the feed went down and the anchors in studio claimed "technical difficulties."

Then the entire channel went down.

I know it's nearly impossible to get across town, and even more difficult to get across the water to Lady Liberty, but I have to try. I have to show her that I'm worried about her safety.

And I have to know that she's okay.

Standing in front of the police headquarters, my first thought is to try to find a helicopter I can commandeer, but just as I'm scanning the sky, I see one taken down by a Tuldarian projectile. The aircraft careens into a building, erupting in a ball of flame and glass. It seems the skies aren't so friendly at the moment—in fact, they're probably the most dangerous place to be.

Fires are raging all over the city and increasing with all the explosions. Buildings collapse as the aliens fire their disintegration weapons at their foundations. Great plumes of smoke rise from a dozen blocks away, and an entire city block crumbles one skyscraper at a time like dominoes.

Desperate, I decide to attempt driving there. I hop into my CVT patrol car, wishing I'd opted for the SUV. I flip the siren on, and gun it... about ten feet before slamming the breaks when a yellow cab pulls out in front of me. I honk my horn, but this only causes the cabbie to lean out the window.

"What do you want me to do, fly?" he shouts.

I growl to myself, but he's right. No one is going anywhere fast.

Obviously public transportation is worthless at this point too.

"Thanks," I say to the cabbie, slapping his hood three

times as I run past him and toward the river. Battery Park is only, like, fifteen blocks away. I can make it there on foot.

I turn onto Liberty Street, gasping for breath, when a squad of alien soldiers appears.

The one in front shouts something, which honestly sounds more like a roar. Then, I almost die when they fire their weapons at me. A Nissan explodes or vaporizes behind me as I swerve into an alley behind a Japanese restaurant. I use the skills that served me so well as Redhawk to push myself off the dumpster and grab the fire escape ladder ten feet off the ground, then climb to the roof. I barely reach the top before the Tuldarians turn into the alley themselves. Apparently, they don't think to look up. Maybe their world doesn't have multi-level buildings. Or buildings at all for that matter.

Time for some good, old-fashioned parkour. I kong vault over an HVAC unit and land in a PK roll. *Ouch*. I'm out of shape after not doing it for so long.

I wonder if any of the ferries are still running—maybe loading up to try to get people out of the city. Then it hits me: the NYPD Harbor Unit. I bet I can get one of them to take me over to Liberty Island if I flash my CVT badge. I cut to the northeast, running and jumping along rooftops like I used to. It takes me a little longer than expected due to some buildings no longer being where they once were, but I finally make it to the water. Scanning the docks, I spot a police boat.

My lungs are burning and my heart is pounding as I approach the Harbor Unit cops and show them my badge. I'm so out of breath, I can barely get my words out. "I need... a ride... to Liberty Island. CVT business."

"Sorry, no can do," a cop with an annoying Jersey accent tells me. "We got our own emergencies to deal with." He hops onto the dock to grab some more supplies along with his partner.

I know it's totally wrong of me, but I can't help myself. As they're loading up their supplies, I untie the rope and hop onto the deck. Since they'd left the boat running, they don't even hear me or notice that I'm in the cabin until it's too late.

Screaming erupts behind me, and they drop all the supplies to run for my new stolen ride.

"You kiss your mother with those mouths?" I shout back as they yell profanities at me pulling away from the dock.

Frank taught me to drive or pilot pretty much any vehicle in existence when I was his partner. I can race a car like a Formula One driver and I'm like Evel Knievel on a bike. I can even pilot a plane or a helicopter in a pinch. However, believe it or not, Frank's not a big water guy. Therefore, I've never had much experience with boats.

It's not complicated, but it takes me a few seconds to get used to the controls. After torpedoing a large ferry, one of the smaller Tuldarian ships notices me and changes course to head in my direction. It fires weapons at me and I catch air in the wake of its missed attack. I swerve through the harbor, and a few more shots barely miss.

It's only about a mile and a half to Liberty Island, but it feels like I'm trying to outrace and outmaneuver the spaceship for hours. When I near the island, it becomes quickly apparent I have a huge problem. I have no idea how to dock this thing. So, instead of pulling in slowly, I pound it to high speed and bring the starboard side of the boat as close as I can to the docks, then dive off the side into the harbor.

Just in time, too. A Tuldarian weapons emission finally hits its mark, and even under water the resultant fireball nearly causes boils on my skin. After a few seconds, I pop above water to get a bigger breath. I make a mental note to apologize for making the police boat into an old Viking funeral ship. I dip back down and swim underwater for as long as possible in hopes I'll lose them if they noticed me jump off the ship. But when I break the surface, I see that they've already moved on to destroy any other watercraft in the harbor.

I think a silent *you're welcome* to the Harbor Patrol guys who were so angry at me for stealing their boat. They'd be dead right now if they'd gone out instead of me.

Soaking wet, I climb up onto the docks and rush for the base of the statue. If Summer's still in the torch, there's no telling how long it'll take me to get up there.

All of that doesn't matter, though, since the torch isn't there anymore. It's gone, along with the entire upper half of Lady Liberty's arm. Smoke rising like storm clouds above tell the story.

I swear. Then another rush of adrenaline kicks in and I make a mad dash for the statue.

The news van from her station is parked nearby, and I

catch sight of blonde hair like Summer's. As I get closer, I'm filled with relief when I confirm that it's her.

"Thank God," I say, falling to my hands and knees.

Looking up, I see something that feels like a kick to the gut when I'm already down. Her cameraman wraps a blanket around her shoulders. He's a big guy who looks as if, somehow, Brad Pitt and George Clooney were able to conceive a love child from their bromance and had a son with a combination of their best qualities. And, from the look of things, he was just responsible for saving her. She plants a huge kiss *on his mouth* and bile rises up in my throat.

Well, now I know why she hasn't called to give me an update on our relationship status.

But at least now I know what that status is: DOA.

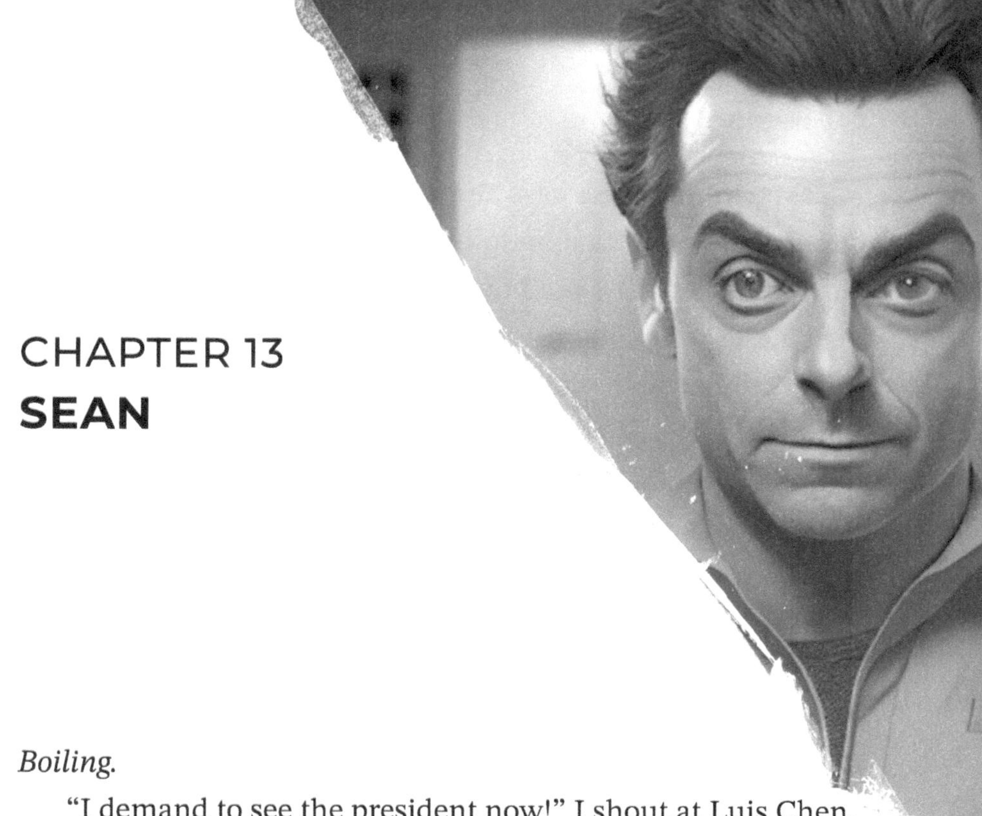

CHAPTER 13
SEAN

Boiling.

"I demand to see the president now!" I shout at Luis Chen.

We're in a meeting room with breakfast laid out on the table, and once again, there seems to be no rush to get this operation underway. Everyone is just standing around finishing up bagels and breakfast sandwiches.

"Perhaps you should step outside for a few minutes, Mr. Meyers," Chen says. "Take a breather. Collect your thoughts."

I'm not having it. I feel anger building up inside of me that will probably get me into a lot of trouble. "You'd like that, wouldn't you? Why don't you just admit that you're all threatened by me? That you know I should be the one running this entire operation?"

For a second, my keen eyesight catches the increased intensity in Chen's expression. But it subsides as quickly as it came and he forces a smile instead.

"Mr. Meyers," he says through gritted teeth. "Under the circumstances, I'm going to let that slide. But only this once. Now step outside before I have you removed."

I'd like to see them try. But not enough to actually allow myself to get manhandled. In case you haven't noticed, I'm not exactly the physical type. With a huff, I turn and storm out of the room. The metal floors clack loudly as I pace the corridor, breathing slowly and counting backward from one hundred. Halfway through, I realize I'm going to need a longer countdown.

If they plan to treat me like a child, and this situation like a walk in the park, we'll all be dead before sundown.

I hear footsteps approaching—how couldn't I? A man I know all too well, Franklin Douglas III, strides around the corner. He's wearing a suit and tie, and truly, I think we'd have been better off with him as president at this very moment.

He stops when he sees me, but only for an instant before he adjusts his lapels and continues.

"Frank Douglas," I say, a small smile on my face.

"I'm sorry... you are...?"

It's a purposeful slight, calculated to throw me off. He knows *exactly* who I am. Still, I play along with his childish game.

"Sean Meyers. Crosscircuit."

"Yes, right. The man responsible for the random robot attack they call the Mega-Mech-Apocalypse several years ago."

Again, part of his ploy. He knows it and I know it, but he's using the opportunity to give himself the upper hand.

"That wasn't a random attack," I say. "And had anyone given me the time of day—"

"People were killed, Meyers. Including a hero named Bullet Train. Did you know that?"

"I did not. I expected a few casualties, but—"

"He would have been very useful in this fight if your robots hadn't killed him. You realize that, don't you?"

"With all due respect," I say in a tone that tells him I have very little of it for him, "if he couldn't handle my robots, what makes you think he could handle the Tuldarians? Oh, right, because my robots are the *only* chance anyone has at defeating them. That's exactly why I should be the one in charge here. What, pray tell, are *your* qualifications?"

He doesn't have to know that I'm fully aware of his time spent as the Black Harrier. Besides, if he wants to play the belittling game, I am an expert.

"Mr. Meyers, one of my companies—one you're intimately familiar with, if I'm not mistaken—is involved in the design and manufacture of arms and other military equipment for the United States government. My foundation supplies food, medical supplies, and other necessities to countries all over the world. Another of my companies is in the business of research and development of technologies to rein in superpowered individuals who choose to use those powers to break the law. Add to that the fact that I served in Afghanistan during the war and have military experience, I believe I'm more than qualified to help with this matter."

I stare at him long and hard, but offer no response.

"Now, if you'd like to start over again," he says. "Frank Douglas." He extends a hand for me to shake.

I consider ignoring it. After all, he's part of the reason I was put in the Trench to begin with. However, if we are to survive this, bygones must be bygones.

"Those people in there are all idiots," I tell him.

He laughs. "If we agree on more things the way we do on this point, I think we can get along just fine. What are you doing out here?"

"Your lackey, Chen, cast me out like a leper for having an opinion."

Frank tilts his head. "And what opinion was that?"

"That everyone in there is an idiot."

Frank laughs again. "Fair enough. Well, I'm heading in. How about we go together?"

I watch him for a second, trying to suss out any deception, but I see nothing obvious. With a nod, we reenter the room, and things quiet down at the sight of the man by my side. He has a certain effect on people. An air. It's no wonder he was so close to mayorship. From what I've heard, just whispers, he threw in the towel. But I, for one, think he had a real chance. Not that any of that matters anymore.

"I believe your team is over there," Douglas tells me.

I follow his finger and realize that the whole room had

been sectioned off into smaller teams while I was "cooling down."

Luis Chen stands at the podium, shuffling through a stack of papers. Frank leaves me where I stand to go find his seat toward the front.

"If each leader will open their envelopes, we'll begin," Chen says. Then he eyes me standing in the back. "Mr. Meyers, that's you. Please find your seat so we can continue."

He motions to a table filled with costumes I've never seen before. It's uncommon for me to be unfamiliar with anyone of this caliber, but I suppose that's par for the course, so to speak. They need everyone. Even the nobodies.

"I work alone," I tell him.

He shakes his head and gives me a look that says "You can go back to the Trench if you'd like." But aloud, he says, "Not today, you don't."

I grit my teeth, and find my seat.

"Thank you. Now, as I said, team leaders, please open the manilla envelopes in front of your seat. There we go. Bastet, you and your team will mainly be responsible for big cities—New York, London, Tokyo, and the like. You've been put in charge of thirty individuals; utilize them using your best judgment. We trust you to assemble the teams to your fullest advantage. Should you require counsel, I, along with my team, Frank Douglas, and Paul Steele will be available."

For the first time, I notice Paul "The Baron" Steele seated beside Frank Douglas. He's sipping on a cup of café-bought coffee and seemingly paying no attention to the happenings in the room. Where in the world did he find a MoonMoney open in the middle of the apocalypse?

Chen goes on to read off similar assignments, which feels entirely redundant considering each of us is staring at the same thing on the papers within our respective envelopes, but I can only assume, being that this is the US government, they are used to working with ignoramuses.

When Chen gets to me, I can't help but smile. I don't know whether it's to appease me or because he finally realized I was the only one who saw this coming, but he assigns my team to my base in Egypt to fully unleash my robot army.

Here's the bit I haven't fully divulged. I placed my control center beneath the Sphinx in Giza, knowing the fools in charge would never risk destroying one of the world's most ancient treasures by just bombing it or even sending in people like Eaglestar to tear the place apart. I know, brilliant, right? I also couldn't risk anyone getting outside access to it, so I completely walled it off in every way. The problem is, it's not going to be easy to get to. Even for me.

I made sure of it.

It's apparent the Tuldarians knew what I was up to and have one of their larger ships hovering above it, along with an army of their ground troops deployed on the ground to guard it.

When I hear this—everything... the devastation going on around the globe—the only thing that comes to mind is how ridiculous it is that we'd all enjoyed Beef Wellington and *fondant au chocolat* made by Chef Gordon Ramsay last night.

All this... people dying, and we were partying. What's wrong with these people?

"Now, as you've likely noticed, your landing left little room for error," Chen says. "This place was designed to fit Air Force One, not a fleet. That being said, we will be departing in waves. Bastet, you and your teams will be first off the runway. If you look at page 12 of your packet, you'll find a list of masked crimefighters already deployed to several of your assigned cities, including a team led by Iguanadon in Cairo. You may also reassign those as you see fit. As a matter of fact, your plane has just arrived. I suggest you hustle. The world burns while we wait."

Oh, now they want to hurry?

Bastet rises, accompanied by most of the room.

While they exit, Chen continues. "The rest of you will use this time to acquaint yourselves with each other's powers and abilities. Training rooms typically used for the US Secret Service will be made available to you this afternoon. They've been outfitted to mimic the actions of both Tuldarian ground troops and their aircraft. However, make no mistakes, these aliens are powerful, and deadly. Team leaders, get to know your new teams."

My dossier promises an international team of heroes, giving me the impression that they've given me the best of the best for my mission. However, when I scan the table at which we are all seated, it's immediately apparent they've tossed me a bunch of random nobodies.

"Well, perhaps we start with introductions," I groan.

There's some Eastern European (or Russian maybe?) meathead whose name I can't recall after reading it.

He speaks with a thick accent. "I am Rockhard." Too much information. However, by the size of him, I knew it had to be some such overcompensation. "I have many powers. I am Baron Eaglestar ability."

"Okay," I say. "I don't know what that means. How about you?" I say to a French woman my notes say is called Whisper.

"Whisper," she says in a French accent. "I am a vibrator."

I cough. "A vibrator?"

"I make things, uh, move."

"She is not wrong," Rockhard says.

"Okay, okay." I let out a sigh. "And… you?"

"Hi, everyone," a little blonde girl says. She doesn't look a day over fifteen. She's bright-eyed and bushy-tailed. That's not a euphemism. She actually has a bunny tail. "I'm Prairie. I can control animals."

"Yeah. That'll be useful," I say under my breath. I point to the last of us. "You, scary menacing guy."

I already know from my files he's the Latin American hero called El Jaguar Inmortal—the Immortal Jaguar.

He's supposed to legitimately be unable to die. As he talks, I sift through reliable reports on him tracing all the way back to at least the 1600s, shortly after the Spanish arrived in the New World, and legends going back even further. He appears to be your typical super-strong, super-fast, nigh-invulnerable fighting type.

I'm still unimpressed.

Although, if it's true he can't die, I suppose that would be quite handy.

"I know everyone is scared, but we can do this!" Prairie says.

"No, *we* can't," I say. "*I* can. And you all can help by doing exactly what I tell you to do and staying out of my way."

"This I believe," Rockhard says. "You say hit things. I do. I make things break."

"Right. If you'll excuse me a moment." I shove the papers back into the envelope, rise, and search the room for the agent who had greeted me last evening.

I can't believe this is it. This is the team they assign the most important person in the room. Three idiots and a vampire cat.

I spot my military liaison in mid-conversation with someone who probably has no real reason to be here.

"Agent Frederick, a word." I start walking away before I'm sure he'll follow. But the sound of his chair moving and the footsteps behind me tell me he's smart.

"What can I do for you, sir?"

"This isn't going to work," I tell him.

"Sir?"

"This… whole thing. These are children playing games. Rockhard? The man's brain is rock hard."

"Sir, Rockhard is one of Russia's finest heroes."

"Yes, and I had one of the best-smelling bowel movements of my life this morning. See how one can make anything sound appealing? While I appreciate the need for assistance, I'd feel better knowing there are *actual* heroes at my side. Not just that which was scraped off the training room floor."

"I didn't make the assignments, sir. However, I know they were well thought-out. I believe you'll find the rest of your team to be up to your requirements."

"The rest of my team?" I can't help but insert a measure of hope into my tone.

"Yes, sir. There are several who are running late due to... the conditions. They should be arriving shortly, from what I've been told."

Chen takes the stage again, interrupting our conversation. We both turn toward him.

"We will take a short recess for lunch. Then, an official mission briefing will occur before you're given a chance in the danger rooms for team building and acquainting yourselves with one another more... violently. You're dismissed to the cafeteria."

"We're eating *again*?" I ask Agent Frederick who I turn to see is no longer beside me.

This is such a waste of time.

As we file out into the cafeteria for what amounts to cold cuts—I guess they blew their food budget on dinner last night —I wonder who will be conducting our briefing.

I'm certain it won't be the president himself. In fact, I'm under the impression he may have already left. Had he been present, he would no doubt have been the one talking, and it would have been a much longer introduction session. In addition, this modest meal would be some elaborate luncheon featuring Justin Bieber or some other such performer.

Regardless, at least those who stand at power realize President Stanford isn't well enough versed in world events or our powers and abilities to handle it himself, despite his bravado last evening. I deduce that it will probably be either the Secretary of Defense—perhaps one of his deputies—or a four-star general.

I'll find out soon enough. Meanwhile, I have some children to get to know... apparently.

I take a seat at the table with my *team*.

"So, with a name like Prairie, I assume you're from Iowa or some such place?" I ask, picking up a soggy tuna fish sandwich.

"Saskatchewan," she says.

"I should have deduced you'd be Canadian. Where in Saskatchewan? Not that it matters."

"Oh my God, it's only the best and biggest city. It's so beautiful. You should totally visit!"

"Saskatoon? Of course you are. At first, I thought perhaps you were from California."

"Why?" she asks.

"You know, the whole *Valley Girl* thing."

"The what?" she asks.

"The nauseating optimism, over-enthusiastic about everything."

"Huh?"

I smile. “It says in your file that you can control people in addition to animals. Is this accurate?”

“Yeah, but it takes a lot of effort and doesn’t last long. Animals are way easier.” She smiles, and I wonder if she’s serious. Either way, I decide she isn’t someone to put to the test lest I be made into some hoppity fool, excited about the prospect of putting my life on the line beside a half-baked team. It’s always the squirrelly ones you’ve got to watch out for.

I take a small sip of milk from a handheld carton. “Is the tail…”

“Real?” she finishes.

I motion for her to continue now that she’s cut me off.

“For sure, and don’t let me catch you, like, checking out my ass or anything. Got it?”

Again, I don’t know if she’s serious. “We have no time for such nonsense.”

“I was just kidding. Geez. Lighten up, old man.”

I sigh. My first inclination is to correct her, tell her I’m not an old man. But, to her, I must look ancient. Instead, I decide to inform them of something they seem to be unaware of.

I look around at the table of wanna-be heroes. “You all realize we are likely going to die in the coming days?” Everyone just stares down at their food. “This is not a joke. I have been preparing for this moment my entire life.”

“Is that why you nearly killed everyone with your robots?” Whisper asks.

“Yes—I mean. I had no intention of killing people—well,

not so many people, at least. I was trying to *prepare* them while testing my abilities against the world's most powerful in hopes that it would yield results enough to know how my creations would handle the Tuldarians."

"My mother died from your *test*," Whisper says without preamble as she takes a bite of her turkey sandwich.

"I..." I don't know what to say. I've spent the last few decades cursing something without a face as the culprit in my own mother's demise. I am unsure how I would respond should cancer itself manifest in front of me. "I am sorry."

"It was a long time ago," she says. "Just prove it was worth it."

I clear my throat. "That's my intention here. And since we are all stuck together, it would be prudent if we learned what one another is capable of."

At this point, we haven't actually had the opportunity to see each other's powers at work. We've been introduced and given our assignments, eaten two whole meals, but we are no closer to being a team then when we'd met over two hours ago. Meanwhile, more people are dying all over the world.

"You eat that?" Rockhard asks Prairie, noticing that half of her tuna sandwich is pushed to the side.

She shakes her head, and the big Russian reaches for it.

"You're not full after two full meals?" I ask.

"Never full," Rockhard says with a mouth full of fish.

No sooner did he finish her half a sandwich than he pulls out a protein bar with Slavic writing on the foil.

"Your briefing is about to begin," Agent Frederick says,

stepping up behind us. "Do you have any questions for me beforehand?"

I wouldn't even know where to start.

Rockhard speaks up first. "This all the food? I require more than this *tunets* sandwich."

"I'll talk to the kitchen and see what I can do," the agent tells him. "Any questions regarding the mission? No? Okay. If you'll follow me."

"The briefing isn't here?" I ask.

"Each team has their own assigned leader."

"I thought I was their leader?" I ask, growing more and more tired of all the government nonsense.

"You're the team leader, yes. But the president has hand-picked some new national security advisors to assess the multiple threats around the world. One of them will be briefing your team on the situation in Egypt."

"And his name is…?"

"Why don't you all follow me and you can meet him yourself."

He ushers us out of the cafeteria, down the hall, and into a small, empty room.

"Is one of his powers like, invisibility?" Prairie asks. And I think she's serious.

Before anyone can respond, the back door opens and none other than Franklin Douglas III approaches us with a stack of binders and hands them to Agent Frederick, who begins passing them out to us.

"I apologize for the delay, but the printing capabilities at this facility are in dire need of an upgrade, to say the least. I thought I was going to have to write these out by hand for a while there."

A giant touch screen at the front of the room lights up with a map of the world marked with hot spots that match the areas Chen had spoken of earlier. Douglas taps a spot in Northern Africa, and the map zooms in on Egypt. The area around the Great Pyramids is highlighted in red.

"As you've apparently been made aware, the Tuldarians have heavily fortified this area because they know that Cross-circuit's main control center is located there. For some reason, they've abducted a former supervillain who called herself the Torturess, a low-level telepath and telekenetic—"

I raise my hand, and he visibly sighs—no attempt to hide it whatsoever. "Yes, Mr. Meyers?"

"What exactly is your definition of 'low level'? Because from what I've experienced, she's much more powerful than you give her credit for. She once literally threw me around a city street with her mind."

He raises an eyebrow in annoyance. "We base our profiles on Guild standards, using the information we have available on any given individual. She's mostly an unknown quantity. Following your experiences with her, did you ever file a C-23 after-action report with the Guild?"

It isn't fun being dressed down, but I'm not going to let it show. "I don't even know what that is."

"So you didn't read your manual when you applied for your masked crimefighter's license... before deciding to operate on the opposite side of the law, of course? I can send you a PDF right now if you'd like to take a look at it."

He's trying to embarrass me, but I'm determined to take it in stride. "That thing is *part* of the reason I decided to 'operate on the other side of the law.' It's hundreds of pages long. I don't think anyone reads it all the way through. It's like reading the terms and conditions before downloading an app on your smartphone. Whoever wrote it was so—"

"I wrote that manual, Mr. Meyers. So choose carefully how you finish that statement." He's leaning over the table toward me with a menacing posture, but I just smile.

I've just basically gotten him to admit to who he really was in front of everyone.

"I'm sorry, Mr. Douglas. I wasn't aware that you had such intimate knowledge of being a masked crimefighter."

I wait for what seems like an inordinate amount of time for him to respond. Finally, one of the corners of his mouth rises. "*Touché*, Mr. Meyers. It seems your level-9 intelligence rating may be well-deserved."

"Level-9? What would I have to do to get to Level-10?" I have no doubt I'm the smartest person in the world, so I feel somewhat insulted.

Now he fully smiles. "I'm not quite sure. We've never given anyone that rating. In the future, assuming you survive this mission, please file the requisite reports so we can update the profiles of your nemeses. And yourself." He looks around the room. "That goes for everyone here. Now, if we can move on, we have a world to save."

I lean back in my chair. "By all means."

"As I was saying, the Torturess has never been considered much of a threat in the past. But from the intelligence we've been able to gather, that may have changed. The Tuldarians appear to be using the pyramids as some sort of conduit to amplify her psionic powers. Whether they'll be able to get her to do their bidding, by force or through some sort of reward, has yet to be seen."

Whisper speaks up. "What exactly are they trying to do with her?"

"Unknown. Part of this mission is to find that out. What's important is how we stop them. And stop *her* if we must."

Prairie looks over at the Rockhard. "He can just throw the pyramids into space!"

The hulking Slav lets out a booming laugh and then speaks in his thick Eastern European basso profundo. "Rockhard can do this."

No he can't. This guy is probably a Level-5 strongman. I glance at his profile in the file in front of me. Super strong, super tough—oh, and he can fly, so there's that.

I cut in. "The pyramids are some of the most important antiquities in the world. I suggest we try rescuing her—or taking her down, whichever the case may be—with as little destruction to them as possible."

Douglas nods. "That's a valid consideration. But if push comes to shove, you need to take her down using whatever means necessary."

"No one is killing her," says a British woman from the back of the room. I hadn't even noticed anyone enter.

"Ah, everyone. This is Annihilatrix." The woman glares at Frank like she could kill *him* for even mentioning murdering Torturess. "She has requested joining your team as she has a... personal relationship with the captive."

"That doesn't sound wise," I say. "What if she tries to—"

Annihilatrix stands beside me in an instant, her eyes glowing red like Eaglestar's used to. I clear my throat.

"Welcome to the team," I say.

She then turns to Frank. "The Guild has clear regulations for murder under Section 3, Paragraph C, in the manual."

"As I told our friend Mr. Meyers, I wrote the regulations. I'm keenly aware that we do not permit murder of any kind." At this, Douglas seems to flinch a bit. I wonder what that emotion is that flashed over his face but decide to catalog it for another time. "However, these are dire circumstances. There are aliens who could very well end life on Earth. We'll have to do whatever it takes to win."

"We are not killing her," Annihilatrix repeats.

"Then I suggest you find a way to stop her," Frank says, brooking no argument.

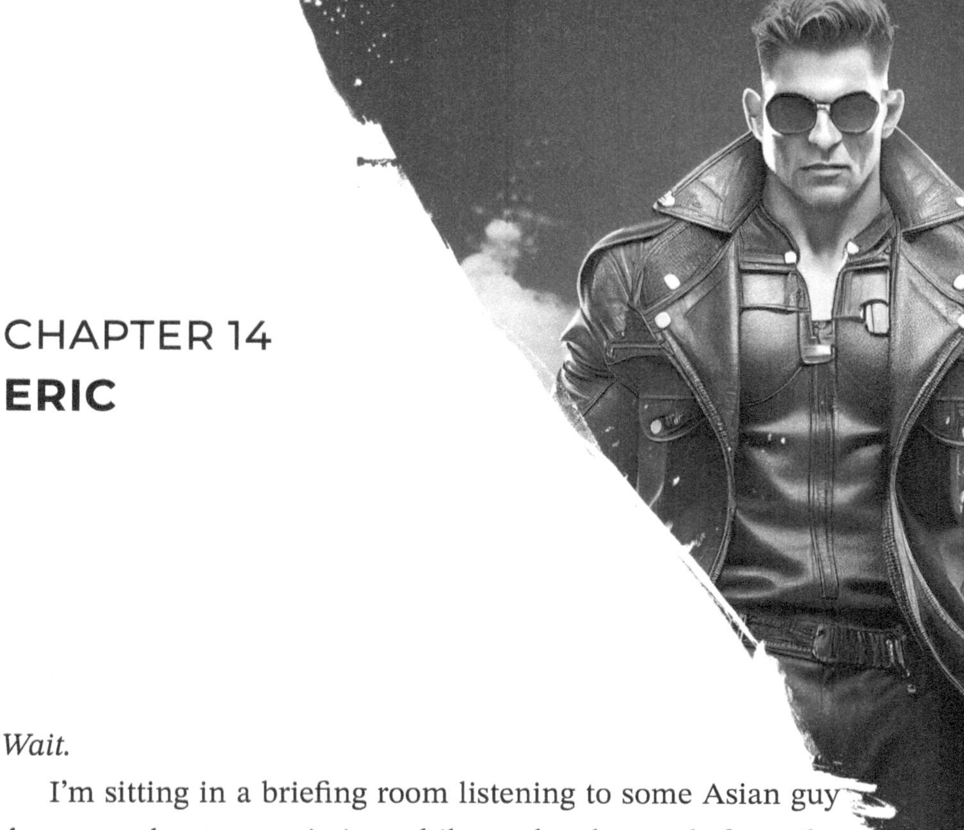

CHAPTER 14
ERIC

Wait.

I'm sitting in a briefing room listening to some Asian guy drone on about our mission while my head pounds from the biggest hangover of my life. And don't get me started on the posers sitting here with me. Weird AF.

First, the cheugiest of all: Royal Rampage—a giant talking gorilla—who happens to be wearing a golden crown for some reason.

Oh, shoot. Royal? Okay, that's kind of clever. Reminds me of King Kong. Alright, props to gorilla man.

Second, Sinsation, someone I used to work with—sort of —when I was a supervillain and it was all the rage to do team ups. She's bussin', as long as you can deal with someone who's a bit nuts. It's a good thing she's so hot, cus that makes me more forgiving of the crazy.

The last guy is someone I helped arrest not so long ago. He

goes by "Justice" and was a vigilante who murdered criminals in cold blood. Probably bonkers, too. I'm starting to see a theme here.

Have I mentioned I used to be a criminal?

And, even with my super-high IQ, I'm not sure I'm following what this—what was it, Chen?—dude is saying.

"So, hold on a sec, man. You saying we're gonna sneak onto the ship where they were able to kill *Eaglestar* and try to rough up the guys who did him?"

"If by 'did him' you mean killed, that's correct, Mr. McCabe."

"If *he* couldn't beat them, then what chance do we have?"

"Well, first, he went in half-cocked with a full frontal assault, so they knew he was coming."

Heh. He said "half-cocked" and "full frontal" in the same sentence and then... well, you know. Nice.

"And, second, he wasn't aware of the device that would rob him of his powers, so he did nothing to avoid it."

"Riiiiiight," I say, looking around the table. No one seems to want to agree. Losers.

"So your team is going to sneak onboard and destroy the device before they can use it on you. Besides, my understanding is that your powers aren't related to the alien artifacts, so the device wouldn't take away your abilities anyway."

"Allegedly," I say.

"Any other questions?" Chen asks as if our conversation is done.

"Yeah," Sinsation says. "Why exactly are we supposed to follow this lunkhead on this kamikaze mission?"

"Because the alternative is to return to the Trench and hope the Tuldarians don't defeat the human race, which would result in you eventually starving to death down there once you ran out of food. Assuming you don't run out of air first."

"Ooooohhh. Okay. Gotcha." She winks while pointing her finger like a gun and makes a clicking sound.

Chen shakes his head. "I'm pleased that I could clear that up for you."

Royal Rampage, the giant gorilla, raises his hand—paw?

"Yes?" asks Chen.

"More food?"

"Certainly. I'll have more food brought in for you."

Rampage hoots and slams both fists on the table, overturning several glasses of water and sending papers scattering. "Me sorry."

A few people snicker. Sinsation appears annoyed. Chen whispers something to some government guy in a suit, and the agent rushes out of the room, presumably to get the gorilla more food before he destroys the place.

After a moment, Chen picks up where he left off. "Even without the ability to sap your powers, the Tuldarian weapons are highly advanced and dangerous."

"We saw that in California," Justice says.

"Indeed. And from what I saw, you're not bad with them yourself."

He takes a few steps to his left and approaches a table covered in a cloth. When he whips it back, he reveals a large metal container. A few flicks of metal clasps, and the box-top flips upward to show the contents.

"After rigorous tests these last days, we've determined these suitable for use." Chen motions for Justice to join him at the front of the room. "By you. We believe it will give us an even playing field."

"And I'll be able to kill these things?" asks Justice. "All of them? I'm tired of having to hold back."

"You certainly will," says Chen.

"Then I'm in," he says, picking up one of the alien weapons, and looking down the sights.

No fair. I want one.

CHAPTER 15
SAWYER

Rusty.

Most of my team hasn't worked together in a couple of years, so while we're waiting for our plane—apparently only one can fit on the runway at a time or something, and the airspace is clogged with aliens—they have us train to get reacquainted with one another. On one hand, it's sort of a nice reunion for us. On the other, it's a nightmare for me because Neith isn't showing any signs of forgiveness. You'd think being sent to the toughest prison in the world would be punishment enough, but she doesn't even seem to care.

I don't know how much of it is me breaking up the team by leaving and how much was me breaking up with *her* without a word—or even a text. But she's definitely not happy. After masked crimefighting was outlawed, I made a conscious decision to keep going, but I didn't wanna be responsible for anyone else getting arrested because of me. I ditched the group, and I didn't say goodbye.

Truth is, I was afraid to say goodbye. I mean, I didn't even text her to explain. I just... left.

Besides, she ended up in the new Resistors without me anyway, so that shouldn't have mattered. It's not like she wanted to be with me anymore. She made it pretty clear we were done—I thought—but I probably should've made sure it was official, especially before starting to date Summer.

Speaking of Summer, I wonder how she's doing now?

I haven't exactly had a chance to catch up with anyone since I sprang the coop, so to speak, but I'll probably skip calling her anyway. She was furious when she found out I was Black Harrier. She's been anti-vigilante for years after her brother was killed during a superhero-villain battle. Yeah, now that I think about it, I'm probably better off letting sleeping dogs lie. I'm sure she'd be happier. With pretty much anyone.

I try talking to Neith all the way down to Training Room Charlie, but she refuses to even acknowledge my existence. We're escorted by our military liaison through the drab halls of "Bunker Base Bravo"—they really like their military-ese here. The room looks like a cross between a low-budget gym and Frank's holographic battle simulation room.

A window on the far wall gives us a view into a control room that reminds me of the place where the sound engineer sits in a recording studio. BlaKat's giant leonine silhouette can just be made out in there. And then there are power dampeners that somehow temporarily take away super-powers, not unlike the ones in the Trench. Probably exactly like the ones in the Trench. That's not such a big deal for me… I guess the worst that could happen is I wouldn't be able to mimic something I see in this particular room. But I can imagine how disturbing it might seem to someone who relies on their powers to fight… like most of my teammates.

"My suit doesn't work," Osprey complains.

"What? You're kidding," Pace says.

"I guess whatever's responsible for you guys losing your abilities also affects my tech."

"So we're just sitting ducks?" White Hot asks.

"C'mon, baby. We ain't useless without our powers," Black Frost says, putting an arm around her and flexing the biceps on his other.

"I don't understand," Osprey says. "If this whole thing is meant to show each other what we can do, why would they dampen our powers?"

"Those in charge believe the first step to understanding one another truly, is to understand one another at the heart," BlaKat says from behind the glass.

"That's stupid," Pace complains.

"Well, let's get this over with," I say under my breath as we enter. I flash a thumbs up at BlaKat. He gives a slight nod in return, then starts working the control board like a virtuoso pianist giving the concert of a lifetime.

I have no idea what to expect, so I don't have a plan in mind.

What I *definitely* didn't expect was for the floor to drop six inches and small drones to fly out from the gap created in the wall. Sixteen or so zip out. Little things with spindly appendages that waggle when they fly. The soft hum—which is pretty loud when multiplied between them—is reminiscent of cicadas in the summer.

They'd be cute if they weren't so obviously deadly.

All at once, they rise to hover menacingly over our heads.

Pace looks back and forth between me and the drones. "So what are these things supposed to—Ow!" A thin beam from one of the flying devices sears his neck. He's so used to moving at super-speed, without his powers, I can only imagine he must feel like he's stuck in quicksand.

I guess that's what they meant when they said we would fight things that would simulate the alien spaceships.

"You all right?" I take a look at his shoulder where the beam ripped his costume and there's a small burn there.

"I'll live, but I really, really want to destroy that little bastard now."

"Me first!" Bash tries to jump up and grab the nearest drone, but without his super-strength, his legs can't make his bulk aerial more than a few inches. The thing zaps him smack-dab in the middle of his forehead, and he tumbles back to the metal floor, groaning.

"Smooth work, team," Osprey says.

Bash lifts his head and it looks like he just went to church on Ash Wednesday. If it keeps going this way, we're all gonna end up injured or even dead before our plane arrives.

I rush to the control room and pound on the window. BlaKat glances up at me. "Can you turn it down a notch?" I'm not sure if he can hear me, but I move my lips deliberately so even if he can't, he'll know what I'm saying.

He heard me alright, but shakes his head. A laser beam draws a black scar across the glass next to my hand, forcing me to pull it back. I'm ready to reply to BlaKat when he presses a button and his voice comes over the training room's loudspeaker again. "Sorry. That's the lowest setting."

Damn.

I think back to our old training practices from a few years ago and try to decide what might work against these flying stingers. We didn't have Frank's battle simulator, so we had to make do with whatever we could scrounge up and haul back to the warehouse we called our headquarters. A lot of times, that meant old punching bags thrown out by local gyms, or even fruit crates.

None of that would do us a bit of good here.

Above, the little machines *fwip* and dash, spraying thin lines of blue whatever-it-is at us.

Bash rises and slams his fist into his open palm. "What's wrong with us? We're the Resistors!"

Pace slaps him on the back. "The big guy's right. We're not gonna be embarrassed by some flying buzzkills, are we?"

"I don't think that means what you think it means," Black Frost says.

"Yeah, yeah. Whatever. Let's take these things out."

Bash falls into one of those poses you see sprinters doing,

one hand on the ground, a foot stretched out behind them. "Time to ramp it up."

Osprey takes the hint and runs toward Bash, jumps onto his back, and launches herself at the nearest drone. She intertwines her hands and uses double fists to bat one drone into another. They smack together, which causes them both to lose altitude. Pace then leaps upward and catches one, and tosses it down to Bash, who smashes it with his giant fist. Even without his powers, he's still strong enough to break it.

This seems to anger the buzzers. They each retaliate with laser blasts, but we all deftly avoid being burned. Seeing what they did to Pace is enough.

"Neith, over there!" I shout, pointing at the other drone which is now pretty close to the ground.

"I know what I am doing," she says, already running at the wall. Planting one foot, she shoves off and upward, grabbing the top of the drone and bringing it hard down on the floor. It doesn't break, but she straddles it while it struggles and shoots at random. Dodging the attacks, she digs her fingers in on one side and pushes with her palm with the other hand until the drone cracks in half. Exposed wires spark and sizzle.

"What's the deal with you two?" White Hot asks me.

"Yeah, now I see why you dumped her," Pace says. "That's one scary chick."

"Quiet, man," I tell him, shushing him. "Things are bad enough. Besides, I didn't dum—"

One dive-bombs my head, forcing me to shut up and duck. The suckers aren't big, but they're fast. And the hits aren't really life-threatening, but they don't feel good. How do I know? The drone zaps me three times as it passes, and now I've now got burn marks on both my legs and one on my butt.

I hop around like an idiot, smacking my rear end like I'm trying to put out a fire. "Freaking A. This is ridiculous!"

"Perhaps you are out of practice," Neith says, rushing by me to tear my attacker out of the air.

These people want us to leave here soon to fight aliens, and they're gonna have us do it with all these minor injuries? Sounds like the government to me, I guess.

Osprey and Bash are able to take down a few more using the same maneuver as before, and Pace does some damage to a couple of low-flyers. And White Hot and Black Frost work together like they're one body. It's pretty impressive.

But I'm not just sitting back getting shot in the backside.

"I'll show you out of practice," I quip back. I mean it as playful banter, but the look she shoots me says she's not messing around.

I quickly disassemble some of the broken drones and use their appendages like boomerangs. Some of the hits are more effective than others. But I manage to destroy four of the units before I spin and notice the others had disabled the rest.

Everyone's breathing hard.

"Good work," BlaKat says into his microphone. "This training course was designed to teach you to avoid the alien weapons and use ingenuity to disable or kill those doing the shooting."

I remove my hands from my knees and look up to see the

Resistors staring at me. I suppose it's a good sign. Maybe that means they've accepted me as their leader again.

I give one of the drones near me a kick. "Well, I guess we're still good."

"Round two," BlaKat says.

"Wait! What? Already?" Pace says. Suddenly, the lights on the power dampeners go off and he shudders like a duck shaking water off its feathers. "Oh, hell yeah. I'm back, baby!"

Not sparing a second, he starts zipping around the room at full speed. He's nothing but a black and gray blur.

"This is gonna be fun," Bash says, cracking his knuckles.

Neith's tattoos begin to glow. Each one gives her a unique ability. I've seen her fly, teleport, turn invisible, and do some pretty crazy stuff with a bow and arrow. Fire sprouts from White Hot's hand, and Black Frost creates a long spear made of... you guessed it, black ice.

Osprey and I are the only ones without any real powers. Then Osprey rises a few feet from the ground. "My suit works again!"

Correction: I'm the only one who has no powers. But that won't stop me from showing these guys what I've got.

Another round of drones exit ports at the bottom of the walls, their metallic bodies glinting in the fluorescent lights. In each corner of the room, stationary guns shooting the same kind of weapons pop out.

I go hard right from the start, making sure I'm the first to disembowel one of the things. I issue a few simple commands, and the team responds without hesitation.

Maybe this really will be good for us. After a few more minutes, I actually start to feel like I can take the lead like I'm supposed to. As far as being ready for a big fight goes, I feel a lot better than I did, like the team is on the same page as well.

The interpersonal stuff, however, still feels awkward. They may be ready to accept me as their leader again, but it doesn't seem like they're ready to be my friend. I'm starting to wonder if that's ever gonna happen, or if I've permanently ruined my relationships with the others.

I nod to Bash, and he steps forward, his muscles rippling as he unleashes his incredible strength. The robots are no match for him, and he takes the front line out with ease, smashing them to pieces with his bare hands.

Osprey takes to the air, using her agility and speed to dodge their attacks and strike back with precision. She's always been a force to be reckoned with, and it's a thrill to watch her in action again. She's like a dancer, her movements flowing seamlessly from one to the next. She's not just going through the motions, either. She's fully invested in the battle. And it's clear that she's not just training, she's pushing herself to be better. As she takes down the last robot in her vicinity, she turns to me and gives me a small smile.

I can tell she's pleased with her performance. And I'm proud of her too. She's come a long way since I first met her, and she was already a badass back then.

Pace moves at lightning speed, cutting through to the robots' weak points. His movements are too quick for the eye to follow—mine or their digital ones.

Neith's tattoos glow to life, giving her the power to teleport around the room, taking out robots with her bow and arrows left and right.

Black Frost creates ice from the air, freezing the robots in place before shattering them with a well-placed punch. And White Hot blasts heat and fire from her hands, melting the robots into nothing but twisted metal and slag.

Before we can even catch our breath, a new batch of robots appears, deadlier than the last group. We work together as a team, each of us using our unique abilities to take down the robots one by one. The training room is chaos, with debris and sparks flying everywhere, but we are all in sync, fighting as one united force.

Together, we're unstoppable, kicking butt like we used to, and it feels good. Finally, the last robot falls to the ground, defeated. We all pause for a moment, panting and sweaty, but triumphant. We did it.

I turn to my team, a proud smile on my face. "Well done, everyone," I say. "I'd say we're about ready to take on the alien invaders and save our planet. Let's do this."

"Round three," BlaKat says.

"What!" I shout.

"Just kidding. Our time here is up, and our plane is en route."

Thank God.

As we leave the training room, I limp up behind Neith as quickly as I can and tap her on the shoulder. She stops, her shoulders slump, and her head falls back. Sighing, she turns around, at which point I can see that she is still in the midst of rolling her eyes.

"What?"

"Wow. Hostile much?" I ask.

"Are you going to tell me why you stopped me, or should I keep going? I'd like to shower before we leave on our mission."

I notice everyone else is slowing way down in an effort to hear as much of our conversation as possible before getting out of earshot.

"We need to talk. If we go into the mission with this kind of conflict between us, we'll be putting everyone in danger. I can't risk that, and I can't risk this mission failing. It could literally be the end of the world if that happens."

"There is nothing to talk about," she says. "I don't have to like you to work with you. I'll do my part, but you can't make me be your friend."

She storms off down the corridor while the rest of the team pretends not to notice what's happening. As usual, my track record with women continues to be stellar.

"That felt good," Pace says.

Despite my disappointment, I repeat, "Good work, everyone."

They all smile at me.

As I near the exit, someone in a costume blocks the door. The costume reminds me of Firefly's but it's more modern and seems to have updated tech.

"Uh… hi?" I say.

"Hello," he responds, his voice filtered by his insect-looking mask, which covers his entire head. "I've been assigned to your team."

"Are you sure?" I ask. "Because we used to be a team and I think they paired us up because we've worked together before."

"I'm sure," he says. He doesn't add anything, remaining mysterious.

"Hmmm. Okay. Well, I'm Black Harrier," I say, holding out my hand.

"Yep, I know. Everyone knows Black Harrier. Cool mask. I'm Firefly."

"Firefly, huh?" Osprey says. "Interesting. Is Mac okay with it?"

The insect man shrugs. "He can't shrink down from giant size right now, so they assigned me this suit that allows me to simulate his powers."

"I don't like this," Osprey says.

I understand, since Mac was the leader of the Resistors after I left. I'm sure she considers him a friend, or at least a mentor of sorts.

"It's fine, man!" Pace says, shaking the new Firefly's hand and introducing himself. "I'm Pace. Welcome to the team, my dude."

Bash offers the guy a fist to bump, then pushes past him to leave.

"You know, it's funny," I say, "we had another team

member before with an insect-themed codename. He went by Cricket."

"Really?" he asks. "What happened to him?"

Osprey and I give each other a concerned look. I really don't know what happened to Javier, and I doubt she does either.

"Not really sure. I was, uh, indisposed up until yesterday and I haven't had a chance to contact him with everything going on. But I assume he's safe and sound back at home. At least I hope so."

God, I hope so.

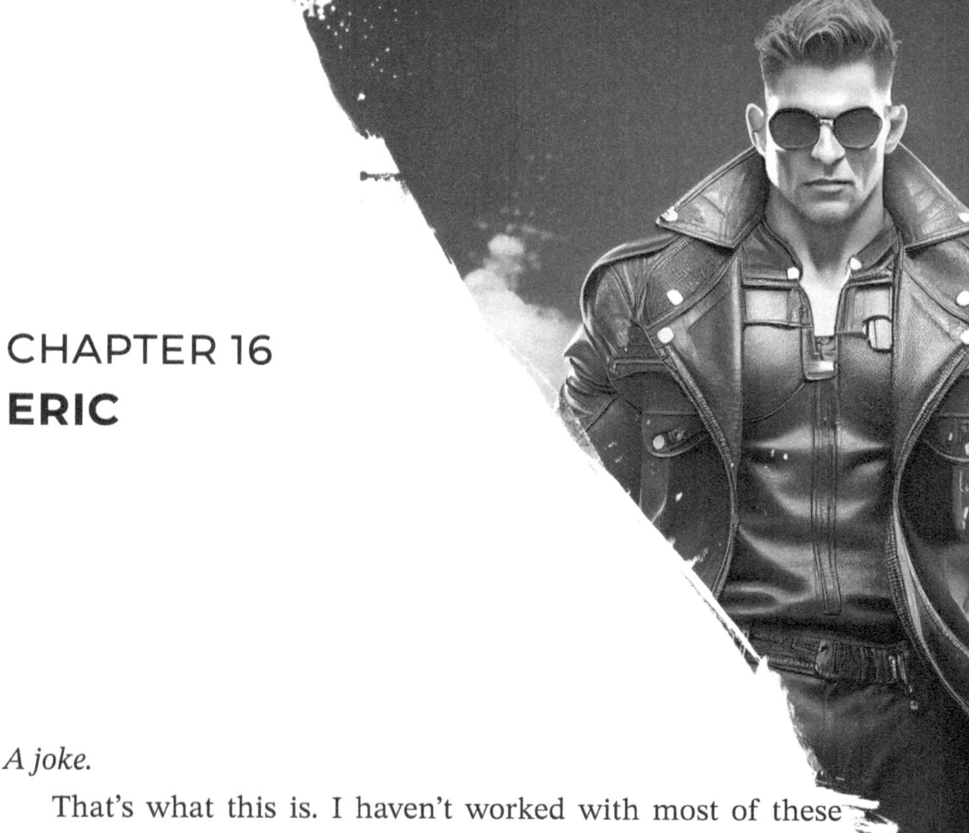

CHAPTER 16
ERIC

A joke.

That's what this is. I haven't worked with most of these fools, and I can't believe how hard it is to get them to gel as a team. Somehow, I'm supposed to prepare these numbskulls for a brawl with alien invaders trying to take over Earth. Oh, and we have an afternoon to do it.

Don't get me wrong, I think taking time out for any kind of team-building exercises when the world is burning is a whack concept. But it's better this than becoming a ghost in a minute because I didn't know one of my team members explodes when they fart or something.

Standing in the center of Training Room Zeta, surrounded by a group of super-powered individuals, I can't help but wish I was still kicking it with the Neon Knights by my side. Those kids were sick. Instead, to my right is Royal Rampage. To my left is Sinsation, practically oozing sex. But she's also a little on the crazy side. Guess that's not always a bad thing.

Justice, a marksman and martial arts expert, stands by himself at the back of the group.

That's right, I read their files. Well, skimmed them.

The group begins our training, running through various drills and exercises designed to hone our skills and abilities. If this was an old, cheesy '80s film, they'd be playing some Joe Esposito song, and we'd only be forced to experience mere seconds of hours or days-long routines. All hail the mighty montage!

We spar, testing our chops against our teammates. We have no powers at first, so it's actually pretty boring, like a karate class for kids or something.

Then we get an alert that the real show is about to begin. Bring it on.

I move to the front of the group, ready to lead my team into victory or Valhalla. Royal Rampage and Sinsation tense up. But Justice still hangs behind us, his eyes flickering around the room. I don't know if he's just one of those prepper-always-prepared dudes, or thinks he's too good for us. But he's starting to piss me off.

"Alright, team," I call out, staring directly at him. My voice echoes off the training room's metal walls. "We've got a lot of work to do if we wanna be ready for the big rumble with the aliens. Let's get started. All of us!" Now it's not only Justice ignoring me. They all sort of do in their own way. I grind my teeth. “Look, guys. We don’t have to be homies. We don’t even have to like each other.”

“Homies?” Sinsation scoffs.

I grunt again. “We just need to throw down together. And if there’s one thing I’m pretty sure we agree on, it’s that we all know how to kick ass. So, what do you say we show these... robots? Is it robots we’re fighting? Yeah, robots. Let’s show these robots what we’re made of. Agreed?”

Sin and Justice nod unenthusiastically, but the gorilla roars and leaps, pounding his knuckles on the ground.

“That’s what I’m talkin’ about!” I yell, patting him on the back. He turns to me, murder in his simian eyes. I back off a bit with my hands raised. “Just excited, my dude. Let’s stomp these metal losers.”

Our first round, we faced off against a group of robots that were apparently programmed to mimic the movements and abilities of our enemy spacecraft. Sure, it’s not the same since they were just little drones shooting plasma bolts. But that stuff hurt!

I flex my muscles and crack my knuckles, a determined look in my eyes. At least, that’s what I’m going for, since Sinsation may be my last shot at any action before I head into the thick of the real battle.

Royal Rampage pounds his chest like a gorilla—’cause, uh, that’s what he is. His strength is almost palpable. Justice calmly readies himself. Despite my initial distaste for the punk, his martial arts training are evident in every deft movement. Sinsation performs a series of quick warm-up stretches. Boooinnng. I've asked her out a few times in the past, but she's always rejected me. She's probably afraid I'd be too much for her.

And we're on!

Panels slide upward into the walls and the robots inside activate in front of us. No one told me this, but just a reminder: I'm pretty freakin' smart. Our first round, without powers, was to analyze our actions and movements. This one's going to figure out our powers.

Sure, they're programmed with advanced artificial intelligence, and were designed to be formidable opponents, but they are stupid compared to the stuff I've developed over the years.

The dummies advance on us, metal bodies glinting in the artificial light, and mechanical limbs clanking against the floor. They're pretty fast and are vaguely shaped like the Tuldarians. Honestly, they're too fast to be great representations of the lizards.

Okay, cue the music, here's the montage. I'll spare the details, since you know what this kind of thing is like.

Royal Rampage roars and charges forward, his massive strength allowing him to take out several of the robots in one blow. Sinsation flips and twists through the air, taking out more of the machines with her acrobatics. And Justice's martial arts skills are on full display as he takes out the remaining robots with lightning-fast kicks and punches.

Now we get a super tight shot on me, 'cause I'm the star of this sucker. *Damn* I look good.

I summon my super-strength, focusing all my energy into my hands. I run forward and *bam!* easily overpower the first robot I run into. I pull it apart like a loaf of bread. One by one, I lift more robots off the ground and toss them across the room like a boss, but I'm reminded again that I really need to work on upping my invulnerability for times like this when I can't use my weapons. This melee stuff hurts almost as bad as getting zapped by one of their plasma beams.

Back to the background actors. Gotta give them *some* screen-time, you know?

Royal Rampage lets out another mighty roar—he pretty much hasn't shut up this whole time. Slamming his fists into the ground, he causes a shockwave that sends several of the machines onto their backs. They roll around like turtles trying to get up, but he pounces, then pounds the robots over and over, shattering their metal exteriors. I make a mental note not to get on that guy's bad side.

Scene change: Sinsation flips and dodges the robots' attacks, striking them with precise kicks and punches. When it comes to robots, her pheromones aren't going to do any good. The camera slows down—extreeeeme slow-mo—as she twirls and somersaults through the air. This one's for the thirsty boys—or girls—out there. She's not all that strong, but she's able to send two of them slamming into each other, and then the sparks fly.

Justice zips by, stealing the focus of the shot. Booo! We follow him as he moves with lightning speed, dodging and striking his opponents like Jackie Chan. His fists and feet are a blur. Bam! Pow! Ooof. He takes a gut punch, but brushes it off like a true hero. Hey, I gotta give him some credit, right?

There's something familiar about that guy, but I can't put my finger on it. Nice to see he can fight without his guns.

I'm pretty shocked. As a team, we're doing pretty good. These robots suck against our combined might. We move with coordination and precision, taking out the mechanical enemies until, finally, Justice and I slam into each other.

"WTF, man!" Justice shouts, shoving me.

Don't worry, I barely felt it.

Behind us, Sinsation takes out the last of the robots.

"Watch where you're going," I tell him.

"*You* watch where you're going."

Both of us face off with raised fists. I'm not sure who's gonna swing first. Probably him. I'm an adult. I've learned to have some patience, whereas he, I deduce, hasn't.

"You saw what I did to those hunks of metal," he says. "Wanna be next?"

Sinsation strides over, wiping grease off her hands. "Okay, boys. We get it. You're both *huge* and there's no need to measure."

"Whatever, man. This guy thinks 'cause they made him the leader we have to follow? I heard he used to be a supervillain."

"So did I," Sinsation says. "It's fun!"

"And didn't you shoot some people in the head?" I ask, ignoring her.

"Yeah, freaking bad guys."

"Well, that's what separates us. I've never killed."

"Oh, so you're an underachiever too?" Justice laughs. "You're nothing, old man. Couldn't even take Eaglestar, and those aliens turned him to sludge."

Old? How old does he think I am?

That comment cuts deep for more reasons than that. Not because I wish I *had* killed Eaglestar, but... I don't know. I guess—I guess Eaglestar's death has hit me harder than I care to admit. And because of that, I hit Justice harder than I probably should have.

He drops to the floor like a sack of stones, out cold.

"Whoa, whoa!" Sinsation says, stepping between us.

Rampage jumps up and down, practically shaking the room. Thankfully, Sinsation raises a hand to halt the gorilla before he tries to avenge his friend.

"I'm sorry," I say. "I didn't—"

"Why don't you just go," Sinsation says, pointing to the door. "You probably shouldn't be here when he comes to."

"But we have to—"

"Go!" she shouts.

So much for getting lucky with her. "Yeah. Alright. Fine. I'll go."

I turn and walk away, but I hear pounding footsteps behind me. I spin, ready to fight, but Royal Rampage skids to a halt beside me.

"Snack time?" he asks.

I nod. "Sure. Let's get some snacks."

This was not how I expected things to turn out.

Crap.

As I head for the conference room for our last briefing before we leave on our mission, Baron Steele is coming my way.

Eaglestar and I had a strange relationship. We were nemeses, but I'd almost describe the whole thing as... fun. We had a special sort of banter between us, which most people find anything from odd to impossible to believe depending on how well they knew him. I've been told I was delusional when dishing about my encounters with him, but I tell it the way I remember it. No cap. I don't consider myself delusional, but who knows? Maybe I've been punched in the head too many times.

But my relationship with Baron Steele has never been anything but contentious. I mean, he hates me. He flat-out hates my guts. Not that I blame him, after the way things used to go between us when he was still in the hero biz, including the most recent: me helping the CVT take him down after he used his powers in public. Needless to say, I definitely don't want to run into him in an empty corridor.

But, if wishes were nickels, I'd be rich.

I don't even have time to brace myself before...

Wham! He slams me up against the wall hard enough to dent the metal. I'm strong, but he's almost as powerful as Eaglestar is—was—probably an eight on the scale. I'm lucky if I'm a five when I've eaten my Wheaties in the morning.

He holds me there—keeps me there. I couldn't move if I wanted to. In fact, I do want to, but it's no use. His forearm is pressed against my neck, but not quite hard enough to hurt me.

"You prob'ly think you're swinging quite the clankers after takin' me down in New York. Let me tell you something, you ponce. You're nothing. Without Eaglestar, you wouldn'ta stood a chance against me, you got it?"

"Yeah. Totally." I stammer the response a bit. You try having a lead pipe like this guy's arm up against your throat.

"I'm leavin' you standing 'cause I need you. And let me tell you, bucko, it's a suicide mission, and I certainly don't want to stand in the way of your demise. But we ain't done, me and you. You somehow manage to survive, we're gonna continue this little chat later on."

"Looking forward to it," I lie.

He stares at me for a few more seconds before pulling his hand away. "Now, get your arse to Conference Room D. We've got a lot to discuss."

Finally able to breathe, I stand there, watching him stomp away.

When I switched sides, I thought all this bullying was over. I told you about the time Eaglestar broke into my house while I was in the middle of dumping my girlfriend, right?

This crap used to happen all the time. Heroes are like that. They like to impose their will, but since they won't kill, I always found a way to escape before being dragged into custody. But now, what chance does a guy have against Paul "The Baron" Steele when we're both on the same side?

I continue toward the conference room, considering my poor life choices. When I reach the door—which was like twenty feet away—I notice it's already open and my team is inside, and Paul Steele is standing at the front of the room.

They're all staring at me, and it's totally obvious that they heard the whole exchange.

Sinsation, her feet up on the conference table, is filing her nails as she says, "*Awk*-ward..."

Distracted, I go to sit in the first seat I find. Before my butt hits the chair, I feel it fly out from beneath me. I don't fall like a kid in elementary school, but I'm confused until I notice Justice across the table for me.

"Not here," he says. His lip is swollen from where I socked him earlier.

"Somethin' goin' on between you two kiddos?" the Baron asks. Justice lowers his head slightly to keep the wound from view. "Ah, I see. Bit of a schoolyard scrap, huh? Well, get over it. This is the fate of the world we're talkin' 'bout. Got it?"

Justice and I meet gazes for a second.

"We good?" I ask.

"Until this is over," Justice promises.

"Good enough for me."

I pull the chair back into place and sit up straight and tall like I hadn't just had my rear end handed to me twice.

"Alright, boys and girls," Paul says, glaring at me. "This ain't my idea of a fun time, and I'd like it to end as quickly as possible. That's where you come in. You've had your little rest while the big boys are out there doing all the hard work."

"I could've been on one of Bastet's teams," I whisper.

Paul throws his binder at me. Papers fly and float to the floor. "That right? Fact is, you're lucky you're even here, *Eric*. Wasn't for Jonathan Powers—rest his soul—you'd have been greetin' him in the afterlife. Can't tell you how many times the Guild's little 'no-killing' rule saved your sorry, pitiful life. So, if you wanna prove yourself here and now, I got time. If not, can I continue?"

I bite my tongue and nod. Whether he likes it or not, I'm not the dude I used to be, and I wanna save the world for once.

"Great. So here's the skinny..."

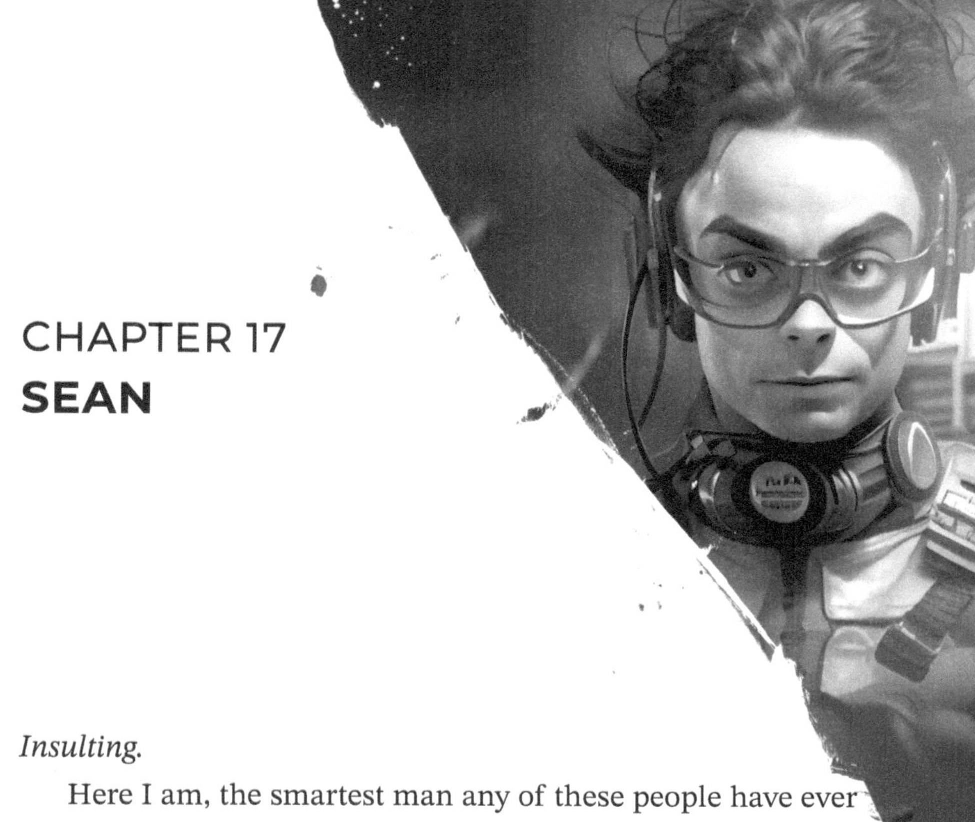

CHAPTER 17
SEAN

Insulting.

Here I am, the smartest man any of these people have ever met, and I'm stuck in training with peons. The leftovers. The bottom of the barrel. The losers.

First comes the Russian meathead whose name I can't recall. It may have been Stone Cold or Piledriver or who cares? Following him is the attractive woman who, despite her modesty, would give Sinsation a run for her money in the seduction department. Her name, I remember: Whisper. Brown hair, green eyes, purple mask and cape. But I still, for the life of me, can't figure out what her powers might be. Something to do with vibrating molecules or some such. But, I suppose that's what this little exercise is all about.

Next up, Jaguar guy, a strong-and-silent type. And finally, the little blonde girl named Prairie. You know, the annoying one with the bunny tail.

Last, Annihilatrix. I haven't figured her out yet, and I don't like an unknown entity. She strides right to the front as if I don't exist.

"I've been in rooms such as these before," she tells us. "They will send low-level bots at us in large numbers. We will be required to work together to dispatch them before a new wave is brought in. Should we succeed, the goal is for us to become acquainted with each other. We've wasted more than enough time here while Torturess is being held captive. Let's make it quick."

"Mmmmm. Yes," I say, stepping in front of her. "Robots. My specialty. You'll find that we will not need to do much fighting." Everyone looks at me, but I turn my attention to the control room. "Commence training exercise."

Whoever sits at the controls behind the glass says, "Whereas the others were paired with robots, and their powers were removed, you will have access to all abilities and tech while engaged. You do not have the luxury of time, given the importance of your mission."

I raise my hand.

"Yes?" the mystery man says.

"If this mission is so important—which it is—why have you not given me… I don't know, anyone useful?"

Without a response from the control room, the faux battle begins.

Everyone stares at me like I'd stolen the last chip from the plate. "It's no matter. I can do this on my own. Just don't get in my way."

The big Russian gives me a dirty look and charges in like a juggernaut, head down, shoulder pressed forward. He might be one of the biggest guys I've ever seen in real life. But you know what they say—the bigger they are, the dumber they look while running.

I raise a hand as he passes me, and like a good little soldier, he stops.

"Why we wait?" he asks in his broken English.

"Watch." I tap a four-digit code into the bracer on my wrist, and with a whirl, all dozen of the flying drones turn to one another and fire. All of them fall to the ground in a smoking heap.

"That's not what this is supposed to be!" Annihilatrix shouts.

"Would you rather waste time fighting?" I ask.

"I would like to understand everyone's abilities and how they can best be used to save Torturess."

"You mean stop the Tuldarians?"

She glares at me. "I meant what I said."

"Ah, well..." I approach her slowly. "It seems our goals may differ."

"Don't you worry," she warns, poking me in the chest. "I'll kill as many as the creepy crawlies as necessary to meet my ends. No cheating on round two. Let's get this over with quickly so we can get the bloody hell out of here."

"Speed was entirely my intent behind my last display of power—which you yourself have said you'd like to see."

"Yes, but aliens not robots, yes?" the Russian says.

"Rockhard is right..." Prairie argues.

Rockhard! That's his name. Silly moniker. Sounds like an adult movie star. I'd say it might sound better in Russian, but I know the language, and *tverdyy kamen* sounds even dumber.

"If that's all you've got, it's not going to do much good against lizards. Duh." Prairie brushes her hair aside.

"Round two," the voice announces over the PA system.

Panels in the walls on all four cardinal directions open up and I reach for my arm bracer. But Annihilatrix stops me, grabbing my hand and giving a stern look.

The bots are menacing enough that I'm jealous I didn't create them. Each one wields knives that look sharp enough to pierce steel—presumably to simulate the talons—and has glowing yellow lights on their chests the intensify as they move. My working assumption is they are charging to unleash a blast of some kind, like the alien guns.

Annihilatrix reaches for her belt and pulls a whip. It isn't part of her powerset, but I do recognize it from the time I fought her partner, Torturess, years ago. I can only surmise she's planning on punishing the Tuldarians with the whip as some sort of vengeance thing.

She cracks it forward, and the metal barbs on the end drive through the chest of the bot closest to us. As expected—and feared—the machine explodes, sending shards flying in all directions.

Suddenly, I'm bleeding.

I don't want to sound dramatic or anything, but it is a lot of blood. I hear a lot of commotion, metal rending, shots fired, and the like. Through blurred eyes—*not* tears —I see Whisper rush to my side like an angel with no wings.

"Oh, that's not good," she says.

I groan while I feel blood gurgle out of my leg. "At what point are we going to be attacked by angry iron chefs?"

"Just shut up and be still." Whisper does something, tending to my wound. Even with the gash in my leg, I'd still managed to put down several of the bladed robots by turning them against each other with my arm bracer.

Whisper's quite a bit younger than me, and more or less my height. She pushes a lock of dark hair away from her face and loops it around her ear. She's seriously close to the gaping wound.

"Not exactly the close encounter I was hoping for," she says.

"Uh-huh. Can you fix it?" I ask.

"Next wave in two minutes." The voice is automated but sounds strangely familiar.

"Was that Bla—I mean, was that Douglas?" I ask.

"That was warning we are dying soon," Rockhard says.

Before anyone can respond, we begin floating as if all the gravity is sucked out of the room.

"You've got to be kidding me!" I shout toward the control room. Murderous butcher robots *and* no gravity?

"Still. Quiet." Whisper leans in and softly speaks something I can't hear. A green globe grows on her lips, then moves toward my wound and wraps around my leg.

"Ouch!" I suck air through clenched teeth. I guess I must have pulled my leg away because Whisper yanks on it hard.

"I said be still!"

A strange sensation envelops me, almost like the pins and needles present when a limb goes numb. The smell of searing flesh meets my nostrils and I turn my head away. Apparently, her powers work like a microwave, vibrating molecules until they heat up. Perhaps she can slow them down also? I'm unsure when that might come into use, but I put it in my back pocket for the time being.

"*Que cobarde*," El Jaguar Inmortal says.

"Hey! *Yo hablo español, pendejo*," I retort.

"Enough!" Whisper says. "You're ready to go. Does it still hurt?"

I think about it for a second. It really doesn't. There's a dull pain, but not the sharp, tingly pain that was there moments ago. I wonder what good it is for us to do this training if we end up too injured to fight for real.

"I can stand on it?" I ask. "Run?"

"Well, running would be easier if we weren't floating in zero gravity, but so would patching you up. I'm believe you're okay to fight."

"Reassuring."

"Would you rather me have let you die here in the bunker?" She crosses her arms and dips her chin slightly.

I grunt and say, "Thanks."

The next wave of mechanical enemies pours out of several openings along the base of the walls. As soon as they roll out, their wheels leave the ground and they begin floating right along with us. The doors in the walls slide shut and I hear a very distinct sound. A click and a whoosh reveal it before even the flame.

"Cool! They have jet packs," Prairie says.

They sure do. They soar in every direction faster than I can track them. I quickly grab hold of one of the handles on the ceiling to keep me in place. The others are still close to the ground. By my count, there are six of the robots. We're outnumbered and way outmatched.

"Anyone have a plan?" Prairie shouts. "My powers don't work on mechanical things."

"Don't die!" Whisper responds.

"They aren't attacking," I say. "They're just... floating there."

"What does that mean?" Whisper asks.

Just then, one gets too close to the big Russian ox. He reaches out and grabs it with both hands and begins convulsing.

"They are electrically charged!" I yell as I kick off the ceiling and torpedo toward Rockhard. "You *sure* you don't want me to disable them?"

My momentum has me slamming into the big Slav hard enough to force him to let go. I experience a brutal shock as well, but not nearly what Rockhard did. And he *is* rock hard. Ramming into him feels like hitting bricks. His hands are red and shaking. I look back over my shoulder to see the robot powering toward us.

"Whisper!" I shout. "He needs attention!"

I try to draw the focus of the robot. Thankfully for Rockhard, it works. Sadly for me, it works. An enemy I can't touch is hurtling toward me and I can barely force myself to move. As I float in zero-g, I stretch the toe of my boot until it finds something solid and gives me a small boost. The robot follows.

El Jaguar pushes off from a wall and corkscrews through the air like a synchronized dancer. As if he didn't just watch the Russian become a sizzling mess, he kicks the robot away from me, and gets a quick jolt for the act. I'm delighted about this until I notice that another robot is coming at me from the other direction.

El Jaguar grabs the robot closest to him—I have no idea what his strategy could be—and he convulses as he holds onto it tight. It starts to smoke and then suddenly he goes limp and the robot's lights fade out and it powers down. I guess that's one way to handle these, as long as you don't mind electrocuting yourself to death.

Then again, he supposedly can't die. I guess I understand his strategy now. If true, perhaps he will be a good addition to our little team. Makes me wish I'd had him with me in the Trench.

Rockhard is out like a baby on Nyquil, Whisper doing something at his side. But it's clear her attention is split between helping Rockhard and finding a way toward the newly dead Jaguar. But all of a sudden, true to his name, the

Immortal Jaguar just jerks back to life, loudly sucking in a deep breath.

Prairie is in a worse situation than I am, with three of the robots surrounding her, closing in.

"What do I do?" she calls.

With a roar that would make Royal Rampage jealous, Annihilatrix soars past me. Where the rest of us flounder around like fish out of water in zero-g, she seems to be flying. When within range, she snaps her whip, grabs hold of the robot closest to Prairie, and sends it shattering against the wall. She rounds on the other two, again in complete control of her actions.

Suddenly, the lights flicker and I'm dropping. I try to flip myself around to land on my feet, but unlike El Jaguar, I'm no cat. Okay, he's not a cat either.

I land with a hard thud on my butt, feeling as if my tailbone smashes to a million pieces. It will at least be bruised. Six loud crashes tell me the machines are no longer rocketing around the room.

Someone had restored gravity to the room.

"What the hell?" I hear Whisper say.

"Lucky for all of you," a voice says over the speaker system. It *is* Frank Douglas. Of course. "We have a situation that requires your immediate attention. Meet me in Conference Room C in twenty minutes."

We all look at Rockhard.

"He'll be fine in a minute," Frank says. "Oh, and wear your uniforms."

CHAPTER 18
SAWYER

Anxious.

They stick us in another conference room for one last briefing before we head off on our mission. As a team, I don't think we're ready, but a few hours—or even a few more days—won't make much difference. Unless we were gonna get a solid week or two together, we're about as good as it gets.

I'm seated next to the new Firefly guy, and decide, since he's the only one I don't know, this might be a good opportunity.

"So how long you been doing this?" I ask. "You know, the masked-crimefighter-thing."

His voice crackles through the helmet. "A few years. I'm not very good at it."

That's reassuring.

"But I had a partner who was."

Still not reassuring.

"I was good at helping him, I think."

He lets out an awkward little squeaking laugh that sounds awfully familiar despite being filtered through his helmet.

Before I can continue, Mr. Chen enters the conference room a couple of steps behind his own air of superiority. Traitor. I was hoping to get someone else to brief us on the situation. I mean, really, really hoping to get anyone but him.

"President Stanford wants to wish you the best on your mission, and wants you to know that all of America—all of the world, in fact—is counting on you." Chen taps a button on a laptop computer seated on the conference table and the large video screen mounted on the wall lights up. The president appears on the screen, wearing a baseball cap and a white polo shirt. Though the background is blurry, there's an awful lot of green.

"Is he playing golf?" someone asks.

"Shhh," a few others hush in sync.

"This on?" President Stanford asks. "Oh, you're ready? Okay. Great. People, friends... I just want to say that I know you will succeed in your mission. America is the greatest country in the history of the world, and we have the best heroes. Good luck."

"Is this live?" I ask.

"No, it's a recording from earlier today," Chen responds.

"Where is he?"

"Excuse me?" Chen looks annoyed.

"Where is the president *exactly*? Is there some reason he can't send us off in-person?"

This is one of the few times I've ever seen Chen become uncomfortable. I've never wished so badly that I could record something, but there's no way I'd be able to get away with it. I'll have to settle for the snapshot in my mind.

"He's unavailable at the moment," Chen says with a note of finality.

I'm not satisfied. "Why? What's more important than these meetings that are determining how we're gonna save the world?"

Chen messes with his laptop again and the still frame of the president on what, indeed, looks curiously similar to a golf course disappears. "The president is no longer at the base."

We all look around at one another in astonishment.

"He left?" I ask.

Chen says something, but it's barely audible. He's actually mumbling... another first, in my experience.

"I'm sorry, we couldn't hear you," I say.

"He's in Florida," he admits.

I stand. "He's freaking golfing at the end of the world?"

A lot of people murmur and argue.

"Yes, *Black Harrier*," Chen says, obviously trying to hide his true emotions. "The president felt a break was in order after days of arduous discussions."

"Discussions," I scoff. "We're putting our lives on the line to save the whole damn world, and the poor president is tuckered out from talking?"

"I never thought he'd get tired of talking," Pace says.

"You will show respect to our president," Chen says, slamming his prosthetic hand on the podium. He gathers himself. Clears his throat. "The president's part in this matter is complete. Surely, you don't expect him to go out on the battlefield. If he were capable of such a thing, do you think we'd have gathered all of you? No. I didn't think so."

Chen is shook. Which is rare, like I said.

I shake my head. "This is not acceptable."

"Are you implying something, Mr. Vincent?" Chen says my name this time, almost like a reminder or something. "Would you like me to put you through to him?"

I nod. "Maybe I would."

"Well, I won't!" Chen shouts. Once again, another first. I honestly don't think I've ever heard Luis Chen lose his cool. "He is the leader of the free world, not one of your InstaBook *followers*. Now, sit down!"

I look around at everyone staring at me. This is decision time for me. One of those adult things I haven't had a ton of time to figure out. Either I do what he expects, be the teenager he's always sort of been in charge of or...

I slowly stand and walk out of the room, ignoring his warning for me to come back.

I wish I could have slammed the door behind me, but it has one of those doo-hickies that regulates how fast it can close. Once in the corridor, I wait for it to shut fully, then let out a breath.

I can't believe how lightly some people are taking this situation. Have they become so complacent? So reliant upon the Guild to save the world that they are this blasé about things?

I don't have a lot of time to ponder over the potential answers to my inquiry. As I turn the corner, Frank leaves one of the other conference rooms. He spots me right after I spot him. It seems like it takes him some effort to pull his eyes away from the tablet in his hands.

I nod at him. "I guess we're leaving soon."

"Unfortunately." He doesn't look happy at all. Not that he ever does, but at the moment he looks especially unhappy.

"Why's that? Something wrong?" I ask.

He looks back at the conference room he just left. "This group they put me in charge of. I'm not feeling very confident about them."

"So you're gonna be coordinating that team in the field?" I point to the room. "Who is it?"

He's looking back down at the tablet again. "Yes." He answers half the question, and I take that as a sign he isn't interested in responding further.

"I was hoping you'd be able to help out the Resistors."

He looks up, raising an eyebrow. "Who?"

I look away for a second, then back at him. "You know... my team?"

"Yes. Right... the Resistors. I'm sorry. I just have a lot on my mind."

"Did you even try?" I ask.

He's even more confused now. "Try what?"

"To get my team. Instead of those guys." I gesture toward the conference room.

"Why would I do that?"

My blood is already boiling from the last few minutes, now it's threatening to poach my brain. But instead of escalating the confrontation, I just turn away. "Never mind."

I feel him grab my shoulder. But gently, not in a hostile way.

"Sawyer..."

When I turn around, I'm confronted with an expression on Frank's face that I'm unfamiliar with. Is it... pride maybe?

"The reason I didn't ask to help out your team is because I'm confident you don't need it. They already have a fully capable leader. The best."

Pow. That hits me like a punch to the solar plexus. But in a good way, somehow. "I, uh... I don't... uh... thanks."

Grabbing my hand, he shakes it, and in a low voice says, "This whole thing... It's you all risking your lives, but I'm the guy deciding who has a chance to live and who's going to die."

He looks down at his tablet again.

"What is it?" I ask.

"Paul's team... they're not coming back. It's a suicide mission. That's why I'm so distracted. We're supposed to be advising these people how best to handle themselves, but it's no use."

"Who's on the team?" I ask, a note of concern in my voice.

"A bunch of murderers. Battlegear, Sinsation, that guy

they call Justice... Just... be careful out there. And make sure you come back to your mom... and me."

Between his worry over me, and the thing that's been burning inside of me for days, I'm so overwhelmed that I can't even respond. Then I feel my eyes welling up with tears.

"Are you okay?" he asks.

I can't let Frank send Justice on a suicide mission, even if it is to save the world. He doesn't know he's his son. At least I don't think he does.

"There's something I have to tell you. And it can't wait."

"I'm sorry, we just don't have time right now."

"Frank, listen to me," I say.

"Sawyer, there's no—"

"You'll wanna hear this!" I shout.

"What is it?" he asks.

"It's Justice." I pause, trying to get a read on Frank's expression. There's none. Just a blank face waiting for me to get to the point. "I found out he has the same abilities I do—that you do. And he doesn't know who his dad is. Frank, I think—"

"No." Frank shakes his head. "Can't be."

"It's true. He has to be your son."

"He's not," Luis Chen chimes in as he approaches from behind me.

"What's this about, Luis?" Frank says.

"Listen to me, Frank," he says. "Justice is not your son. He's Andrew Garner."

I can't even keep track of all the revelations.

"Alex's brother?" Frank asks.

"Yes."

"So does that mean you're Alex's dad too?" I ask, mind racing. I turn to Mr. Chen. "Wait... Frank, don't trust him. He's been spying on us for years."

Frank nods. "I know."

"You knew?" Mr. Chen and I say at the same time.

Frank laughs. Actually laughs. "Of course I knew. Did you think I was just some dumb playboy billionaire?"

Mr. Chen runs a hand through his hair. "Frank, I'm sorry. It's not what it looks li—"

"We can discuss that later. Luis, what's going on here? Andrew Garner?"

Chen sighs. "Your father made sure he was adopted by one of his... lady friends after the massacre at the restaurant. She was basically a full-time nanny whom he lived with, but Drew was so young, he thought she was his mother. Big Frankie Jr. wanted to keep him safe but out of the way. But then when you... took him out... nobody else knew about Drew. And Kayla, your father's maid and Drew's guardian—did everything she could to keep it that way, afraid that she and the boy would be next. With the money cut off, they didn't do well."

The whole thing sounds way too familiar. Not the exact same thing I went through, but close enough to hit home with me.

"I don't understand," I say to Frank. "Why would your father take care of Alex's brother? Since when was there a connection with our family before you found Alex at the orphanage?"

"We don't have time for this," Frank says.

"*Make* time. I want answers," I say.

"I'll tell you," says Chen, to Frank's chagrin. "Alex and Andrew's mother was your grandfather's illegitimate half-sister, Sawyer. She was your great aunt."

"What? How can that be?"

"Your great-grandfather, Franklin Douglas Sr., had an estranged daughter. He took care of her and kept her close, as did Frankie Jr. after Franklin died. And hired her husband, Alan Garner, to work for Douglas Industries."

I press two fingers against the bridge of my nose. I'm getting a headache. All this time, I thought this meant both Alex and Justice were Frank's sons, and maybe when Frank learned of Alex's whereabouts, he rescued him from the orphanage, similar to how he'd brought me onboard.

Never did I expect this to become some weird daytime soap opera story. *Murder and betrayal, tomorrow at noon.*

"Someone found out who she was," Frank picks up, apparently okay with it now that so much is out in the open. "And had her and her family killed as a message to my father. Much like they did with my mother."

"So Alex is, what, your cousin? Some kind of nephew?" Admittedly, those kinds of familial ties confuse me. "Does he know? Why would—"

"He is unaware that anyone knows Andrew's whereabouts," Frank interrupts. "Or was, until Luis decided to tell him recently."

I glare at Chen. "Is that why Alex refused to come here?"

But Frank is the one to answer. "I don't know. It may be part of it."

"We need to tell Justi—Drew everything," I say. "It's not right to keep it from him."

"No," Chen says. "His team has already left for their mission. If you tell him now, it will only mess with his head and increase the chances of him not making it through alive."

"What are his chances even without that?" I ask.

"Honestly, not good," Frank responds. "But neither are ours."

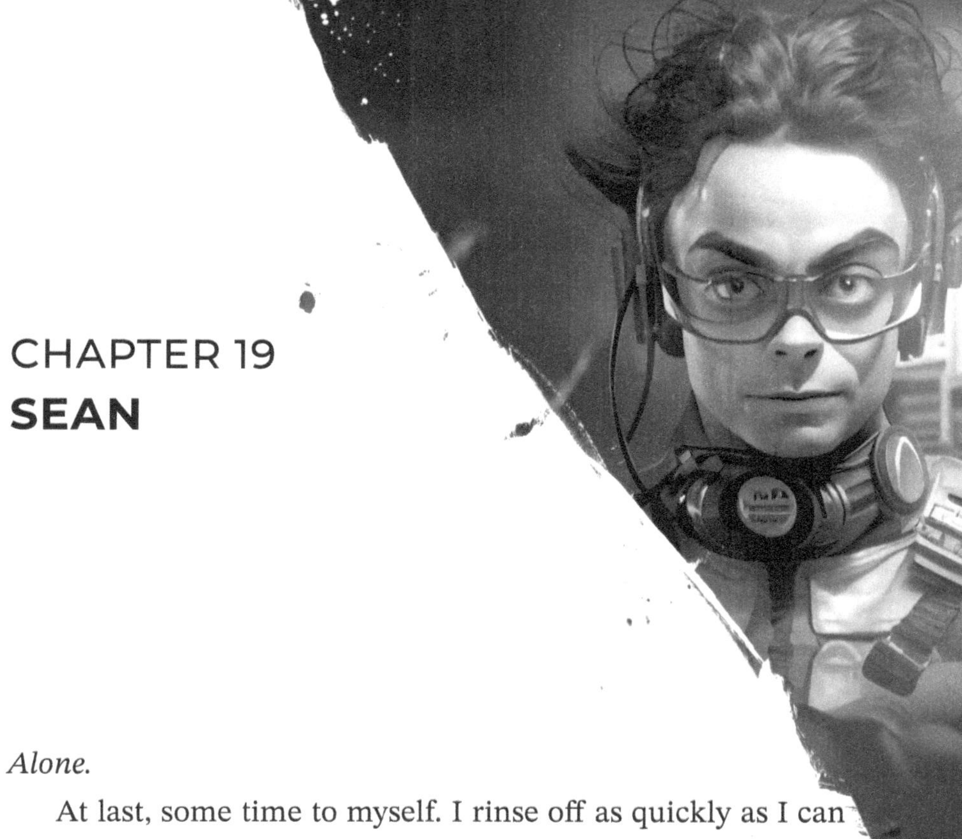

CHAPTER 19
SEAN

Alone.

At last, some time to myself. I rinse off as quickly as I can and put on a fresh costume. Ah yes, I forgot to mention these people outfitted us with new costumes and gear. I suppose it makes sense that Frank Douglas wouldn't want me heading out to fight for the government in the orange jumpsuit I've worn in the Trench for all these years.

There's a fancy helmet. I slip it on and it emits a high-pitched screeching. I squeeze my ears shut, but it dissipates quickly. I give myself a once over in the mirror. The visor covers my whole face. It's less a visor and more a form-fitted segment of glass that I hope is stronger than it looks. A little loading symbol flashes in the corner of my visor and in a sudden burst of color, the HUD lights up with all kinds of information about my surroundings. What a distraction. I search for an "off" button but can find nothing. Instead, I remove the helmet altogether, deciding between the potential for another squeal and the vision impedance, I'd be better off without it. I haven't needed a helmet so far, so why start now?

Leaving my assigned quarters, I make my way toward Conference Room C. I'm not sure what I expected from a room designed for a conference, but it's small. I thought we'd be meeting with all the supers who were present in the facility, but to my surprise, it's just my team.

Rockhard looks like he's completely recovered. He sits with his arms crossed over his barrel of a chest, slumped back in his chair. He looks embarrassed, and for about a second, I feel sorry for him. But then Whisper slinks up next to me and our elbows and hips touch. I take a side step to place a buffer between us and she scoffs, then moves to her seat and plops down.

Jaguar sits in silence, looking none the worse for wear despite the fact that he died no less than an hour ago.

Franklin Douglas III enters through the door on the other side of the room and steps up to a podium. How many times are we going to go through this?

"Sean." He nods. "Team." Nodding again. "Things have escalated a bit faster than we'd expected. Luckily, your plane is only twenty minutes out."

"What's going on?" I ask.

He sighs heavily and looks me in the eye. "It turns out, you might have been right."

I fight back a smug look but can't help myself. "That surprises you? What was I right about this time? I've become quite used to never being wrong; it's hard to guess what you might be referring—"

"The Torturess was last seen in Egypt, as you know," he cuts me off.

"Did you see her again?" Annihilatrix asks.

"No, but we don't believe what transpired this morning is a coincidence."

"Which is?" she says, sitting forward in her seat.

"Turns out, the zombie apocalypse has truly come earlier than expected." Douglas taps his tablet, and the screen behind him lights up.

There they are on the screen: *actual* zombies. I don't mean people mindlessly staring at their phone like you'd see on any subway or DMV waiting room. I mean corpses rising from their graves and walking the Earth once again. Rotting, ambling, undead people.

"How is this possible?" Rockhard asks.

"I was going to ask the same thing." Great. Now I'm asking the same questions that moronic Slav is. I hope that doesn't mean I'm losing intelligence just by being around him. Maybe that's one of his powers—intelligence-sink.

"I'm pretty sure all of us were thinking the same thing," Whisper adds. She smiles at me when I look over at her, but I'm not quite sure why.

"That's the $64,000 question." Douglas looks at us, but we all return blank stares.

"Why 64,000?" asks Prairie.

"Because that used to be—never mind, it's not important.

What I'm saying is that nobody knows yet, and we're still trying to figure it out. It could be some new manifestation of the Torturess's powers, or she may have come across some ancient artifact that's allowing her to do it. Certainly the Nazis didn't uncover every supernatural artifact in existence during World War II."

"Why are we still sitting here?" Annihilatrix demands.

"We're in a tough position here. We needed a bunker safe enough to house the most important people in the world—including you all—but that has limited our ability to get planes in and out. As I've said, your plane will be he—"

"We don't have time for this," Annihilatrix says, standing. "I can fly, and I don't need you or some aeroplane."

It's nice to not be the one storming out of rooms. But I can't blame her. If I could fly, I'd have left long ago.

"You're just gonna like, let the most powerful member of our team leave without us?" Prairie asks.

"You're welcome to try to stop her," Douglas says. "I'm not going to waste my time attempting the impossible when we already have so little of it."

Prairie crosses her arms and slumps back in her chair in a huff.

"What about the rest of the team I was promised then?"

"They're not coming," says Douglas.

"Why is that?"

"Their plane was destroyed by the Tuldarians on their way here," he replies.

The rest of my team members give one another a *"This is*

all there is?" look. Or maybe I'm just projecting my own feelings about it.

Douglas clears his throat. "As I was saying, your plane is moments away. Bastet's teams were vital to saving lives in the here and now. While the Tuldarians have been content in guarding the pyramids from airspace, now that this—whatever it is—has occurred, your roles have become priority number one."

"They should have been our first plan of action from the start," I say.

"While that might be true, the streets in every major city in the world have been overrun for a couple of days now. We felt stopping the mass slaughter was of utmost importance."

"That's always the problem with you heroes. You can never see the big picture, can you?" I'm getting frustrated. After all, this speculation isn't really helpful to solving the problem. Time to move on. The hardest part for me is not saying that out loud.

Douglas ignores me, listening to someone in an earpiece. "Congratulations. Your plane is here. Just be aware, you'll need to parachute down, as landing isn't a possibility."

The others share a look of concern, I assume because they're afraid. Me, I'm just worried about these people being my only backup. What I've seen so far hasn't inspired a lot of confidence.

"Surely you cannot be serious," Whisper says.

"It's very rare that I'm not," Douglas says.

"You expect us to fly in, untrained and blind, then leap out of a plane to figure out how to deal with *zombies*?" Whisper asks.

"What is to figure out?" Rockhard asks. "Double tap in head, right? We have all seen in movies, *da*?"

I roll my eyes. "Not to mention someone who may turn out to be one of the most powerful supervillains in history?"

Frank raises a hand. "I told you, she—"

"I know you *think* the Torturess is not that powerful, but I happen to know otherwise. With the aliens tapping her true potential and amplifying it, you're only now starting to comprehend it. As time goes on, you'll find more and more just how mistaken you were. I just hope it's not too late for us by then."

"I hope this is one case where you're wrong, Mr. Meyers," Douglas says. "Now, you won't be without backup. While your mission is yours and yours alone, you'll have others there to even the odds."

"Yippee," I say sarcastically.

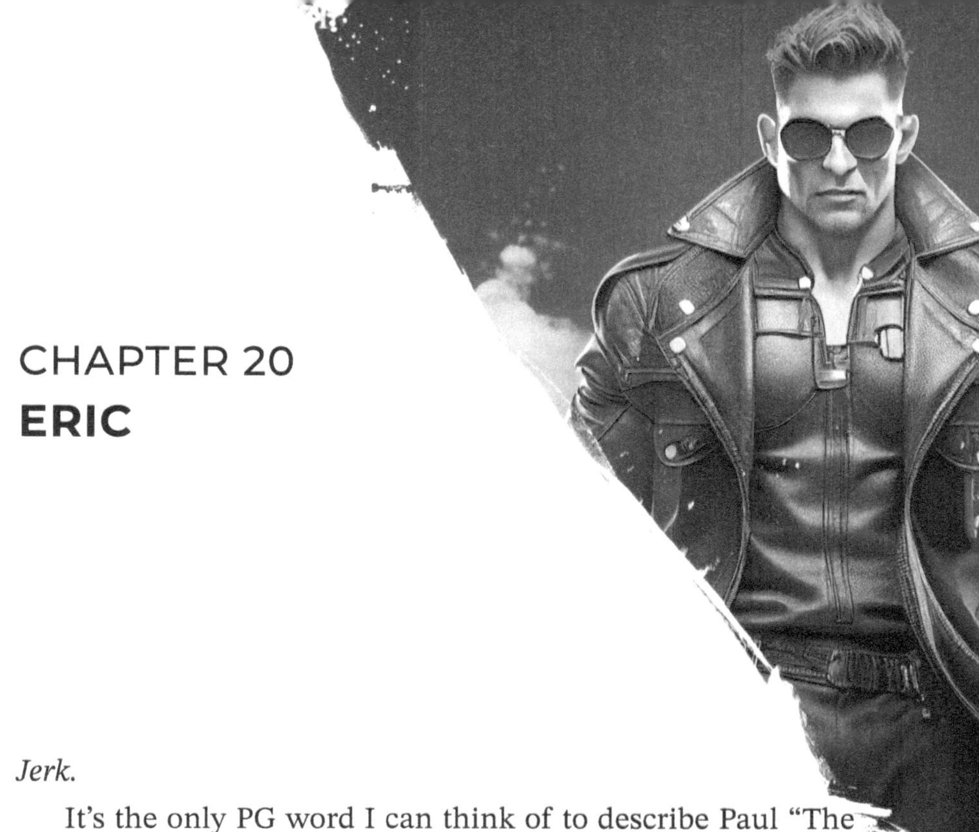

CHAPTER 20
ERIC

Jerk.

It's the only PG word I can think of to describe Paul "The Baron" Steele. What a stupid name. Baron. "Oh, look at me. I'm royalty in a country that lost the war and no longer matters."

Jerk.

All I know is if he ever comes at me like this again, he's going to catch these hands, if you know what I mean.

One thing I know for sure: he's wrong. This isn't a suicide mission. I feel like this'll be easy.

My team of super-powered individuals has to board the enemy alien mothership. Yeah, they killed Eaglestar, but I could have too, if I'd wanted to. But I couldn't do that. We were friends, you know? Played on different sides of the field, but neither of us were out for blood.

Everyone keeps reminding me that time is running out.

Sure, but we still have to be careful not to rush in. Then we would get killed. And I'm not planning on dying at all. First on the agenda, we take out that damn machine that siphons away everyone's powers. If we don't stop it, the entire planet will be in danger.

Our mission is to infiltrate the ship, destroy the power-sucking machine, then make our way to the control room, where we'll plant a bomb and blow the whole ship to pieces.

Cake.

I've pulled off more complicated bank robberies.

Plus, I'm not alone in this mission. I'm sure they gave me the best for this important mission. We got this.

I've got my new main bro, Royal Rampage. For a gorilla, he's super smart. Then there's Sinsation—ow *ow.* Have I mentioned she's a bombshell, and has the sickest acrobatic skills I've ever seen? I feel like maybe I talk about her a lot. But, she's just as deadly with her bare hands as she is with a weapon. The best part about her (other than the obvious) is that even if the aliens manage to bleed her of her powers, the pheromones she uses to seduce humans probably wouldn't work on them, anyway. Those fighting skills aren't superpowers—just A+ badassery with a little bit of not giving any effs thrown in.

And finally, Justice. Apart from our little tuss-up, I feel the guy. We get each other. He likes guns. I like guns. I heard he can pop a tomato from a mile away with precision.

Like, I said, cake.

Since receiving the call from the Veep and before being

flown out here by the US military, I had time to gather up some things I knew would come in handy. That includes my sky-gliders (trademark pending), hovercycles that work like a charm. Just like I knew they would. Fortuitous timing, for reals. I just finished developing these for the CVT after perfecting my prototype over the past couple of years. I'd even had to build one big enough to handle Logan Andrews, and he's not much smaller than old Roy here. The gorilla can't move quite as fast as the rest of us, but that sky-glider can handle him.

The one thing I'm bummed about is I had this whole thing planned to unveil them for the CVT. Had some dope plans involving a staged attack on the annual gala and everything where I'd zip in on one and show everyone what it could do.

Freaking aliens ruin everything.

The cargo plane took us *back* to New York—which is pretty stupid. Duh, I was already here. But I get it. The little guys needed to get filled in on the what's-what by the bigwigs in the Colorado bunker. Just kind of a waste of time taking all my stuff out there just to bring it right back here.

However, flight over was so relaxing, I actually caught some Zs.

We debark and I take the team down the runway to the rear of the plane. Even from here we can see the massive mothership hovering above the city.

"Man, it's huge," Justice says.

I snicker. Can't help it. "That's what she said."

Sinsation groans.

"What? Like I could pass that up."

The rear hatch is still lowering as we reach our position. I stop, waiting while everyone else can't take their eyes off the Tuldarians. Little spaceships zip all over the city, firing crazy cool weapons.

"Dude, isn't that where the Empire State Building is supposed to be?" Justice asks.

I turn to follow his pointed finger. He's right. Where one of the world's most iconic buildings should be is nothing but empty air and pillars of smoke.

"We have to stop these things," I say.

"And how do we plan to get there?" Sinsation says.

"I'm glad you asked, my dear. Check these babies out!" I point to the now open cargo hold where nine of my specially designed flying machines are parked.

"What are we gonna do with motorcycles?" Justice asks.

I laugh, picking up a satchel from within the ship and tossing it over my shoulder. "These aren't like your little crotch rocket. They fly."

"Dude, my Kawasaki's pretty damn fast."

"Nah, bro. I don't mean speed. I mean they *fly*."

"*Fly* fly?" Sinsation asks, already throwing one leg over the seat. "Oh, I'm gonna like this."

Her sentiments aren't shared by Royal Rampage, who whimpers and backs away. "Me no want to fly."

"You're going to love it, big man!" I say. I take a few steps toward him, but that only makes him shrink back more. "Hey, I'll be right beside you. I won't let anything happen to you, cool? You're like family now, and we all know it's all about family."

The gorilla looks up at me with a pair of eyes I've gotta admit are pretty cute, and nods. "Cool." The word sounds really odd and forced coming through his giant lips.

"Yeah, buddy!" I shout and put my hand up for a high-five.

Now he smiles, showing me giant fanged teeth. He slaps my palm so hard it pushes me back a step. Man, I'm glad he's on our side.

I show everyone, including Roy, how to mount the machines, turn them on, and give a quick overview of the controls.

"Yeah, yeah. We got it," Justice says. "I'm ready to get this thing going."

"Right, but if you're not carefu—"

Suddenly, he and Sinsation gun it, blazing down the runway at speeds I wouldn't recommend.

I swear, pausing only to help Royal Rampage. But even he has the thing firing down the runway before I can even get his seatbelt on.

I swear again, then swing my leg over the bike. Pulling the throttle feels like sitting on a subwoofer at an Eminem concert. The wind stings as I breeze down the runway, but they're going too fast and have too far a head start for me to catch up.

Finally, Justice and Sinsation start to rise from the runway, and the gorilla follows. He's shaky, though, turning almost horizontal at one point.

I shout for him to lean, but it's no use. There's no way he can hear me over the rushing wind and the sound of his engines. Luckily, he slows as he loses control, giving me a chance to catch up. Once beside him, I can see his face. What I expected to be a look of sheer terror is absolute, unadulterated elation.

He spots me pulling up beside him and removes his hands from the controls to pound his chest. The sky-glider immediately begins to plummet, but he reaches forward and snatches the handlebars in time to pull it back.

His expression turns momentarily to fear, then another huge grin takes its place.

I coach him a bit until I'm confident he's got a handle on things, then focus on getting us to the mothership.

Like I suspected, our gliders are so small, the aliens don't even pay any attention to us as we get near. And the gaping hole in the side of the ship that Eaglestar apparently made is still there.

You mean to tell me this advanced race doesn't know how to patch a hole instantly like they do in the sci-fi movies?

Justice and Sinsation finally slow down. Actually, they've come to a near complete stop, just staring, mouths open and eyes wide.

Hovering, the gliders make barely any noise at all. But it's not exactly quiet up here. With all the smaller vessels racing around, all the plasma fire, the buildings exploding, we can still barely hear each other.

"This thing feels *great*!" Sinsation shouts with a look of ecstasy overwhelming her face.

"This could be a trap," I tell them. "Let's find another way in."

Instead of just waltzing in through the opening in the hull, we decide to infiltrate the ship through a small purge vent on the underside of the vessel. Using our various powers, we're able to pry open the metal and crawl inside.

It's dark and the shaft is almost too narrow for Royal Rampage to follow. As it is, he's pretty skittish. However, he follows us as we creep through bowels of the enemy spaceship, our senses on high alert.

"Light up ahead," Justice says. We crawl another thirty feet or so and stop. "It's a grate."

"Can you see what's on the other side?" I whisper.

"Negative."

"Only one way to find out," Sinsation says.

Have I mentioned she's a bit unhinged? She falls to her stomach and donkey kicks the thing. Metal slams against metal as the grate goes flying across the room.

"You want to announce our arrival?" I ask.

"I'm ready to get the party started." She's the first to climb through. Justice and I quickly follow, and Roy isn't far behind. He gets stuck halfway, his legs dangling and kicking. He begins to freak out, grunting and whooping.

"Hey, calm down, big guy!" I say, grabbing one leg. I

motion for Justice to get the other and we slowly help him squeeze through. Finally, he topples in. You know what hurts? A six-hundred-pound gorilla landing on you.

Justice and I push futilely until Roy rolls to the side. We all stand, Justice and me gasping for air.

"Sorry," Rampage says, looking down at his feet.

I pat him on the shoulder, and this time, he takes the affection. "All good, dawg."

"Me no dog. Me gorilla."

"I know. I know." I turn back to survey our current location.

Thankfully, the room is empty. Three odd-looking glass beds stand upright in the middle of the room, all sorts of tubes and wires hanging from the ceiling above it, and everything gives off an eerie blue glow. There's only a single door on the opposite side of the room, and I signal to move toward it.

Justice stops and gives the door an inspection. "No doorknob or anything."

"They don't have hands like us," I tell him.

"Ah." He nods.

"Just push?" Sinsation offers as she presses her hand against the door and it swings open. "Men..."

The corridor on the other side has the same blue lighting, though I can see no bulbs or anything. It's as if the metal itself is providing illumination of some kind.

"Right will lead us toward the bow," I say. "We're already close to aft. No sense in going left."

"Right it is," Justice says, before taking the lead.

Sinsation is at his side in an instant. Is something going on between them? I hope not. I thought I had a chance with her after all this. She's gonna be so impressed when I lead this team to victory.

Whereas I would use a bit of caution, Justice moves at a rapid pace, alien weapon in hand. His hand raises. He's found someone or something. A flash of bitterness courses through me. At first, I don't understand it. Then I realize: I'm the damn leader here. Beneath it all, I've been kicking myself for losing my cool with the guy back in training, so I haven't really asserted myself. That'll end.

I move to the front.

"I got this," I tell him.

He gives me a look, then extends his free hand, motioning for me to take his spot.

I turn back to the team. "Three bogies ahead."

"Doesn't that mean an airplane?" Justice asks.

"Whatever. There's three enemies. One for each of us with one to sp—"

Before I can finish my sentence, Roy sprints ahead, fists against the ground. The aliens don't even see him before he's on top of them, literally tearing them limb from limb. Dinosaur blood spatters everywhere, painting the walls in a sickly shade of red.

I rush up to him, the others padding along behind me. I take in the carnage, which is complete, and shake my head. "That's not how we're going to do this."

"But bad guys dead," Rampage says.

"Yes, but we could have been more discrete."

Roy tilts his head, obviously having no idea what the word "discrete" means.

"Oh, let the big guy have his fun," Sinsation argues. "He's not lying. Look at this place. Good job!" She reaches up and ruffles the fluff on top of the giant gorilla's head like he's a puppy.

"Yeah. Fine. Good job. *But* we're going to take the rest of this ship with a bit more... tact."

"I agree with Battlegear," Justice says.

That's a surprise. Maybe he can let bygones be bygones and all that.

"Good," I say. "Justice, after you."

"You sure? What about all that—"

I shake my head. "You're good at what you do. Lead us."

That was awfully humble of me, if I do say so myself.

Justice nods and crouches, moving low down the next corridor. Everyone but Sinsation steps over body parts and smeared blood. She just wades right through like she's at the ocean. She even gives one of the horns a little kick as she passes by.

The ship is large and complex, with technology far beyond anything I've ever seen. I find myself gawking more than once. If we survive this—which we will—I'll be on a scavenging trip for a long while.

As we make our way deeper down blue-lit corridors, we

stumble across another group of alien guards. Up close, they do bear a striking resemblance to our interpretation of old dinosaur bones. Honestly, I always thought if we could see a dino with skin on, it would look way different from *The Land Before Time.* Then one turns our way. He still doesn't spot us, but with his face turned toward us, I realize this isn't some cute '90s cartoon.

They're bigger and even more menacing. For a moment, I wish I hadn't called off our primate friend.

Silently, I give orders.

Justice's gun takes a few seconds to reload between shots, so he'll only be able to pop off on one of the Tuldarians before the other two catch wind of our attack. That means the rest of us will have to get dirty.

Oh, did I mention I brought a little weapon of my own? Hmmm. Must have forgotten that detail. Wait until you see what this puppy can do.

The plan is simple: Justice takes the rightmost guard, while I take the one on the left. That'll reduce the concern that our gunfire will cross, and allow Rampage to take the alien in the middle.

"So, what, because I'm a woman, I have to sit back and watch?" Sinsation asks after I whisper the plan.

"Would you rather go?" I ask.

"The big guy just took out three," she says. "My turn."

Royal Rampage grunts a little too loudly, clearly disappointed he might miss out on the fun.

Alien sounds come from around the corner. We can't

speak their language, but my best guess would be translated to something like "What was that?"

"Now or never," I whisper.

"Who's going, me or the monkey?"

"He's actually not a monkey," I say.

Sinsation gives me a look.

"I don't care who goes. Just decide," I say. "Now, on the count of three." I look at Justice and count.

On three, we both slide around the corner and fire. While Justice's Tuldarian firearm practically evaporates his target, my weapon—a handheld pistol that looks like something out of a steampunk comic—sends a projectile straight into the Tuldarian's forehead.

Their skin is tough—really tough. But when it hits, it sticks. A small red light blinks twice, then a whirring sound echoes through the hall.

I call it the boregun. You can imagine what it does. No? Fine. The drill-shaped bullet is equipped with a super-powered electrical engine about the size of quarter, which sends the tip deep through the armored skin and into whatever these things possess as brains. By the matter that sprays out all over the walls, I deduce it's not far off from the contents of our own skulls.

While explaining all that took a bit, the attack was over in less than ten seconds. Now, I watch as both Sinsation and Royal Rampage barrel down the corridor, directly at a stunned dinosaur. To be fair, I have no idea what their facial expressions mean. But one can assume when eyeballs turn into bowling balls, the possessor of said eyes is pretty shocked.

Sinsation drives a wicked kick to the Tuldarian's stomach —which does very little but double the alien over. However, when followed up by what amounts to an uppercut from a gorilla, the result is devastating.

"Move!" Justice shouts. His weapon has recharged. Mine doesn't need to do that, by the way.

Sinsation slides out of the way, but Roy stays put, effectively blocking Justice's line of sight. The gorilla is incensed, or at least bloodlusty. He snatches the dino by its feet and swings the creature around.

I can't aptly describe what this looks like. Imagine the most brutal thing you've ever seen on the Discovery Channel —maybe an alligator twisting the neck of a deer that got too close to the swamp, or a lion taking down a gazelle. Doesn't compare.

A four-hundred-pound lizard whips through the air and slams headfirst into the bulkhead. But Rampage isn't done. He brings the thing back around the other way and smashed it again, then again, and again. Finally, he stops and drops the reptilian extraterrestrial to the metal ground with a thud.

Its face is gone. No more. Nothing to identify what it was it once was. Just a pinkish, cauliflower type mess of flesh.

"This is too easy," Justice says.

"Dude!" I whisper shout. "You never say that."

"What? Why?"

"You're gonna jinx us!"

"That's stupi—"

Suddenly, alarms go off, and the bluish tint to the walls goes yellow.

"Dammit, man," I groan.

"Oh, you think that was me? I'm sure it was the gorilla playing drums on the walls."

"It doesn't matter," Sinsation says. "More fun, heading this way."

A sound like a thousand horses charging down the hall meets our ears. Then, from around a far corner, the noise is given a visual. At least ten of the aliens are en route to us.

As soon as I see their guns raise, I shout, "Find cover!"

Everyone steps aside just in time as half a dozen sprays of plasma zips past us. The heat given off by the blasts is enough to give us sunburns. They all miss and hit the wall with a sizzle. But strangely, it has no major effect on the ship's interior surfaces.

In the video footage of what happened back in California, when one of these guns was fired on a building, rock erupted everywhere. This ship must be made of some pretty heavy-duty stuff. Which makes Eaglestar having torn through it like Christmas wrapping paper all the more impressive.

"Now!" I shout to Justice.

While the alien weapons are recharging, we whip around the corner and fire. Justice is able to nail two of them in one shot, while I loose three burst rapid fire and return to safety behind to cover. I listen as the engines from my projectiles spin up. A satisfying series of thunks tells me three more of the creatures went down.

That leaves about half of them.

But they aren't stupid. They're not just going to sit there and wait for us to come back for another round. Problem is, I don't know what they are capable of.

A *tink-tink-tink* draws my attention to the floor of the intersection. Something round and metal, and—*KABOOM*!

The explosive flashes light unlike anything I've ever seen before. To say I'm blind doesn't begin to cover it.

"I can't see," Sinsation says with no more urgency than someone ordering a drink at a bar.

"Me either," Justice says.

Then we hear a roar, and the slamming of fists and feet on metal. I feel the air whip past us, and the sound of alien gunfire.

Oh, man. The gorilla is too stupid to realize what's going on.

The sounds of battle last for what feels like hours, then finally stops. We stand there, blind and waiting for the aliens to capture or kill us, but nothing happens. After long seconds, my vision begins to return, though blurry.

I spare a glance around the corner to find a lot of dead aliens, and a tall, lumpy pile of fur.

Justice—clearly having regained his sight as well—swears and tears off down the hall, sliding on his knees to a stop beside Royal Rampage's body.

"He dead?" I ask.

Justice looks up at me and shakes his head. "No, but he's missing an arm."

I reach his side, and look down at a smoking elbow, cauterized by the plasma weapons.

"We have to keep moving," Sinsation says.

"And just leave him here?" Justice demands.

"She's right," I say. "We don't have a healer here. He's no good to us. We'll have to come back for him."

The gorilla's eyes are closed and his breathing is shallow. It looks like quite an effort, but Justice finally stands.

"We *are* coming back," he says.

I nod. "Agreed."

Problem is, I'm lying. There's no way we are risking our lives for an overgrown Curious George, no matter how smart he might be for his species. We have a task, and that includes destroying the weapon housed within this flying machine, and getting the hell out of here with an exploding ship in our wake. None of us can carry a gorilla on our backs.

Reluctantly(ish), we continue down the hall. The yellow lights are still blinking, and I have to hope most of the Tuldarian troops are not onboard. Why would they be? They're busy taking over a planet and surely doubt anyone would have the balls to fly up here after what happened to Eaglestar.

Finally, we reach a set of double metal doors: the secure room where the weapon we have been tasked to destroy is being kept. I'm sure of it. As we close in, we can hear more thunderous footsteps coming from behind us.

That means they'll pass, and probably kill Royal Rampage anyway.

"Hold them off," I say.

Justice and Sinsation make a wall behind me. Reaching into my pocket, I retrieve a device approximately the size of a business card, and lay it flat against the control panel beside the door. Then, I roll up my sleeve and access a bracer on my wrist, trying a variety of hacks I've developed over the years. But nothing works.

The enemy footsteps grow louder.

I keep trying, but it's no use. Finally, I aim my gun at the panel and fire. The bullet drills into the screen, sending sparks. But the door doesn't budge.

I hear gunfire behind me, and angry alien noises.

Desperate, I try my bracer again, and am shocked that the door opens this time.

"Hurry! Inside!" I shout.

Still firing his Tuldarian rifle, Justice backs in after me, followed by Sinsation. We all dive to the side, and I spin quickly, and tap three buttons on my wrist—the same three I pressed to open the door—and it slides shut.

"Everyone alright?" I ask.

"Yeah, we didn't even see anyone," Justice says.

"Then what was with all the gunfire?"

He shrugs. "No idea. Wasn't us. Wasn't them."

"Probably them killing Royal Rampage for good," Sinsation remarks.

"Don't even joke about that," Justice says.

"I'm not joking. This is war. War is fun, but it can also suck."

"What's this?" I ask, interrupting and pointing to a hub at the far end of the room.

At the front of the room, a viewscreen hovers above a console. This is clearly the bridge of their ship, where I would've expected to see a captain or leader of some kind. But like most of the ship, it appears empty, with everyone down below, causing chaos.

"Crap," I say.

"What's the problem?" Justice asks.

"This isn't where the weapon is," I say as if he's an idiot.

"Yeah, but the secondary mission was to blow this place to hell, right? So what if we destroy the weapon by destroying the ship? Same goal."

Honestly, that makes sense. It also begins to make me wonder why that wasn't the plan in the first place. Doubly, it upsets me that I didn't realize that immediately, and this numbskull did.

I slide the satchel off my shoulder, and set about divvying up the explosive devices. I make my way to the controls. It's a massive console with odd-looking sliders that are clearly designed for Tuldarian hands, not ours. Wires and tubes run the length of it in every direction, humming with alien power. I can feel the energy emanating from it.

Imagine what could be done with this kind of technology? It feels like a shame for us to blow it up. But that's the job. That's how we save the world.

I'm about to set the explosives to detonate, when the door to the secure room slides open. I turn, gun raised and ready to kill them all or die trying.

Instead, I see something I wasn't expecting at all.

"What the hell are you doing here?" I ask.

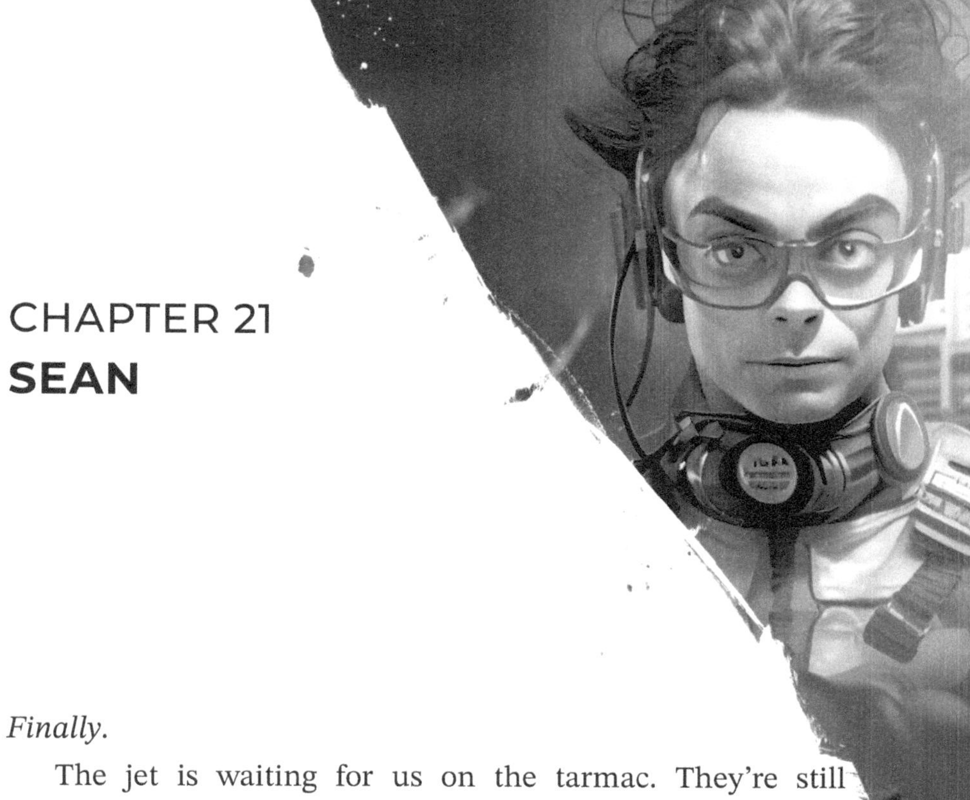

CHAPTER 21
SEAN

Finally.

The jet is waiting for us on the tarmac. They're still clearing the snow away, and there's a new storm brewing, ready to dump a whole lot more. If we don't leave soon, there's a good chance we won't be able to get out of here and save the world—literally the only thing I've been trying to do since the first day I laid eyes on the alien vessel hovering just outside of my hometown.

Just saying it in my mind sounds stupid. "Save the world."

All I needed to do was get to my control center in Egypt, but now, the place is overrun by... the undead? If I wasn't the one telling this story, I'd be suspicious. However, if you remember, I told you long ago that the truth is very important if you are to understand the actions I will take in the near future.

Looking around at my ragtag team, there's no chance of us

winning in a fair fight against the aliens. At least when that freak with the whip was with us, we might have had a flying chance.

We have a rabbit-girl, for heaven's sake. Harrier—that's right, I'm calling *him* Harrier now—needs to smarten up about the Torturess. She is a killer. She is a powerful, dangerous killer.

Here I was thinking Franklin Douglas III was smart. I never fell for the "Lifestyles of the Rich and Famous" act. But now, I'm not so sure.

"They're ready for you, sir," Agent Frederick says. "Good luck. The world is depending on you."

I sigh, holding in the comments about irony and ignorance, and approach the airstairs.

It isn't a very big jet, but there are plenty of extra seats. For some reason, Whisper sits down right next to me, which I don't like one bit. I prefer to stretch out and get comfortable. I know to keep quiet because anything I say would probably sound rude, but I do give her a curious look.

"Maybe I fly beside... uh, *samolet*?" Rockhard says as he enters and has trouble fitting into his seat.

"You can fly?" Prairie asks.

"*Da*. I fly all the time. Like to fly. Feel like bird."

I shake my head. "We can't afford to lose you before we even get there. You're the brawn."

Rockhard huffs. "You cannot tell me no. I don't answer to capitalist bastards like you."

I make a show of looking around like he must be talking

to someone else. "In case you forgot, I'm team leader. So you *do* in fact, answer to 'capitalist bastards like me.'"

Besides, Russia hasn't been communist since the Soviet Union broke up decades ago. What's with the old-time Cold War shtick all of a sudden? Don't tell me they keep this guy on ice and unfreeze him when they need him or something ridiculous like that. Or maybe he's just much older than he looks like Eaglestar was?

And, truth is, I don't know how his power works, including how much energy he expends when in flight. However, it doesn't take much calculation to realize he would probably be exhausted by the time we get to North Africa, and we don't need our strongman out of juice before the battle even begins.

"Do you even know *where* Egypt is?" I ask.

He points vaguely. "I go that way. Or I go that way. World is round. I get there either way."

Well, he's not a genius, but at least he's not one of those flat-Earth nut-jobs.

"I fly faster than this." He pounds a fist against the plane's bulkhead, making a small dent.

"Geez, man! Be careful!" Prairie shouts.

"You're not flying. That's my final word." I turn my attention to the tablet I was given before we left the base.

As it boots up, I consider the zombie situation. It certainly would be easier if we could all fly at super-speed. It's going to take hours to reach Egypt. I'll have to use my time wisely, and have a solid game plan by the time we arrive.

The tablet's homepage pops up, and I navigate to the folder marked "Top Secret." I punch in the passcode I was given—Admin1234!, if you can believe it. Well, it's the government—of course you can believe it.

Sifting through photos and video, I decide these aren't the type of zombies depicted in movies and TV shows. They aren't ravaged and starving for brains due to some virus, or being controlled by a bizarre fungus that overtakes their wills. They're something else entirely, all wrapped up tight in yellowing bandages.

"These aren't zombies," I say to no one in particular.

Mummies...

I think back to my Ancient History classes. I was twelve at the time, and working on my third master's degree. I imagine some of these creatures might be the remains of long-dead pharaohs and it saddens me to know what we're going to have to do. So much for peaceful resting.

So how do you defeat foes who are already dead? And if we do manage to "kill" them, is it still murder?

After watching a video of them shambling around the Sphinx, I realize they're not actually walking. See, that's what people don't realize. Zombies, mummies, skeletons—all those scary monsters we see in horror films—they can't walk if they have no muscles. We won't even begin to discuss how bones stay together without the proper ligaments.

These undead abominations are being remote-controlled. I can tell by the way they move jerkily, like my robots did before I'd perfected the little babies.

This makes much more sense. Torturess is basically creating a swarm of scarecrows using her telekinesis, puppeteering them. No murder, then. We just need to cut the strings on these marionettes. But just the fact that she's capable of controlling so many at once is terrifying in itself. Whatever is going on with her, she's become exponentially more powerful. And that's scary considering she was already dangerous.

I thought the argument was over, but Rockhard apparently doesn't agree. "You let other lady go."

"For all we know, Annihilatrix is dead," Whisper says, a grimness to her tone I haven't heard before.

"It'll take a lot to put her down," a familiar voice from the doorway says.

Just as they're about to shut the doors for takeoff, Frank Douglas boards the plane.

"You're coming with us?" I ask, not even bothering to hide my disdain.

He stops his trek down the aisle between the seats. "You have a problem with that?"

I shake my head. "Me? No. No, not at all. I'm just somewhat... surprised, is all."

"Really? Why's that?"

I make a show of eyeing the cane he's used to assist with walking since he quit the hero game a few years ago. "I just thought we'd all be better served by you staying here at the base and offering support *remotely*."

"You thought wrong. We are still unaware of how the

alien presence might react to long-range transmissions, and can't take the chance of disruptions." He points toward the rear of the plane. "We set up a small command center in the back."

I glance at the door several feet away at the back of the cabin. I've never had the opportunity to travel on Air Force One, but I have toured the old version at the Reagan Library (virtually from prison of course), and this jet reminds me of a smaller, updated version of that.

"Whatever suits you and the mission," I reply dryly.

"I'm always glad to hear that my decisions meet with your approval."

I'm not always the best at picking up on emotional or verbal cues from others, but I can tell his statement is dripping with sarcasm.

I don't feel like I need to say this, but just as sarcasm evades me, I often forget how people of normal intelligence might deduce situations I find simplistic. Regardless of what they tell me, I am *not* leading this team in the bunker *or* out. They've just sent Black Harrier along with us, and that makes me angry.

He hobbles to the back row and lowers himself into a seat with the sort of grunt I've witnessed from injured or older individuals. After a second, I unbuckle my seatbelt and join him. He clearly wanted to be alone, since he sat a few rows back from the rest of us, but I occupy the seat directly across the aisle from him and buckle in anyway. This elicits the desired effect: a sigh from Douglas as he leans his seat back and closes his eyes.

I decide to point out the obvious. "You shouldn't put your seat back. We're about to take off."

"I'm not worried about it."

"Well, you should be. Every time I've ever flown, they forcibly advise everyone to place their seats in the upright position before takeoff." I look down. "And your seatbelt?"

"Like I said, I'm not worried about it."

"Why not?"

"Because that's not going to happen."

"How do you know?"

He peels open one eye and looks over at me. "Because I own this plane, and I sign the paychecks. That's how I know."

"Ah, yes. What privilege."

While I have trouble discerning sarcasm, I am keenly aware of how to apply it to my needs.

However, if Douglas recognizes the dig, he doesn't acknowledge it. Instead, he nods, then turns his head forward and closes his eyes again.

I know he wants to rest, but there's something I've always wanted to talk to him about if I ever got him alone, and this could be my only chance.

I lean halfway across the aisle, and whisper in a conspiratorial tone. "So, how did you do it?"

He doesn't bother to open his eyes this time. "*It?*"

I spare a glance at the others to ensure no one is paying attention. Every one of them has earbuds in, listening to music or watching videos on electronic devices—which, I note, no one told us to turn off or place in airplane mode. Not that I've flown during the time of personal handheld devices —since, as I like to point out often, I've been wrongfully locked up.

Still, I speak softly just to be on the safe side. "How did you become the world's greatest crimefighter without any powers?"

Now he opens his eyes again. Check. "I don't know what you're talking about."

"Don't worry. Your secret is safe with me. You'd be shocked how much research one can do while in a place with very little to entertain. My conclusion is irrefutable."

He sighs again. Eyes open, he presses an elbow into his chair's arm, and leans in toward me until our noses nearly touch. "You realize if I ever found out you told anyone, I'd have to murder you in your sleep."

I know he has to be joking since the Black Harrier would never do something like that. Even in retirement. But it doesn't sound like a joke, and I know that if he *was* serious, then he's probably one of the few people on Earth who could actually pull it off.

I nod once. "Yes."

The conversation pauses as the pilot's voice comes over the speakers with the typical announcements—nothing about seats or belts or trays or airplane mode still, though—and we take off down the runway.

I'm not sure if we're going to continue conversing until he

speaks up again. "What... specifically... do you want to know?"

I think about what I really want to ask him. I already know his history—that his mom had died when he was a baby, and he was raised by his father, who was a business tycoon. I've also figured out from my own research that his father had also most likely been the head of a criminal empire, but there's no way I'm going to bring that up. At least he's using those ill-gotten gains for good now.

I settle on a simple question. "How did you manage to fight all of those criminals and keep up with your super-powered teammates when you're just an ordinary man?"

From his expression, he actually seems somewhat wounded by that last part. However, being the eloquent public speaker he is, he doesn't let it show in his words. "The truth? It was mostly through sheer force of will. I was determined not to let anything stop me, and nothing did." He lifts his cane. "Well, until recently, at any rate."

Surprisingly, the answer gives me a new respect for the man. I'm impressed even, and I'm not impressed by much. "Interesting."

"The money didn't hurt either." He winks. "I have a lot of... stuff to help me out."

Unwilling to lose my opportunity, I continue the questioning. "When did you decide you were going to start fighting crime?"

His eyes suddenly become distant, and I can tell he doesn't

want to answer this particular question. Just when I think I've lost him completely, he responds.

"It wasn't until I was almost an adult. Much older than when you first tried to, before breaking bad."

"I never 'broke bad,'" I argue.

"Listen, Sean, while I'm sure you had your delusions about why you were doing the things you did, the fact remains, many people died because of your actions."

I don't miss a beat. "And no one has died because of yours?"

"That's different and you know it."

"Collateral damage. Another privilege afforded only to some."

He looks away. "Death is never a privilege for anyone."

I consider telling him there are many who would prefer death to living pain-filled lives here on Earth, or better yet, buried under the ocean, but I don't believe it will further our conversation.

"So, nearly an adult, yes? I am truly amazed you were able to become such a proficient hand-to-hand combatant after starting at such a late age."

"There are some secrets I'd still like to keep."

He closes his eyes and leans back again. I suppose it wouldn't serve any purpose for me to mention that I already know he most likely inherited his father's and grandfather's mimicking abilities.

I decide to open up to him, perhaps reel him back in. "My parents... they died when I was young."

There is a beat before Douglas answers. "Yes. I know. I'm sorry."

"Everything I've done, I've done for them."

"I'm sure they'd be honored," he says.

Sarcasm again. I let it go.

"Believe it or not, I'd really like to save the world in their name."

"I'm sure you would," he says.

"Did you ever bring your father's killer to justice?"

Douglas clenches his jaw, and I would swear his eyes are tearing up. "No. That's not possible." I'm about to ask him why, but he speaks first. "We're done here."

Shaking.

A violent tremor startles me awake. My eyes snap open and struggle to adjust to the darkness. Something isn't right, and I don't need to be a genius to know it. Lights are blinking and I feel both tremendous heat and blowing air.

"Harrier?" I shout, not even realizing I'm using Frank Douglas's former crimefighter moniker.

"Sean, that you?"

I can tell it's Whisper, and her voice is somewhere behind me, but I'm facing the wrong way, and now that I'm fully awake and aware, I see I was staring directly into a gaping hole at the side of the plane. I immediately deduce that we've been hit by Tuldarian weapons fire and are about to go down just like most of the other aircraft in the world the past couple of days—including the remnants of my team who never it made it to the base.

Most of what was inside the plane that wasn't bolted down has already been sucked out. I wonder if Frank Douglas is included in that category, since he's no longer sitting across the aisle. Perhaps he should have heeded my warning about seatbelts.

I seem to be securely fastened to my seat for the moment, but if my calculations are correct, my entire seat may soon tear loose.

"We need to cover that hole!" I shout.

"With what?" I can barely hear Whisper over the cacophony of sound.

Frantic, I scan the plane, studying what's left—which is not much. My mind races as I calculate the size of the opening and measure it against any and all options for covering it up.

The door to the control room at the back is slightly larger than the gash in the side of the plane. I point. "There! We can use that!"

"But how?" El Jaguar asks, rushing over to it. He deftly avoids being sucked through by clinging to the walls and ceiling as he passes. "It is not moving."

I search the cabin for Stone Cold or Rock Gnome, or whatever he's called. The big Russian. He seems to be unconscious a few seats up from me, sitting across the aisle from Prairie, who is shaking and curled up in a ball. Her big eyes are filled with terror, and tears stream down her cheeks.

"What happened to him?" I ask her.

Prairie looks at the mass of muscle, then nods at a big, crimson laceration on his forehead. "A big, metal case full of like, equipment or something hit him in the head as it flew out of the plane. Hard."

He may be incredibly strong and able to fly, but from everything I've seen, he's definitely not invulnerable. I try to figure out how to wake him. He's our only chance and we're quickly running out of time.

Then it clicks. Something always clicks.

"Prairie, I'm going to need you to use your powers to wake him up."

The terrified expression momentarily leaves her face as a look of total confusion takes over. "Me? How? Doing people is tough."

"Yes. But you can do small animals, things like that?"

She nods.

"Good. There are tiny creatures living inside of everyone. Little... bugs. Okay? You need to control the ones inside Blockhead's body to wake him up."

"Blockhead? Bugs?"

"Just do it!" I shout. Then, noticing her shrinking back, I lower my voice to just above the rushing wind. "I don't know exactly how your powers work, but reach out and find them."

She squeezes her eyes shut, and everything is silent for a

few moments. Except for the deafening sound of the air rushing through the plane, of course.

It's not working.

It's too late.

After everything I've been through to get here, I'm going to die. All these years preparing to fight the Tuldarians, and I'm going to die in a plane crash on my way there.

Suddenly, Boulderholder sits up in shock, taking a loud, deep breath.

It worked! I knew my plan would work.

Never doubted it for a second.

Prairie looks as if she just ran a mile. The big Slavic guy shakes his head and looks around, then winces in pain as he grabs the bloody cut on his forehead.

"You!" I shout, grabbing his shoulder. "I need you to rip that door off and put it over that hole!"

He's still somewhat dazed as he looks back at the control room, his eyes glazed over.

"Snap out of it!" I slap his face, and I think all it does is hurt my hand. "We're going to crash!"

He growls at me, then rips the seatbelt off with one yank and starts dragging himself to the back of the plane using the remaining seats as an anchor. Even as strong as he is, the vacuum is stronger, and it takes tremendous effort for him to not get sucked right through the hole.

Reaching the control room, he grabs the edges of the metal door, then pulls. It comes off easier than I expected, considering the type of reinforced material they had to have used. Maybe the adrenaline is making him even stronger than usual.

He carries it to the hole, but just as he is about to cover it, I remember he said he could fly. "Wait! You need to be on the outside. We need you to try to keep the plane aloft as much as possible so I can try to land it."

He shakes his head. "*Nyet*. I am not so strong as that!"

Oh, wonderful. *Now* he decides to be honest about his real strength level. He's close enough that I can reach across and touch the back of his arm. "Yes you are, man! Yes. You. Are!"

No, he isn't. At least I don't think so. But it's worth a shot. Either he dies trying, or we all die anyway.

He grits his teeth, then turns around just as he gets to the hole. As nature rips him through, he secures the door over the hole. Though the worst of it is over, there's still a whistling rush of air around the edges. It'll have to be enough.

Suddenly, Whisper starts moving toward the newly sealed hole.

"What are you doing?" I ask.

"Shhh," she says, moving quickly but with intent.

After a moment's hesitation, Whisper's lips glow and she leans in. The edges of the door shake, her words apparently vibrating the molecules until they stitch together. It's not much, but it's enough to seal everything shut for now.

Time itself stops. Or, at least that's how it feels. I spring to the front of the plane, throw open the cabin door, and see Harrier—sorry, Douglas—trying to pull the plane up as the pilot and co-pilot flop around the cockpit. I think the pilot is just unconscious, but there's a hole in the windshield and I realize that the co-pilot is missing a head. Plus, the desert is coming up toward us at startling speed.

Of course the original Black Harrier's trying to save us. How could I have doubted it?

He glances back and sees me. "Whatever you did seems to be helping, but we're still descending way too fast."

I unbuckle Sleepy Hollow's belt and push his body out of the seat, then sit down and look around the control panel for anything I might be able to do to help. The plane slows somewhat and I give a silent thank-you to Crunchbreaker.

"It's no use," Harrier says. "Everyone, hold on!"

We're about to collide with the ground, and it's possible we may survive if the big lunk can manage to slow us enough as Douglas pulls up the nose of the plane. Out of caution and self-preservation, I pull out a device I've been hoping to keep secret until I absolutely needed to reveal it, and slap in onto the front of my chest. Because that moment won't happen if I die in a plane crash.

As the plane's nose continues to rise, Douglas smiles. Actually smiles. "We may just—" His eyes go wide as he looks over at me and I activate my device. "Sean! You're not buckled i—"

Everything goes black pretty quickly after that.

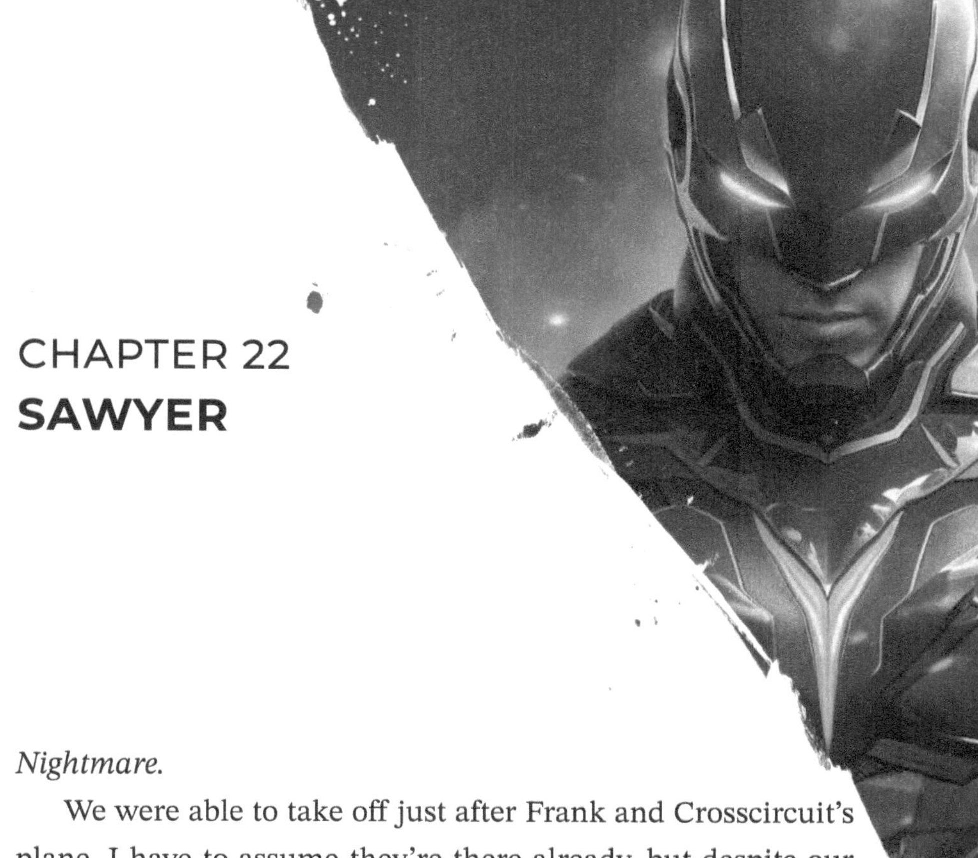

CHAPTER 22
SAWYER

Nightmare.

We were able to take off just after Frank and Crosscircuit's plane. I have to assume they're there already, but despite our attempts at communication, we've been unable to get in touch.

And now for the nightmare part: below us, strangely glowing creatures roam around in such large numbers, we can even see them up here. It's nighttime, so sort of extra eerie.

At first, we thought they were alien vessels that had landed. But they sort of... oscillate. I think that's the word. It's not a solid, unmoving object. It was Neith who first suggested they were alive. It didn't take long for us to deduce that they were indeed hundreds of individuals moving at seemingly random.

A door in the rear of the plane opens. "Alright, children."

Oh, right. At the last minute, we found out that instead of Mr. Chen accompanying us, it would be Baron Steele. I can't say I was upset. The less I had to be around Luis "The Traitor" Chen, the better. Hey, that wouldn't be a bad villain name for him. Maybe I'll suggest it.

"We're flying over the DZ in six minutes. Time to put your purses on." With that, he goes back into the command and control room and shuts the door.

"Looks like we're here," I say, already strapping on my parachute.

"Hell yeah," Pace says, not even hesitating to throw his on as well.

While the rest get suited up, I stare out the open sliding door. I count at least four large alien vessels, but none are as big as the one in New York. The combined might of these is probably stronger, though.

I sort of can't believe Crosscircuit was telling the truth about his robots in Egypt. It just sounded so ridiculous, I thought it had to be a lie.

Shows what I know.

"We dive so the world survives," BlaKat says.

"Is that our new catchphrase?" Neith asks, adjusting her buckles.

I move to help her but she slaps my hand away.

"I've got it," she snaps.

"Okay, I'm sorry. I was just try—"

"I know what you were trying to do. It is not going to work, Sawyer William Vincent. Now, let us focus on our mission so we can move on to never seeing one another again."

Ouch.

"Yeah. Alright. If that's what you want," I say.

I turn back to the team to find they've all got their packs on and have lined up in somewhat of a single file to take the plunge.

Only Firefly seems a bit afraid. As a matter of fact, he hasn't even strapped up yet. I glance over at Neith, afraid to ask my next question for fear she might accuse me of trying to pull a fast one on Firefly too.

"Can I help you with that?"

"It's just… I've never skydived before," he says.

"But isn't flying one of your powers?" I ask.

"It's… sort of a new one. I only fly after I shrink down, and never very high. And definitely not out of a plane. I would probably get pulled into an engine or something."

"First time for everything."

"How are you never afraid of anything?" he asks.

"What are you talking about? I'm afraid of a lot of things. You just haven't known me long enough." I offer him a smile, but he can't see past my bird beak. "Come on, I'll help you."

I grab his bag and he slowly turns his back to me. Then, like I'm helping a little kid put a jacket on, he places one arm through each loop. Arms that are shaking.

I'll be honest, it doesn't make me feel too confident fighting alongside him.

When done, I pat him on the back. "Ready?"

"*Supongo*," he says.

"What's that, Spanish?" I ask, but I know it is. Not only did I take a really cool course on Duolingo on my phone—and remember every single word I learned with superpower-like clarity—but Javier used to speak it all the time by accident. Oh, and I took it in high school, but my Spanish teacher was pretty hot, so I never really paid attention. *Ah, Ms. Morales.*

That makes me think about Javier—not the Ms. Morales part—and a little pebble hops up and down in my stomach at the thought of whether or not he's alive. And I guess Ms. Morales too. I wonder what ever happened to her?

"Sorry, I mean I guess," Firefly says, but his slumped shoulders tell a different story.

"How about we jump together?" I offer.

He perks up.

"Let's stop messing around, huh?" Pace says as he rushes for the open door and jumps without another word.

"Holy—" Bash starts.

"Are we even in the right place?" Firefly asks.

"Doesn't matter now," Osprey says as she blazes past us, not needing a parachute since her suit can fly—unlike Firefly's apparently—all the way from a plane thousands of feet in the air.

After a small peck on White Hot's cheek, Black Frost follows. Soon, it's just me and Firefly left.

Since we have no tandem jump equipment, I'll have to just hold on to him until it's time for us to pull the cord. I quickly explain to him what that'll look like.

"If we don't go now, we could lose them," I say. "Stand here." I move him to the door, feeling his body trembling under my grip. "On the count of three, okay?"

Firefly nods.

"One... two..." I grab him and we fall out before I say three, catching him by surprise before he can object.

Just as we leave the plane, a deafening whooshing passes by, followed by an even more deafening explosion. My suit can withstand serious heat, and I hope Firefly's can too. I can only assume an alien ground-to-air missile is responsible as the plane goes up in a bright flash that lights up the night.

Oh, my God. Baron Steele and the pilots are still in there. I have no doubt the man and woman flying the plane are dead, but I wonder if Paul could withstand that kind of hit?

I don't have time to think about it, since we're falling even faster from the force of the explosion. Even over the whipping wind and through his helmet and mine, Firefly's scream is so high-pitched, I can hear it.

I've never actually been skydiving either, but it's not much different from leaping from the top of the Empire State Building before snapping my cape out and gliding. Actually, it's sort of easier. I'm not worried about smacking into brick walls or shattering through glass.

When we reach what we were told is the proper altitude, I shout for him to hold on, then pull the line on his chute. Once he's safely soaring above me, I get a real picture of how fast I'm actually going.

I open my chute. The snapback is about the same as my

glider cape too. As we draw nearer to the ground, I can hear the sounds of battle.

The plan is simple enough, but not easy. While one team tries to get Crosscircuit to his base under the Sphinx, the Resistors—my team—are supposed to take on the army of aliens and... zombies... on the ground, keeping them busy until Crosscircuit's army of robots can be activated to finish the job.

What an absolutely crazy thing to say, and I've said a lot of crazy things over the years.

The Guild and Bastet's teams are off fighting in the major population centers of the world to protect as many people as possible, so it's up to us to keep these lizard aliens busy. It actually says something about Frank's trust in me—us. Just a few short years ago, most of us were just sidekicks. Now, we're being trusted with literally saving the world.

As my feet hit the ground, I hear metal debris raining down around me and sand flies up from the impacts. Again, I think about the pilots as it fully sets in that the plane we'd just jumped from is utterly gone, blown to smithereens. Thirty seconds later and Firefly and I would be minced meat.

I swear, and let out a sigh. That was closer than I'm comfortable with.

"Harrier to the Resistors," I say into my helmet. "Report. Everyone landed and okay?"

"10-4, good buddy," Pace says.

"Safe and with White Hot and Black Frost," Osprey says.

"Bash, Neith, and I are good to go," BlaKat says. "You got the bug?"

Firefly...

I look around but he's nowhere in sight.

"You read me, Harrier?" BlaKat says.

"Yeah, I don't see him. Looking..." I spin a circle, calling out for him but receive no response. "Firefly, you there?" I ask into my helmet.

A soft groan comes back. "I think... I think I landed in a hole."

I let out yet another relieved sigh. At least he's alive.

"Okay, I'm looking for you. Did you see anything before you landed that might help me find you?"

"I—no." That's all he says.

Mr. Harrier, a male voice in my ear says.

I turn, but see no one. "Uh, yeah?"

My name is Steve. I am your helmet's built-in AI. Would you like me to scan for heat signatures that may lead to finding your friend?

Steve... wow. I have an AI that's *not* a sexy, seductive bombshell. Oh, duh. Chen made this suit, not Frank. The thought that a computer programmed by a man who had been lying to me for as long as I can remember is practically in my brain upsets me. But I need to find Firefly. What other choice to I have?

"Yeah. Thanks, Steve."

Scanning... I have found and highlighted a reading approxi-

mately thirty feet below ground and six hundred yards north of your position. Compass activated.

In my Heads Up Display, a little red, orange, and yellow dot appears precisely where Steve told me it would be. Breaking into a run, I head toward it. After about six minutes, I get there, slightly out of breath.

Hey, you try sprinting in all this gear. This new armor is better than ever, but I swear each time it gets better, it gets heavier also.

"Firefly!" I shout down.

"Down here!" he shouts.

"Thanks, Steve," I say softly.

You are welcome, Mr. Harrier.

"We aren't in a plane now," I shout down. "Can't you fly out?"

"Something's wrong with my suit. I can only fly when I shrink down, and I'm not able to do it. Must have been the hard landing. I'm stuck!"

Of course he's stuck.

"Okay, hold on. I'm gonna shoot my grappler down. I can't see you, so I need you to get as far to the east as you can!"

"Which way is east?" he asks.

Crap. I guess his helmet doesn't have a super-cool compass built in. "Just put your back to one of the walls!"

"Okay! I'm there!"

Well, here's hoping I don't impale one of my teammates. I pull the trigger, and the familiar sound of my grappler unloading reaches my ears. I feel it hit the bottom of the hole, and then I can sense Firefly grabbing on.

"I've got it!" he shouts, confirming.

"Here we go!" I retract the line, and the little mechanism reels the line back, with him on it.

As he nears the light, I notice his helmet is off and in his hand. There's something else I notice, but I sort of can't believe it. Not until he's out of the hole and safely standing beside me.

"Javi?"

Javier Martinez, my partner, my man in the chair, smiles at me. "Thank you, Sawyer. *Gracias.* Thank you. I thought I was dead down there."

I shake out my head like I'm seeing a vision or something. "Javier, is that seriously you?"

He nods. "I haven't just been sitting around since you got arrested. I've been training. I was actually working on a suit just like the one Mr. Chen gave me. That's how he found me. I bought some pretty specific tech from a site on the dark web, and he tracked me down. I guess my VPN doesn't work against Douglas Industry spyware."

He laughs.

"Dark web? Who are you, really?" I ask, laughing.

"Like I said, I've been working hard to live up to your legacy. Anyway, that's when Mr. Chen found me. I was scared at first, but he offered me a job taking Firefly's place. I said 'yes' immediately. Are you proud of me?"

"Of course I am! Did he remember you?" I ask, then feel bad about the question.

"Not at first." He shakes his head. "But that's okay. After a little bit, he did."

"What about your family?" I ask.

"Hopefully fine. I had to do something, right? You taught me that. If we don't succeed, everyone dies anyway. This is how I help. I just wish the mission didn't start out with me messing up again."

Head hanging low, chin against his chest, he kicks the sand.

I put a hand on his shoulder. "You didn't mess up, Javi. You did something super brave. You jumped out of a freaking plane!"

"Well, technically, I didn't jump."

I smile apologetically. "Sorry about that."

"Don't be sorry. You did what you've always done for me. Pushed me to be my best. Just happened to be out of a plane this time."

"Harrier, you got him?" BlaKat asks.

Shoot. I forgot to update the team.

"I've got him. We're good to go. Everyone, meet up on the marked location."

After a series of "copy"s and "got it"s, I turn back to Javier. "Alright, Javi. Just like old times. Let's save the freaking world."

CHAPTER 23
SEAN

Pain.

I wake up face-first in the sand. I've always wanted to return to Egypt, but this isn't exactly what I'd had in mind. Apparently, I went straight through the hole in the plane's windscreen as we hit the ground. Even worse than how stupid I allowed myself to be after saving everyone (except the co-pilot, I suppose), I'm embarrassed that it happened in front of Harrier.

Well, the *real* Harrier, I mean.

I'm not going to let it happen again.

I groggily stand, hearing the soft whir of my exosuit guiding my limbs. Luckily, my last act before slamming to Earth was to attach and deploy the exoskeletal armor that now covers and protects me head-to-toe. It's made up of the best technology I am capable of, not just acting as a defense against all manner of attacks, but allowing me to tap into supernatural strength and speed. Almost like I'm inside one of my most powerful robots.

One might say, with this, I have most of Eaglestar's powers with none of his weaknesses. Sure, I can't fly. Believe it or not, containing enough fuel within a piece of equipment like this creates an unwieldy balance that I can't justify.

Problem is, I hadn't been prepared to unveil this until the perfect strategic moment, when the enemy believed me to be as scared and weak as I'd been back in California. I hadn't been able to use it then, since I hadn't completed it until I had the resources at the bunker. You didn't think I was actually wasting time sleeping with all that's happening, did you?

All that to say—I didn't expect to deploy my suit so soon.

Self-preservation is a grandly underestimated character trait. However, when I saw the Egyptian desert rising up to greet our plane at an incredible rate, I figured being jettisoned through the windshield of a large aircraft is about as harrowing an experience as one can find oneself in. So it had to be done. No use grousing about it now.

Whisper and Prairie rush toward me, shocked that I'm still alive. Walking behind them more casually, El Jaguar wipes sand from his face and clothes, and pops his arm back into its socket.

I wonder if he died again? Probably not, since he's up-and-at-'em already.

Prairie stutters as she talks. "B-but I thought—I thought you were dead."

"I'm fine." There's no time to waste discussing it. We're

already here and ready to fight, and I'm not even sure we landed in the right place. It was a crash-landing after all.

"What's with all the metal and wires?" asks Prairie.

"None of your business," I tell her. "Just keep doing what I order you to do."

"I'm just saying, it would have been nice if you'd used it to help in training..."

"In training? *In training?* I was belittled by *She*aglestar back there for using my technology. How dare you question me?"

I give her a stern look that quiets her immediately. She's not happy, but I don't care. If I can't be in charge of the entire operation, I'm definitely going to exert what authority I *do* have over this small team.

This small, pathetic team they stuck me with... I can only hope they don't turn out to be more of a hinderance than a slight asset. Or simply mere cannon fodder.

As fortune would have it, we've landed next to the Giza Plateau, within a couple of miles of the Great Pyramids and the Sphinx, although it's obvious something is off.

Way off.

A cold blue energy swirls like a hurricane over the massive, noseless head of the Sphinx. Lightning strikes every few seconds, and the dull roar can be heard even from this far.

"Where is Mr. Douglas?" Whisper asks, drawing my attention from the obviously more important subject at hand.

I jab a thumb over my shoulder, not bothering to care if the guy survived.

Whisper rushes over, climbing up the nose of the plane—a nose that now looks strikingly similar to that of the Sphinx. "He's alive!"

"Joy," I say under my breath. The man used to be one of my heroes. I couldn't have been more disappointed now that I've finally met him.

"He is breathing. I may be able to..."

"I don't care," I tell her. "Heal him. Don't. It doesn't matter. We have a job to do."

"He is too badly wounded," she shouts down to us.

"Then leave him!"

"What is your malfunction?" Prairie asks. "The guy is dying and—"

"The *entire world* is dying," I tell her, biting off each word. "If we don't do what we came here to do, Franklin Douglas III will be the least of our worries."

Whisper leaps down. "I hate to admit it, but he is right. And we have no communications, so there is no one to tell. The good news is, I do not think he actually *is* dying. But he is not in good shape. If we survive tonight, he should too."

"Wonderful," I say, sarcasm dripping. "Now, let's go."

"Wait, what about Rockhard?" Prairie asks.

"For Pete's sake! He's probably dead! He did his duty. It's time to move."

Whisper and Prairie give each other a look they don't know I saw as I turn away and start off in the direction of the pyramids. I'm immediately hit with a smell so putrid it can only be described as death warmed over. Which, if I'm not mistaken, is what it actually is.

I can't imagine what had tipped the Tuldarians off that something was awry in Egypt. Perhaps they could sense my superior technology. Perhaps not.

All told, it isn't just the aliens we'll need to get through. There are bodies everywhere—dead, but not dead. Undead, I guess? Zombies are all the rage, right?

Okay, let me just qualify that we're not talking about anything that is *truly* undead here. As I surmised earlier from the video, Torturess's greatly magnified power is animating these corpses as if they're alive and turning them on us. Still, the effect makes it appear that the dead are back on their feet and coming for us. Watching the video was unnerving, but no more so than a scary movie or television show.

In person, it's quite terrifying.

Far as they might be from us, their attention—or rather that of their controller—has been drawn by the sound of our very eventful landing. Wind picks up, sending dust billowing in all directions. But it's unnatural—a result of the event above the Sphinx, no doubt. I turn to the others.

"Anyone want to argue that we shouldn't go find out what's happening up there?" I point to the blue cloud. "I didn't think so. Be careful, we don't know how dangerous these mummies are."

"Mummies?" Prairie asks. Her face contorts in a form of terror with which I'm unfamiliar.

"What else do you think they are?"

"I don't know... my eyesight must not be as good as yours. I just thought they were... tourists? I don't know! But certainly not mummies! Is there even such a thing as mummies?"

I bend over and look her in the eye like she's a child. "You can speak to animals and they do what you ask them to. Are you really unsure as to whether mummies could exist?" Her face turns red and I return my attention to the rest of the group. "Are you all ready?"

A thundering boom cracks down so close to us that I nearly lose my footing. I spin quickly, gearing up for a fight, but it's just the giant Russian juggernaut. Guess he didn't die. A shame. However, he had helped put down the plane, even if a little too fast.

Prairie forgets what we were discussing and wraps her arms around him. He's so big, her hands don't even reach his sides.

"We are dating now?" he asks.

Prairie pulls away. "Huh? What?"

"Settle down, Crag Mountain," I tell him. "We've got to figure out what's going on up there." I point to the Sphinx.

"I fly and go look," he says.

"No!" I shout, but it's too late; he's already off.

We watch, helpless, as he flies into the eye of the preternatural light show. His form becomes awash with a blue glow and a deafening clap gives way to a flash of white. Lightning converges on him from all directions. An enormous explosion of light, sound, and presumably biological matter brightens the night sky. And he's gone. Possibly dead. I can tell you with all confidence he's probably dead.

I swear. "This is why we don't go off willy-nilly on our own!"

Prairie giggles. "Willy-nilly?"

I give her a look that shuts her up again, but make a mental note to refrain from using that idiom in the future. We're down to the four of us.

A voice behind us draws our attention. Douglas has crawled out onto the nose of the plane. "You already lost your powerhouse?"

"Mr. Douglas!" Whisper says. "Do not move. You are injured!"

"I've been through worse," he says.

Show-off. Always looking to impress the ladies.

I don't spare him a glance. "He didn't really leave me much choice. Still think Torturess is only a minor threat?"

"Obviously the Tuldarians have developed a way to greatly amplify her powers. Regardless, you'd better get a handle on your team, or you'll all be dead within the hour. And the rest of us, not long afterward."

His chastisement grates on me, but I don't have time to dwell on it. I take a few steps back toward him. "You're here to monitor the situation. If you're going to live, at least do so with purpose. We able-bodied folks will go put ourselves in harm's way."

"Do your job, and I'll do mine," Douglas says, grimacing.

"I'm trying!" I shout, though I didn't mean for it to come

out so petulant. I turn to Prairie, Whisper, and El Jaguar and say, "Try to keep up."

I lurch forward, letting my exosuit's speed carry me hundreds of yards in only a few bounds. It's not long before I meet one of the undead creatures. Stretching out a mechanical arm, I deliver a clothesline across its neck. The thing flips head over toes several times before cracking down on its skull. I'm grateful to see that it doesn't try to get back up.

El Jaguar has no trouble maintaining speed with me, and as I engage with another mummified corpse, he makes quick work of a third. Truth is, I'm unsure what threat these things pose. Their faces are wrapped, their hands too. Unless they could—

My unspoken question is answered when one does what I can only refer to as "casting a spell."

A heavy gust of wind hits us with the force of a freight train barreling out of control. I dig my metal boots into the sand, but still slide back at least a dozen feet. El Jaguar, however, is blown away like a fluttering leaf.

When the mummy notices I wasn't dispatched, it comes at me fast—unnervingly fast. Grabbing hold of my arm, it wrenches back. I find myself shocked at how powerful the creature is, moving me almost as much as the wind had. I have to remind myself that it's the amplified power of Torturess doing this, and not some Walking Dead creature.

I decide it's best to give in and let the momentum spin me so I'm facing King Tut again. Before it has time to reach me again, I piston my fist through its head.

It's almost a pity, thinking about the history I just destroyed.

There's no blood, just fractured, brittle bone and cloth exploding beneath the impact.

El Jaguar has found his way back just as the ladies arrive on the scene. They are swiftly surrounded by several more of the undead puppets. The cat-man is a whirlwind of punches and kicks, but there are simply too many of them.

In my distraction observing how my team handles themselves, I end up in one of the mummy's grasps. Two wrapped arms envelop me. The fingers don't exactly clasp in front of me, covered as they are, which makes it simple enough to break free. As I do, one arm shatters beneath the power of my suit.

Spinning, I thrust a stiff-fingered metal hand through its chest cavity. I don't know what my intention is, but it certainly isn't to be elbow-deep in a mummy. Destroying the head of one was successful, but now, this thing still thrashes and grunts, beating me relentlessly with its padded fist. Now I'm far too close for comfort, with one arm lodged between broken ribs and the other at too awkward an angle to do any real damage.

I put my head down and shoulder into it. Above, I hear a sizzle and look to see that its head has been completely disintegrated. I shove the mummy's remains off of me and turn to see that it's Whisper, standing with her hand where the corpse's head used to be. That's quite a power, being able to do anything from heal to make body parts disappear. It's a wonder I hadn't heard of her until now.

Where we'd just had things under control moments before, someone has decided we are threat *numero uno.* Hundreds of mummies approach at speeds unlike the lumbering, groaning animated corpses we are all so used to imagining around Halloween.

El Jaguar, Whisper, and I back up to one another, forming a three-sided defensive posture.

"Where's Prairie?" Whisper asks.

Looking around, I can't see any sign of her. Poor girl must've been overwhelmed. Who in their right mind thought someone with such weak powers should be on the front line like this?

Then I hear a dull roar steadily growing louder and higher in pitch. I look up to see thousands of birds—falcons, eagles, osprey, and other predators—moving together in unison like so many synchronized swimmers. They swoosh and swoop and then rise high into the sky, almost disappearing from sight. Without warning, they come back down like a mighty rush of wind and tear through the battlefield, pecking and clawing. The avian cries are all that can be heard, as if I've been buried under the sea and the pressure of the ocean is berating my ears. I watch as dozens of mummies are whisked off the ground and carried to some faraway place. And then there is silence. Not actual silence, but the kind of silence that occurs when a storm settles.

When the dust falls, Prairie stands there with her hands

on her hips, looking quite satisfied with herself. To think, I was just about to dismiss her entirely. If she can control that many birds at once, I re-calculate how powerful she really is.

The birds haven't performed a complete devastation of our enemies, however. A few stragglers remain, but El Jaguar whips around like a man possessed, picking them off one by one until the path before us lies clear. Every time I start to feel impressed by him, I realize that the confidence that must come from not being able to be permanently killed must in turn fuel a combination of fearlessness and audaciousness. If he weren't so stupid, I might envy him.

"Let's go!" I shout.

As we draw closer to the Sphinx, it becomes almost impossible to stand. The whipping wind is relentless, and whatever the cause of the blue glow coaxes my hair to stand on end. Some sort of static electricity.

We're almost to the small opening at the rear of the Sphinx.

"Teflon is dead!" I hear someone shout. I don't think his name was actually Teflon, but that's what I hear and I don't bother to seek correction.

I turn to see Prairie kneeling beside the half-buried remains of the Russian meathead. Frankly, if it weren't for the remnants of his costume, I'd be hard-pressed to know it was him.

So now I know for certain it's only me, Jaguar, and the two women left.

"That's a shame," I say. "Keep moving. We're almost there."

"You're heartless," Prairie says, rising slowly.

"I am pragmatic." I turn to Whisper. "I presume your powers don't extend to bringing back someone's head and limbs?"

Whisper's eyes water as she shakes her head quickly, looking a little sick to her stomach.

I hear noise behind us, and spin to find El Jaguar absolutely destroying a pack of five mummies. A pack? A gaggle? A murder? Oddly, no one has ever had to define what a grouping of mummies should be called.

One of them glows blue again.

"Watch out!" I shout to El Jaguar, but it's too late. Wind hits him again, sending him reeling. However, he was ready for it this time, and drops low to the ground. He rolls beneath the blast, and comes up with a savage uppercut that cracks the head off the last one.

"He'll catch up with us," I tell the girls. "I wonder if he actually feels pain when he dies?"

"He does," says Whisper. "I asked him."

Okay, now I'm *slightly* more impressed.

We start moving toward where I know the entrance to the Sphinx resides.

"How do we go inside?" Whisper asks, looking at the giant wall.

I recall everything I can about the monolithic statue before us.

"After the renovations in the '70s, everything we thought could have been entrances were sealed shut. My control room is deep underground, but the other entrance is through a tunnel running all the way from Cairo, which we don't have time to get to."

The girls look at me, wide-eyed, as I speak. I like to think they're impressed with my knowledge, but as it turns out, I have a large gash on my cheek and it's starting to bubble.

"I'll deal with that when we're done," I tell them, pulling a bloody hand from my face. "Whisper, behind these stones—"

Before I can tell her what's behind the stones, one of the Tuldarian weapons cracks and a chunk of the Sphinx is blown away.

I spin on the dinosaur, who is apparently waiting for his weapon to charge and try again. "Do you have any idea how precious this monument is!"

"I don't think he cares," Prairie says. "Let me try something."

She hunches over, squeezing as if trying to have a bowel movement. I hope that's not what she's doing. Then, with a loud scream, she rises, ramrod straight and hands outstretched.

Suddenly, the Tuldarian goes rigid. The look in his eyes tells me he is terrified. His weapon slowly begins to move, trembling wildly in his grasp.

"Everyone, get ready to move!" I shout.

Then the weapon turns in his grip, the barrel aiming straight up—

His head explodes like a watermelon. Prairie stops screaming, and the Tuldarian falls headless to the sand.

"I guess they are more like animals than people," she says, shrugging. "That's good to know. I wonder if Mr. Douglas assumed that when he sent me here?"

"Yeah, me too," I say, seething a little. I hate to think Douglas had actually developed a strong plan in teaming me up with these fools. "As I was saying, the old entry point should still be useable. Whisper, can you blast us in with your vibration power?"

"I do not know. I have used a lot of my strength. Besides, are you sure you want to destroy the largest statue on Earth?" When I don't respond, she adds, "What? I cannot know things too?"

I don't bother to correct her—the Statue of Unity is the largest, and several more are bigger than the Sphinx.

"It's already ruined. Just blast us in!" I say with more frustration than I intend and less certainty than I desire.

Whisper closes her eyes and presses her hands to either side of her mouth. I can hear her muttering something in French under her breath and a small, green object begins to glow between her lips. It grows exponentially over the course of the next few seconds and then, with one final whisper, it bursts forward.

Rock shatters and explodes. The green aura acts as a forcefield around Whisper, and subsequently, us. When the devastation is over, the shield dissipates and before us looms a large, jagged doorway.

After a quick glance behind me to see if El Jaguar is on his way—he is, finally—we enter into the heart of the beast, so to speak. I activate the headlamp on my exosuit, providing much needed light.

"Crosscircuit?" I almost forgot about the earpiece I'd been fitted with before leaving for the mission. It appears Douglas got the communications back up after the crash. He doesn't sound too happy.

"Go for Crosscircuit," I say.

"There's a massive storm heading your way, and based on what little we understand on what's happening, it may be that the aliens plan to use Torturess to harness its energy for something huge. Better stop her fast."

"Did you think this intrusion would somehow expedite this process?" I ask, annoyed. "We're doing the best we can. We've just entered the Sphinx. Searching for her now."

"Copy that," he replies. I can hear the pain in his voice. "Try not to cause too much damage, if possible."

Prairie gives me a worried expression. I look at the hindquarters of the Sphinx that we sheared off and decide to change the subject.

"Are you all right?" I ask him.

"I'll survive." He makes a probably unintentional, pained groaning sound. "Good luck."

If I had to guess, I'd say he's going to pass out in the next three-and-a-half minutes and we'll have to do without his 'support.'

"I don't need luck. I just need the ability to do what I do best."

When he doesn't reply, I assume I was far too generous in my estimation of his time left in the land of the conscious.

Inside, there's another barrier at the end of the short shaft in the rump of the Sphinx.

Whisper looks a bit weary, but I don't even have to ask before she performs another breach with her powers. I don't know how much juice she has left, but we may be out of luck if any of us need to be healed later on. Within, a corridor descends below the colossal statue.

"Those creatures are quite powerful," El Jaguar says, making small talk. "Perhaps they are mere bone, but whatever mystical powers they have... they are formidable."

"Remember, they are not the ones with the power," I say. "It's Torturess. She must be stopped."

The shaft breaks into a fork. After a short deliberation where I allow my team to feel like they are part of the decision, I choose to go right. It might have been a while since I've been here, but I still know my way around.

A squeak up ahead startles us, followed by others. Bats.

"Prairie, can you make sure those don't give us any trouble?" All I hear is silence as a reply. "Prairie? Whisper, where's Prairie?"

"I do not know," she says. "She was right behind me. We must go to look for her."

"No!" I shout. "We don't have time. You heard what

Douglas said. Say a prayer for her or send good thoughts. Whatever you have to do. But we must keep going."

She nods somberly, and I think she understands. Then she bolts back up the shaft.

"Whisper!" I shout.

Jaguar goes after her.

My head slumps and I swear. The last thing I want is to be left alone in here, so I follow them. They'll pay for their insolence later.

"Oh no!" Whisper's voice carries from the darkness ahead.

When I arrive, I see the source of her lamentations. Though Prairie wasn't far behind us, she's also no longer with us.

"Is she..."

"Dead," Whisper says softly.

"*Dios mio*," El Jaguar says, and I wonder which god he's referring to.

"How?" I ask, though something tells me I don't want to know.

"I am unsure. There's no sign of struggle or fight," Whisper explains. "No marks or cuts. It is as if she just... dropped dead."

Her last words come out stunted, as if she's holding back tears.

"We have to go, Whisper," I say. "We can mourn later."

"*Eres despiadado y malvado*," says Jaguar. Something about having no heart and being wicked.

Something I've been accused of twice now.

Whisper's expression has as much anger as it does sadness when she looks at me. "Don't you care? How can you not care?"

"I do. But the fate of the world is at stake. We just don't have time for this now." I wish I believed my own words, but the truth is, I'm no more affected by Prairie's death than I was by Crunchmaster's. In fact, my biggest concern is that our team is down to just three now, and my confidence is dwindling.

Whisper hugs Prairie's body and stands. When she pulls her hand away, blood coats it. She turns Prairie's head and from her ear, a steady stream of red pours.

"Torturess," I say. "She did this. I don't know how, but she did. And she could do it to any of us. Except me, probably. My mind wouldn't be as hard to break. We need to go."

Whisper takes a deep breath as she pulls herself together and walks ahead, refusing to look at me.

El Jaguar kneels beside her and performs some kind of ritual, reciting words in some ancient-sounding language. He too stands and walks past me as if I'm not there.

"Am I the only one who understands the gravity of this mission?" I ask no one in particular.

My exosuit whines as I begin to follow them. The corridor delves deeper into the Earth to the east, below the nearby temples. The path narrows, forcing us to walk single file before opening into a giant chamber. It isn't made of the dusty orange stone you would expect. Instead, its walls are solid metal and covered in hieroglyphics. In the center of the room there's a large spherical contraption.

That's when I see her—the Torturess, standing on a platform in the middle of the sphere. I haven't seen her since the last time she kicked my butt, back when I was a teenager attempting to be a hero. All I can think about is how helpless I was then, and how much more powerful she is now. I don't know if this is all her or if she's being controlled by the aliens, and I don't care. All I know is that she is going to die.

Other than her eyes being completely white, she looks the same as she did last time, like she's barely aged. Long, dark hair and curves for days. I can see why Anni would switch teams for someone like her. A choice between her and that oaf Battlegear? Please, it's not even a contest.

I hear a chattering in my ear—another warning from Douglas that the storm is closing in. But I barely hear it. It's just me and her. With all I've been through in my lifetime, I hadn't realized just how much I've been waiting for this moment. Incredible how a brief moment from one's formative years can shape one's future self.

Had it not been for her, I might have still been trying to play the hero side of things. It's possible, even, I would never have known of the alien threat, never would have built my robots, never would have tested them on the Guild, and we would now have no hope whatsoever of beating the Tuldarians.

Though the memory of her flinging me around the city stings, perhaps it was for the best.

"Torturess!" I shout before rushing toward the sphere. Something external stops me in the middle of the room, though I see no signs of it. I hit something invisible—as hard as any wall—and crumple to the ground. Even my exosuit is unable to withstand the telekinetic force.

Straining, I rise to my knees and place a hand out in front of me. It connects with something solid where there's nothing visible at all.

Whisper speaks through her hands, and hurls green balls of vibrating energy—I truly don't understand her powers—and they collide with the force field, sending sparks raining down on me. El Jaguar throws himself up against the barrier repeatedly, seemingly being rebuffed with more force each time. I know he'll probably just get better again if he dies, but I may need him for this fight.

"Stop!" I say, getting to my feet. I slowly walk the perimeter, feeling with my hand, looking for a break. No joy.

"Sean," says the voice in my ear again. "The storm is right above you. It's now or never."

"Torturess, it's over," I say.

Her head snaps to me. "Thieves. You have stolen this land, and it shall return to us." Her voice doesn't fit. It's too deep, guttural, like the aliens.

"This isn't you!" I shout, feeling stupid even saying it. Now I'm one of those morons trying to reason with someone who's been possessed.

In response, she says, "We are many, and we are staying. You will be exterminated like vermin."

I turn to my remaining team. "Okay, I don't know what else to do. Just hit it with everything you have."

I pick up speed, beginning to run around the sphere now. It rotates to follow me, the Torturess at its center. Her eyes being completely white like that is unnerving.

I retract a long blade from my forearm, letting it scrape against the invisible wall. El Jaguar likewise rages against the forcefield while Whisper's energy balls continue their relentless attack.

Nothing manages to make Torturess's defensive magic waver for even a moment.

Then there's a high-pitched squeal and the room becomes white—solid white. First I can't see anything, and then there's nothing at all.

CHAPTER 24
SAWYER

Hope.

It's a funny concept. Something like faith, I guess? I've never been to church or anything, but I can figure it out. While faith exists in some kind of higher power, hope is more… grounded.

I hope we make it out of this alive, but I don't have faith we can.

Another funny thing—if we aren't alive, did we really make it out at all?

I hope Mom is okay. I have no control over her fate at all. I have no control over anyone's fate except maybe my own. And even then, I was ten seconds away from being blown out of the sky by an alien missile. Is there a god making sure the good guys win? I really don't know, but even if I can't have faith, I have hope.

Hope that Battlegear's team made it onboard okay and is succeeding in their mission. Otherwise, the Tuldarians will be able to de-power most of the heroes on Earth and then we're pretty much screwed—or, hope*less*.

I'm also worried about Justice even though I know he's not my brother now. He's still family, and if we make it through this, I wanna make sure he knows it and has all the advantages of being a member of the Douglas clan.

My team moves ahead toward a pack of Tuldarians. By the look of the massive missile launchers, I would put money on it they were the ones who took out our plane. Ducking behind a sand dune, I drop to my stomach and the rest of the team follows my lead.

"Okay, this is it," I whisper into my helmet. "You've seen what these things can do, but they don't know what we are capable of."

"What are we capable of against a force like that?" Bash asks.

"Speak for yourself," Neith says—one of the rare times I've heard her speak since this whole thing started unless it was chewing me out. "This is my world, and they are not on theirs."

A sad look passes over her, but mixed with something else... determination maybe? Then it clicks. I'm not sure how I missed it before. She hasn't been quiet because she's mad at me—though she is. Her stoicism stems from the fact that her powers are shared with a literal Egyptian goddess. This must feel more personal to her than to any of us.

"Hell yeah," Pace says. "They won't know what hit them."

"Let's not get cocky," Osprey says. She looks at me. "You've got a plan, I assume?"

"Don't I always? BlaKat, you got eyes?" I ask into my helmet.

"Fourteen dinos, fully armed." He's holed up in what we deemed a safe location based on Frank's early recon. The guy is a force to be reckoned with himself, but we'll only need his raw power should we find ourselves in a tough position. For now, he's most useful as the man in the chair.

I look to the kid who formerly occupied that role for me. Javier Martinez. How crazy it is to have him here by my side. And all things aside, he seems ready to put a hurting on these lizards. Odd timing as it is, I suddenly remember that I used to have plastic dinosaurs as a kid—one of the few toys I owned. I think Mom grabbed them out of a box of stuff someone was giving away outside our building. But I loved those things. Now these ugly aliens are ruining another one of my favorite childhood memories. Figures.

"About two for each of us," I comment. "Not bad odds."

"It is for them," Bash says, rolling onto his side and flexing his biceps.

"That's what I'm talking about!" Pace says. "There's that big D energy I'm looking for!"

"Gross," Amy says.

"D?" Neith asks.

"You don't wanna know. Trust me," Amy says.

"Drones out," BlaKat says. "Transmitting to your optics."

"Aahhh, 'drones,'" Neith says.

"That's not—uh, yeah, it totally means 'drones,'" Amy says.

Suddenly, several feeds flood my helmet, allowing me to see what BlaKat sees. I'm used to looking at lots of data on my helmet's HUD, but this is crazy. It's almost overloading my senses. I don't know how BlaKat keeps track of all this.

I give the team their assignments, which includes an airborne distraction by Osprey. Unfortunately, with Javi—I mean Firefly—being unable to use his propulsion system, that'll put us at a small disadvantage. No pun intended. But he can still shrink down.

"This won't be like robots in a danger room," BlaKat says. "These things are armed to the teeth. And they have actual teeth, too."

"We got this," Black Frost says. "Right, babe?"

In response, White Hot snaps her fingers and a small flame grows from her thumbnail. "Roast gecko on the menu tonight."

BlaKat's not wrong, though. The real thing could be more difficult than the training. The aliens are better fighters than the robots who simulated them. However, it might prove a bit easier because it's out in the open, and the fact that it's *not* a simulation has our adrenaline really pumping. Already, I'm feeling hyper-aware.

"Ready?" I ask the team. Everyone agrees except Neith, but that's only because she's in kill mode. I wouldn't wanna be in her scopes. "Resistors on three?"

"Let's just slaughter them," Neith says, standing.

"Okay. Let's just slaughter them on three. One, two, three..."

"Let's just slaughter them!" we all shout.

With that, the operation is on.

I charge at the lead into battle against the Tuldarian army. Since my martial arts skills aren't all that effective against such large enemies, I'm equipped with a bunch of tactical weapons along with the super-cool new suit Chen provided me with. It also improves my strength and speed, which I definitely need against these aliens.

Even my helmet is a weapon, with a five-inch graphene beak sharp enough to stab through the Tuldarians' natural armor.

While Osprey flies above, gathering the dinosaurs' attention, Black Frost focuses on disarming as many as he can by freezing their claws to their weapons. His ability to control the battlefield by slowing the enemy is a crucial component to our potential victory. He gets two of them stuck before the others figure out what's going on.

Once they start firing, he changes his tactic to creating an ice wall around a few of them. Osprey uses the opportunity to drop a few stun grenades into the center of those trapped by his powers. The explosion creates the intended effect, confusing the aliens into firing their weapons with no sight. I can't see if any of the plasma bolts did friendly damage, but it doesn't matter. Not yet.

I move around, using sonic devices that send false signals

across the battlefield to distract them. And, for once, I'm not afraid to use real weapons. I pick up one of the dead dino's weapons. Now that I know how to use it, it's on like Donkey Kong. I fire, hitting one in the leg. The limb explodes in a shower of alien mist. The Tuldarian topples over, but isn't out of the fight.

Out of seemingly nowhere, Bash crashes down on the creature's prone form, crushing one of its arms against its chest and the other into the sand. Then, with force I think might rival Baron Steele—God rest his soul, maybe—his fist pistons into the lizard's face.

As I instructed him, he picks up the dead Tuldarian's weapon. He doesn't know how to use it, and the learning curve is a bit too high in the middle of the fight, so he cracks it over his knee and tosses it aside.

I tried to give everyone a crash course on using the guns while on the plane, but without a way to practice, it was like teaching someone how to cook with no ingredients.

My own weapon now reads blue—cocked, locked, and ready to fire. Just as I'm about to unleash hell on one of the mini Godzillas, Neith steps into my field of view, and directly into my line of sight. I quickly raise the weapon so I don't kill my ex-girlfriend.

"Careful!" I shout, but she isn't listening.

Tattoos all over her body glow, making her more radiant than she already was. All at once, six of the aliens rise into the air, weapons first, as if magnetically drawn to some unseen force. They converge on a singular spot, legs kicking and thrashing in a vain attempt to get free of whatever ancient power Neith used on them.

This was something I'd never seen her do, but that doesn't surprise me. Each of her tattoos has a certain ability, and I've only seen her use a few of them. Meanwhile, she's covered in ink.

Have I mentioned how hot that is?

Not the time, I guess.

Pace zips by her like a blur, disarming others who are not caught in her snare. Osprey dives down from wherever she was flying above, feet first and nails one of the floating aliens square in the face. The speed at which she connected sends the Tuldarian caroming into the sand. The resulting eruption is like a meteor strike.

Which is kind of funny considering that's how their ancestors likely died.

Then, Neith releases them. In my head, I can hear "Let the Bodies Hit the Floor" play. Then I realize it's not in my head at all. Drowning Pool is playing in my speakers.

I hope you don't mind, Steve says. *But I have taken the liberty of creating a playlist based upon your musical tastes.*

"Mind?" I shout. "This is awesome!"

Now my blood is really pumping.

While Black Frost and White Hot do their thing, either frying them alive as promised, or freezing them and letting Bash shatter them into a million pieces—which is pretty gruesome, honestly—I go to work on a squad that just arrived.

Aiming between two runners, I blow a hole that superheats the sand like glass. The rushing Tuldarians don't exactly slip and slide like the Three Stooges, but it does throw them off their game long enough for Neith to step in.

She's a force on a whole other level. Another tattoo glows and she flickers out of view. This, I've seen her do. Teleporting is one of those things most people wish they could do. Imagine being in one place one second and somewhere else the next? She appears behind the newly arrived prehistoric aliens—is that a thing? Devastating explosive arrows explode all around them, striking from all directions and leaving them disoriented, confused, and most importantly, dead.

"All fourteen down," BlaKat says. Then he cuts off our celebration. "Another twenty coming in from the south."

I spin to see a cloud of dust coming our way.

"Here we go again," Pace says, coming to a grinding dust-laden stop beside me.

"More from the north," BlaKat says.

Suddenly, we're surrounded.

A circle of aliens closes in on us and we are trapped. There are simply too many of them. All weapons are trained on us.

"You fought well, humans," one voice says, sounding like grinding gears. Its owner steps forward. "Your fight has come to an end. Surrender."

I glance around at my team, totally outgunned and outnumbered.

I know no one wants to go down without a fight, but given the choice between certain death and possibly being taken prisoners with the chance to escape, I'll take the latter. Especially since I managed to get out of the Trench. Wherever they bring us can't possibly be that bad.

Then, without warning, the Earth begins to shake. A massive shadow covers us. I turn to see where all the Tuldarians are already looking and firing their weapons.

Firefly has swelled to full size—which is like two stories tall. With size thirty or so boots, he smashes down on half of the approaching army, then we are all forced to duck to the side when he kicks with his other foot, sending the rest soaring and scattering.

Then he fires a blast from both wristbands simultaneously. Normally, when Firefly is shrunken down, these are like very precise and painful stings. At this size, they're six-foot wide blasts of powerful energy. He shoots at one of their smaller transport ships full of reinforcements that's just landed, and when the smoke clears, there's nothing left but a crater.

Definitely a welcome addition to the team.

We all cheer, and I run up to him as he shrinks back down to normal size. "Javi! That was amazing!"

I realize I'm shouting over the music. "Steve, volume down by thirty percent."

Volume reduced.

"Yeah. I'm sorry. Sometimes when I'm scared, the suit doesn't respond to me."

"Well, it was just in time," I tell him, patting him on the back.

"Still not time to celebrate," BlaKat says, sending a new feed to my helmet.

As effective as we are against the aliens, there seems to be an endless supply of them. For every Tuldarian we take down, several more take its place from one of the transports arriving from the mothership. We can only keep it up for so long. And I can only hope—there's that word again—that Crosscircuit gets his robots up and running soon before we run out of steam.

Then, the unthinkable happens. A squad of dinos approach White Hot from the rear, but she doesn't see them coming and can't hear anything over the sounds of battle. I fire my weapon at one of them and vaporize the thing, but now it needs to recharge.

Black Frost turns and sees what's happening and throws up an ice wall to protect White Hot from the Tuldarian fire, but their weapons disintegrate it quickly. Next, he creates an ice path and slides to get between her and the lizard aliens. Just as he gets near, White Hot finally realizes what's happening and turns around.

They each try to sacrifice themself to save the other. And, in so doing, the aliens hit both of them simultaneously and our Icy/Hot duo disappears in a red spray.

The entire thing happens in seconds, but I feel like it takes hours. I feel like I should scream, "Nooooooo!" like I've seen so many times in movies and TV shows. But instead, I freeze up and feel helpless as the Tuldarian troops move their attention to me.

Next, I notice a bright white light on the horizon, almost like the sun is starting to rise early. It spreads so fast that there's no time to react, and I assume we're all about to die.

Everything goes black.

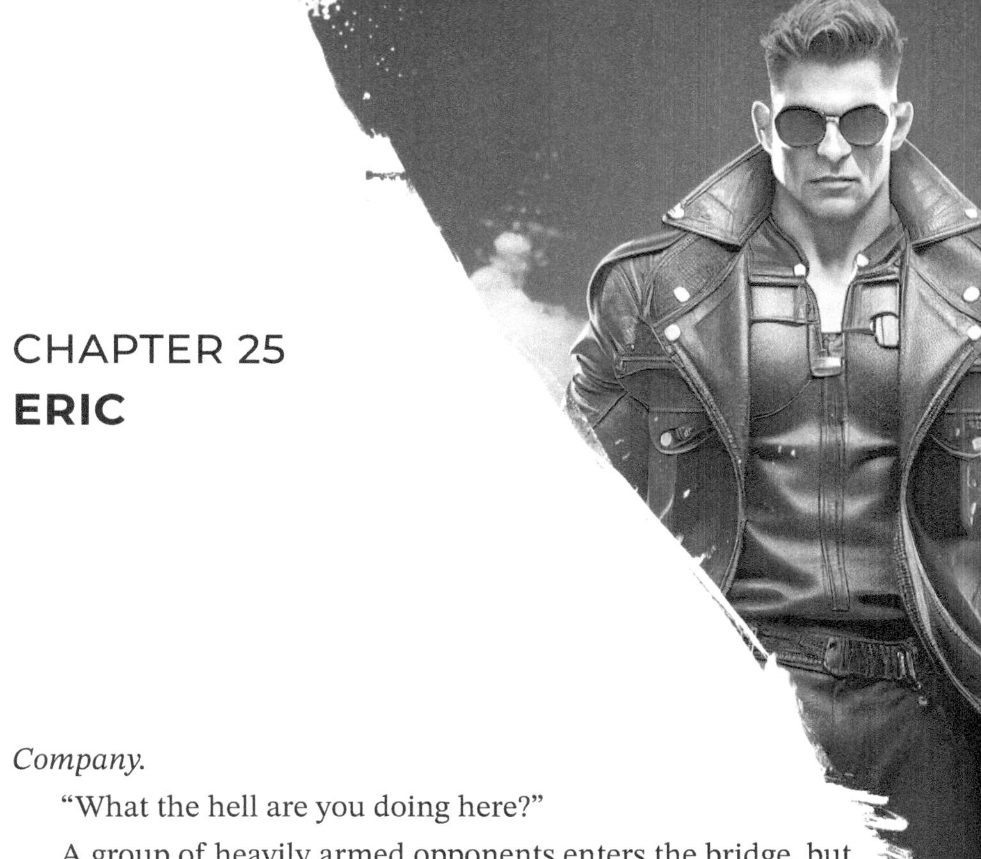

CHAPTER 25
ERIC

Company.

"What the hell are you doing here?"

A group of heavily armed opponents enters the bridge, but they're not aliens; they're human. My heart soars when I realize they're another team, one made up of elite operatives. First, Deadeye, an incredibly accurate, never-misses-his-target assassin who never seems to enjoy his work.

Next up, Bullshark. Let me tell you, having both a giant sentient ape and a half-man-half-shark up here with a bunch of dinosaur aliens might be the cheungiest thing I've ever experienced. He's gotta be seven feet tall, and every vicious thing a shark has, he does too. Add clawed hands and a human brain into the mix, and that's all kinds of scary.

Rush—of all present, I hate him most. He's arrogant to the extreme. That stupid smirk he always wears makes me want to slap it off. Or maybe just melt the face around it with one of the weapons I *didn't* bring. Stupid me for not bringing the melty-melt.

Then again, we're on the same team.

Darkstryke has a mullet, if you can believe it. But his glowing white eyes make up for it. I wish I had glowing white eyes.

The last party-crasher is a young woman I recognize only by reputation. She's a young Asian girl who goes by the code name Shuriken. She may be decent at fighting if she lives up to her name.

"Glad to have some backup," I say, but they immediately open fire on us.

"What the fu—" I take a bullet to the forearm and it cuts my cursing short. "Everyone, find cover!"

I duck behind—something. I don't even know what it is, but hopefully it's not flammable or highly explosive. The way they're shooting, anything that can blow up will.

"Why are they shooting at us?" Justice asks.

"We'll take it from here, McCabe. Stay out of our way," Deadeye barks.

"Screw you, Mason," I shout back. "You just shot me!"

"Wasn't me," he says. "I wouldn't have missed."

I growl, putting pressure on the wound. "We've come this far. We're gonna finish what we started."

If you told me this morning that we'd be locked in a fierce firefight with our own side… No, I guess I'd believe it.

"We were set up," Sinsation says, laughing. "Kind of brilliant."

"Huh? How?" Justice asks.

"Don't be stupid," she says. "We were a distraction while the real team did the job. You seriously never questioned why they'd pin the hope of saving the planet on a bunch of criminal losers like us? They never expected us to survive the first wave."

That realization cuts deep. But it doesn't matter. I set out to save the world, and dammit, I'm going to do it.

I shout out orders to my team, trying to coordinate our efforts.

"Sin, can you... do your thing?"

"On Deadeye? Never," she says. "His mask filters out my pheromones. After what happened in London, he got smart. You ask me, I showed him a good time, but whatevs."

"London?" Justice asks, and I think some jealousy shows through.

"Worry about that later. Or never," I order. "Justice, your time to shine, buddy."

"Oh, yeah." He repositions his alien weapon. "Set phasers to kill."

I close my eyes for a second. For that split second, I feel bad about ordering my team to kill some peeps who are supposed to be our allies, but they were villains before all this, right? And so was I. But I turned... right?

Why am I asking you? Of course I did.

I'm about to speak when Justice rises from his cover and unleashes a blast that sends Rush soaring against the far wall. The floor where he just stood should be a smoking pile of slag, but the way this place was built, it's clearly designed to stand up to their own weapons.

However, the speedster's feet… my god. They are gone.

"Hell yeah, bitches!" Justice shouts, falling back to recharge. "Hope whatever supervillain organization you belong to pays disability! Who else wants some?"

"I wish you hit his face," I say.

I go to make a move, but Deadeye's marksmanship is deadly, and I'm pinned.

"Where's the monkey?" a deep voice roars. Bullshark. Has to be. "Where's the freaking monkey!" he shouts.

"He's dead," Sinsation responds like it hardly matters.

"No!" Bullshark's protest is so loud and filled with rage or pain—I can't tell—it hurts my eardrums. "I wanted to kill him!"

I guess either emotion would probably cover it.

Sinsation rolls and cartwheels from cover to cover toward the enemy. Darkstryke's electricity powers give him an advantage over anyone trying to get near him—but Sinsation is not just anyone. He tries to blast her with his electric pulses, but he's only as good as his aim. She activates her strobe light—a small drone-like object that hovers a few feet over her head, and makes her even more difficult to hit than usual. Then she executes a few flips and somersaults, runs up the side of the bulkhead, and lands on his shoulders.

"You like that, big boy?" she asks, then grabs him by his long hair and yanks him to the ground. I hear a thud from yards away as his head hits the metal floor. I bet he's going to be out for a while.

Shuriken's abilities make it hard to keep up with her, but her throwing stars aren't having much of an effect on Justice, since he's wearing body armor. A couple of the pointy weapons stick into him between the grooves, but it doesn't seem to bother him.

"Finally!" he shouts as the light on his alien weapon turns blue. "Bye-bye." A massive pulse of plasma erupts builds at the barrel. The shot, aimed at Shuriken, goes wild as the seven-foot-tall land-aquatic monstrosity caroms into Justice. Together, they crash into the ship's bulkhead.

Justice wouldn't stand a chance against Bullshark hand-to-hand under the best of circumstances, no matter how good his martial arts skills are. But right now he's dazed and stumbling to get up, so he's sure to be toast within seconds.

Bullshark lifts him by his shoulders and opens that giant maw of his—holy crap, he's going to bite the dude's head off!

My brain barely registers a giant brown blur, and I have no idea what it is until I see a one-armed Roy plow into Bullshark just as he's about to chow down on Justice's face.

No cap, this is bananas.

Oh, shoot. Gorilla, bananas? I didn't even mean to do that.

The shark-man goes down as the injured gorilla literally starts beating on him with his own severed arm. If these guys were fifty feet tall, it would be like watching a kaiju movie or something. He drops his arm and raises Bullshark by the ankle. He attempts the same maneuver he pulled on the dinosaurs, slamming him into the metal floor over and over again, but poor Roy's lost too much blood. He collapses onto his knees first, then slumps over onto the deck. A puddle of blood pools under him and gets bigger. If he wasn't done for already, he definitely is now.

Unfortunately, though, Bullshark isn't down for the count. But Royal Rampage's last breath effort afforded Justice the time needed to crawl away and get to cover before the monster gains his wits back about him. Also unfortunately, I know from past experience working with him, the guy heals fast.

I'm not an idiot. I know when we are on the losing side, but I refuse to give up. I take cover behind a bulkhead, trying to dream up a plan. That's when I see Deadeye reloading his weapon. I realize that if I can take him out, the rest of his team will be disorganized and vulnerable.

He probably doesn't know about my forcefield. I was hoping to save its limited energy, but I turn it on now and stand, then rush toward him as fast as I can. Sure enough, he gets reloaded and perfectly aimed shots whiz toward my face. I won't lie, I flinch. Bruh's got skill. But the bullets are met by blue energy and a loud crackling as my forcefield lights up.

I quickly make my move, firing my weapon and closing in on Deadeye.

"Cheating bastard," Deadeye says.

He does three things at the same time. Man, he's incredible. One, he dodges my attack completely, almost effortlessly.

Two, he shoves his weapon into a holster at his side. And three, he pulls a katana blade from the sheath on his back.

The problem with my forcefield is that if I want to shoot, my weapon needs to be on the other side of the barrier, or else I'll cook myself alive. That means that with one swift movement, he's able to slash and knock my gun out of my hand.

We are inches away now, and if I'm going to end this, I need to be able to hit him. So, I lower my forcefield and we engage in a brutal hand-to-hand combat, both of us determined to come out on top. He's a way more skilled fighter, but he's only at maximum human strength and speed, whereas I've made myself superhuman. Sure, some of that is now jeopardized by the fact that he shot me and I can barely move my arm, but hey, that's how things go sometimes.

His sword pounds my armor. I block the next strike with the forearm of my injured arm, then throw a punch of my own with the good one. It hits his left shoulder pauldron. This opens me up to a kick to my midsection that steals the air from my lungs. I'm vulnerable to him driving that blade straight through me.

If I'm going to make my move, it has to be now.

Pulling my secondary weapon, a small pistol that packs a huge punch, I swerve to the left, then rise and aim it at his forehead.

"Tell them to stand down," I shout, turning my attention briefly to Bullshark, who's about to tear Justice apart again.

"No. What are you gonna do, shoot me?" Deadeye scoffs.

I shrug. "The thought had crossed my mind."

"Is it worth it? We have to finish our mission or the Earth could be done."

"You're the ones attacking *us*! What the hell is your problem?"

"We have to execute our plan precisely, and your team could screw it up. Besides, they didn't think you'd make it this far. You're supposed to be dead by now."

"Sorry to disappoint you," I say through my teeth.

"It's nothing personal."

"Right," I say, showing him the blood leaking from my forearm.

"Don't be a child," he says. "It'll heal. If you get in our way or throw us off in any way, it could prevent us from completing our mission."

"Yeah? And how's that working out for you so far?" I point at the fight going on between the members of our team. "Call off their attack and we can work together."

Then the decision is made for us when a squadron of Tuldarian soldiers shows up and begins firing their weapons at us.

CHAPTER 26
SAWYER

Yaaawwwn.

I open my eyes to the sight of a strange hotel room. An overwhelming feeling of disorientation gnaws at me.

What's going on?

The only feeling I've ever experienced like this was when the warden of the Trench got me drunk on his awful whiskey. But I can't be drunk. I don't drink. I've seen what it did to Frank.

The first thing I notice is I'm completely naked, which is odd because I never sleep that way, not even in my own room at home. Pieces of my uniform and armor are strewn about the room, including my underwear hanging from the lamp on the nightstand next to the bed. That's when I realize I'm not alone, and quickly roll over to see a woman lying next to me, facing the other direction.

Black hair.

Neith? Did we…? Why don't I remember anything?

I reach over to touch her bare shoulder—bare shoulder… no tattoos. So… the woman starts to turn over, still half asleep. Not Neith. Osprey without her blonde wig on.

"Amy?"

Her eyes pop open and I can immediately tell she's just as confused as I am. She jolts up and springs out of bed, wrapping the covers around her nude form, which leaves me—

I grab a pillow and cover my crotch.

Amy spins, looking around the room, and that's when I notice for the first time that pieces of her costume are everywhere also, intermingled with mine. She spots her wig hanging from the ceiling fan.

"What the hell? Did we—?"

I lift my hands in the universal sign of surrender. "I have no idea. I don't…"

My words trail off as flashes of memories return, like images and video clips appearing on a screen almost too quickly to follow. My mouth goes dry. "Um… yeah, I think maybe we did."

"But how—why…" I can tell the same images are probably streaming through her brain, too. "Oh, God. We did, didn't we?"

With the initial shock wearing off, I start to feel it. The urge to grab her… to continue what had apparently started last night. But that's not me. I would never…

I see the same hungry look in her eyes that I'm feeling

myself, and the compulsion is almost too much. She shakes her head and rushes to the bathroom, slamming the door.

After a few agonizing seconds, I slide out of bed and pull on my underwear and pants. I know I should be worried about Amy. The logical part of my brain says I should knock on the bathroom door and try to talk to her—figure out what happened. Find out what's going on.

But I can't bring myself to care. In fact, it takes everything I have not to kick down the door and pull her into my arms. It's like there's something missing from my soul. My conscience… it's just… gone. Or at least buried. I still know right from wrong, but it's like all of my willpower has just vanished.

I finish putting on the rest of my clothes and suit, barely keeping myself in check. As I'm leaving, the bathroom door to my right flings open, and there she is, standing in all her glory. Her smile says that she's no longer upset, and her demeanor tells me she's fighting the same dilemma.

I take a step back.

The sixteen-year-old me would've given anything to be in this situation. Like, literally anything. But she's not herself. She's acting primal… almost animalistic.

The one last shred of decency I have left calls out to me from somewhere deep in my psyche.

This is wrong, Sawyer. There's no going back after this.

I know in an instant, I'm right. If I give in to these impulses, I may never be able to become myself again. And even if I do, will I be able to forgive myself for whatever I do?

I can't go out the door, because that'll bring me close enough to her that if she grabs me, I'm convinced I won't be able to maintain any semblance of self-control. I look behind me and see from the view that we are probably thirty stories up in a tall building.

There's only one option.

I grit my teeth and throw myself through the window, smashing a Harrier-sized hole in it like a cartoon character. It's only after I'm hurtling through the air that I realize I should have checked to make sure my grappler was in working order before taking the plunge.

I fumble for the grip at my waist, pulling in free and spinning to aim for the stone wall. Thankfully, it *thwips* out and *clinks* into place. I don't immediately pull the locking trigger, allowing myself to plummet far enough that the tension won't just hurtle me into the building.

When I finally do, the grappler sends me arcing downward. I call on my years of practice to guide myself to safety on the street below, then click another button to detach and retract the wire.

Above, I see Osprey staring down from the broken window. For a moment, I think she's gonna follow, then she ducks back inside.

So there I am, standing in the middle of a crowded street after just escaping a woman's bedroom as if her father had been chasing me with a shotgun.

That's when I realize this isn't an isolated incident. Everyone around me appears insane.

A cab driver to my left is beating mercilessly on one of his customers, while to my right, a woman waving a rolling pin chases after a young man.

What the heck is going on here?

I consider how many people need my help, then decide I'm in no condition to help anyway. I need help myself. All I can think about is climbing back up to Amy. The urge is almost unbearable.

Using every ounce of determination in me, I turn and run through the streets of Giza, just outside of Cairo. My mind is a fluttering mess, trying to make sense of what's happening around me. Evading speeding cars, dodging out-of-control people, I leap and parkour over and under anything that won't move.

The streets are chaos. People are everywhere, running and screaming, their eyes wild with fear. I can't imagine this is what Egypt is always like. They're acting irrationally, pushing and shoving each other, completely disoriented.

"Steve, what's going on?" I ask into my helmet.

There's no response.

I swear.

Suddenly, I see a group of men charging toward me, their eyes wild with rage. I stop to reason with them, but I can tell immediately, it's no use. They're like animals, completely consumed by whatever is driving them to act this way. I rush forward and dart to the side, narrowly avoiding their grasping hands and push my way through the crowd. I can feel them getting closer, their fingers brushing against my skin, but I don't let it slow me down. My heart is pounding in my chest. My breathing is ragged and taxed. But these people are too panicked, too frenzied to make way.

I limit myself to moves that are least harmful, but I have to use my martial arts skills to clear a path. Guilt floods me to crippling levels.

Another group of men in the distance, armed with guns and shouting, loot a store. Glass shatters as they make their way in and back out again, stealing whatever they can. Again, I know I have to stop them, but I'm disoriented and unsure of where to begin.

Dozens watch, many cheering them on. But none of them are standing still. Fights break out, fists and feet flying with abandon. I finally manage to push through the crowd, and make my way toward the looters. They turn toward me, their faces twisted in rage. Guns rise, and one fires. It hits me in my helmet. A headshot. Whatever Chen made this thing out of, it's tough.

But here's the problem. That trigger pull was the last bit I needed to lose control of myself.

"Bad move," I tell him as he fires three more times.

I bolt to the side, anticipating where the bullets will land. Screams ring out behind me, and I know someone just died. Fiery rage fills every inch of my body. I strike out with my fists, and where I had just used a measure of my will to hold back, now I have none of it. I wanna kill them, destroy them for what they've done. They represent every single villain I've ever fought, every thug on every street corner who thought they could take what didn't belong to them.

In a matter of seconds, they are disarmed and bleeding under my graphene gloves. Blood sprays everywhere, but I don't care. They deserve this. Every bit of it.

"No killing," I hear in the back of my mind. Frank's voice. My father. My mentor. "No killing."

"You killed!" I shout as my fists drive into the bridge of someone's nose.

A vision of Frank stumbling through his apartment enters my mind. Tie loose, shirt untucked and stained. It somehow serves as a reminder that I can't allow myself to travel the same road he has.

The crowd around me boos when I let up, and some are incensed into madness that I didn't deliver a fatal blow. I hear them closing in all around me, which forces me to hop to my feet and take off again. I easily break through those blocking the sidewalk, but as I pound through the chaos in the streets, I realize this is only the beginning.

Turning a corner, I see a figure floating in the middle of the road, surrounded by crazies, nut-jobs, madmen. I can tell she's a villain by the way she's completely calm and collected while everyone else is losing their minds. Her eyes glow bright, hot white as she slowly moves through the streets.

Vaguely, my mind tells me who it is: the Torturess. Even more vaguely, I remember something about fighting in the desert...

What is she doing here?

I recall why I was fighting in the desert. To create a pathway for Crosscircuit's team to do… something.

What were they doing?

And whatever it was, did they fail at their mission?

Suddenly, the ground shakes beneath me, sending me stumbling into a parked car. The alarm blares, and eyes turn toward me. Specifically, her eyes. There's a flash of recognition there.

She knows me. And for some reason, she hesitates.

But I don't.

Launching myself at her, fists clenched, I brace for an impact. But I jump right through her, landing on the street in a sprawl.

A mirage?

I rise, catching my breath and trying to make sense of what's happening. Though my mind is racing, I know one thing for sure: I have to stop Torturess before she can cause any more harm.

I set off on this heroing thing when I was, like, thirteen years old. Since then, I haven't always thought of myself as one of the best. Sure, Frank instilled in me the confidence to believe I was someone who could make a difference in the world, but if you'd told me all those years ago my powers would lead me to going head-to-head with someone with the ability to turn an entire city into slobbering fools, I'd have said you needed to be thrown into a padded room.

Furthermore, I don't think I've ever found myself fighting

crowds of civilians—much less in the middle of an alien invasion.

But there she is. Am I gonna have to kill her to end this? To save the Earth?

A sonic boom cracks and a figure in crimson descends from the sky like a meteor. Her landing causes the already shaking ground to quake. The vision of her brings back a bit more: something Frank told me about Annihilatrix, fighting the aliens, trying to get to Torturess.

Then, like a tidal wave, the memories of days past flood over me. At the bunker, Annihilatrix was in a state of rage. She was devastated, and determined to take revenge after discovering that her partner, Torturess, was being used by the aliens for all sorts of things. It appears along with creating zombified mummies, she was also being forced to control people's minds.

She stalks over to the projection of Torturess as people continue to scatter in all directions.

"Telia. It's me. Please stop this," Annihilatrix says.

"It's not really her," I shout. "It's some sort of projection. I think she's still in the Sphinx."

Annihilatrix spins on me, her eyes glowing red, and I wonder whether she's as out of her mind as the rest of these people. Is she gonna kill me? She's so angry, I don't even know how to interpret her expression.

Before either of us can say anything else, the mob of humans parts and dozens of Tuldarians show up from all directions and surround us. They train their weapons on us, and I'm afraid they're gonna fry me.

But I manage to get out one sentence. "You guys made a huge mistake."

Hell arrives in Egypt as Annihilatrix unleashes her powers on the aliens. Her strength is way beyond human and her laser eyes are like nothing I've ever seen before, including Eaglestar. His are focused beams of light that cut and sear. But hers? It's like a solar flare or something—a six-foot-wide swath of pure energy bursts from her eyes. The blast tears up asphalt, cars, and anything—or anyone—in its path.

The aliens don't stand a chance. Without regard for any of the humans present, she whips her head around, vaporizing dozens of the dino-creatures within seconds, her anger and pain fueling her powers.

"Everyone, down!" I shout, but it's really no good. The people are either still under Torturess's control, or so frightened they can't respond to reason.

Just like that, hundreds are left dead in the streets of Cairo by Annihilatrix's rage-infused power.

I fall to the ground, doing my best to avoid her devastation. I can't help but feel a sense of awe and admiration. I also can't help but feel a sense of guilt. My powers were useless to prevent this from happening, and now I can't even help clean up the mess.

No one could possibly stop her. A five-story building crumbles a block away, the entire bottom floor being blown out from beneath it.

"Annihilatrix, stop!" I shout.

How could I possibly expect her to hear me over everything?

But then, something shifts in her. I can see it in her face, a moment of clarity and understanding.

She looks toward the projection, but Torturess's visage is gone. Something's happened and I have no idea what.

As dust and debris cloud the street, Annihilatrix seems to realize that this isn't just about her, or even just about Torturess. This is about all of us, about the fate of humanity. And in that moment, she appears to make a decision. She's gonna do what Eaglestar was unable to do and end this war, once and for all.

Annihilatrix turns her attention to the alien ships hovering high above Cairo. The ground shatters under her feet, and her determination is palpable as she pushes off and flies toward them, her laser eyes focused on her targets.

The rending metal can be heard even down here. The ships erupt in a brilliant display of light that paints the entire sky neon blues and purples.

When she's done destroying them, she faces west for a moment, then disappears in a blink as a sonic boom rings out. My guess is she must be headed back to New York and the mothership, the source of the invasion.

All I know is, I wouldn't wanna be on that ship right now.

CHAPTER 27
SEAN

Bright.

Harsh sunlight pours in through a crack in the drawn shades. I open my mouth to yawn. A maniacal cackle catches me completely off guard. Leaping out of bed, I spin in a quick circle. Apart from me, the room is empty. It's at that moment I realize the laughter had escaped from somewhere deep within my own belly.

I'm in a hotel room with no memory of anything that occurred leading up to this moment. Already standing, I pull the curtains fully open, basking in the sunlight. I can tell I'm in Cairo, or maybe Giza, but the last thing I recall is being at Bunker Base Bravo. The streets below are a mess. The Middle East is always a war zone, but this seems worse than normal. Fires blaze from rooftops and people frantically run around in the streets. At second glance, they appear to be rioting, fighting, destroying everything they can get their hands on.

A smile creeps onto my face, and a feeling of great joy comes over me. I like it. Like a kid in a candy shop, I need to be part of what's going on down there.

Breathing deep, then letting it out, I look down. Naked. Interesting. A few steps take me to a sliding mirror. Inside, a fully stocked closet. I've never been one for fashion. Most geniuses have a sort of uniform. Black shirt. Jeans. Thin hoodie even, regardless of the season.

I find something in black and throw it on. Black is inconspicuous. Menacing. I stroll into the bathroom to find a toothbrush in a plastic wrapper, and a small travel-size tube of paste.

As I'm about to leave, I remember my exosuit and find the disc device that issues a command for the nanobots to build the suit. Attaching it to my chest, I exit the hotel room and tear down the seven flights of stairs, not wanting to wait for the elevator. I smash open the front door and allow the mayhem to overtake me.

It's beautiful chaos. I couldn't have planned it better myself.

Maybe I had planned it. Was this all my doing? I sure hope so.

I enter the throng, pushing past several men wearing business suits. They turn and try to attack me, but I slap the device on my chest, and in seconds I'm inside of my exoskeletal battlesuit. Their eyes go wide just before I level them with little more than a thought. My mechanical arms slam outward with almost enough force to shatter their sternums.

I don't even bother to look at them once they hit the ground. I assume they're dead, and that's fine. The next moments are disorderly and unrehearsed. I flip cars end over end, bash in a man's skull for bumping into me. There's no rhyme or reason to my actions, but I know it needs to be done. I feel it inside of me. I'm doing the right thing.

Somehow, over the din of it all, I hear the groaning of the manhole at my feet. I stop and watch the cover as it rises slightly, almost imperceptibly—but not to my keen eyes. A cold, wet hand wraps around my ankle. Fast as my reflexes might be, before I can stomp down on it with my other boot, I'm being yanked into the sewer. Water splashes all around me. When I rise, a creature with large fangs stands before me—a creature I know well and have fought before, prior to being sent to the Trench. Iguanadon is a humanoid lizard-man with incredible strength and speed.

But he's not very intelligent. He lets out a primal roar, sending spittle into my face.

Where most would assume he's a villain, he's not. Part of the Guild he might not be, but he'd accept the position in a heartbeat if it were offered.

I hate these goodie-goodies—no idea what they're doing. They don't even consider what the world deserves, they just fight for what they think is justice. *What* I *do is justice!* I nearly scream as the thought rises up inside of me.

And then I do. "This world deserves judgment!"

The reptile swats me like a bug, sending me flying against the wall. I feel a crack and hope it's the stone and not my spine. I stand, thankful I'm not paralyzed. I never could defeat him when I was in his element, in the sewers, with the damp, musty air making it hard to breathe. But that was before I created my exosuit.

Iguanadon is fast, and he uses his speed to try and outmaneuver me, darting around the sewers, launching quick strikes and trying to catch me unawares. But I'm not. I am in full control of myself and my suit. My armored boot kicks forward, driving deep into his belly. Ever see a flying lizard? He lands in the disgusting sludge, sliding a dozen yards before landing with a thud.

For a moment, I think I might have won. But he quickly gets back on his claw-adorned feet.

"You idiots never know when to stay down," I say, stomping forward, water sloshing in my wake.

I leap at him, landing a flying kick to his neck. He roars and swats again. But I'm no fool. He's used all his tricks. He misses, and I let out another swift kick to the side of his knee. Iguanodon drops, his scaly leg fractured.

Grabbing him by his tail, I whip him around, but suddenly find myself holding only his severed fifth limb. Gross.

Despite his broken leg and now missing tail, he comes at me, using his good leg and arms to carry him at full speed through the tunnel. We collide, and though my boots are planted, the ground is slippery and he gains ground.

I punch at his head, neck, and chest, but he ignores it, snapping sharp teeth at my face.

"Enough!" I shout. With a thought, a piston in my forearm fires and a foot-long dagger running the length of my ulna pierces the soft flesh around his neck.

Though he doesn't let go, he thrashes wildly and falls, landing on top of me.

I'm submerged in Egyptian excrement and sludgy water. I don't have time to take a breath, and with his heavy frame on top of me, I am fighting not to suck in a lungful of poopy death.

Finally, using every ounce of mechanical strength my suit allows, I manage to shove his corpse off of me and climb back to my hands and knees.

Now I do take a breath and immediately regret it. How am I supposed to look threatening while covered in this stuff?

I shout loud and the echo returns to me. "This world has abandoned itself! It does not deserve life, but I will be the one to give it what it truly deserves."

I climb back through the open manhole, away from my interruption, and tear off through the streets at my superhuman speed. Passing by shop after broken shop, I catch my reflection in the mirror. What stares back at me is someone I barely know. My speed begins to slow as I look into the eyes of the thing who wears my eyes.

Before I know it, I'm stopped and begin walking toward the front window of a storefront. Pain and hurt glare at me. But I see something else there as well... Through clouded deception, I see my mother's eyes. They slowly go white with death.

"The Torturess," I whisper. "She did this."

She's convinced the whole world that nobody deserves to live.

With the help of the Tuldarians, she's done it—the thing every villain from small brainiac mice to giant brainiac machines had tried to do. She's finally accomplished world domination.

Touching the side of my exosuit's helmet, I say, "Bunker Base Bravo."

The phone to the private line rings. No answer.

I take in my surroundings again now that I have a bit of clarity, and remember that feeling I got looking down from the seventh floor hotel window. The thrill and excitement. The knowing that what I did matters—but not knowing why. I've become a villain, but I don't feel like it. I feel... good. More than that... I feel like I was doing good.

I consider what I'd just done to Iguanadon, killed him in cold warm-blooded blood. How could I do such a thing? And those businessmen. Were they dead too? Panic grips me, and I start to sweat.

I shake my head free as I can. I would have time to explore my feelings after the Torturess is stopped.

My bionic legs take me toward Giza. Once I clear the city limits, the Pyramids loom in the distance. I keep pushing, faster, harder until the silhouette of the Sphinx grows. The same blue cloud of energy pulses above it.

Where the Russian hulk had died. Where Prairie had died. Where so many more are on the brink of dying. How did I get to that hotel room in the first place?

My thoughts are interrupted when a green ball of energy lands in front of me, the heat of it burning as I dive to the side. Following the trajectory of the blast, I spot Whisper standing atop the great cat-man statue's head.

She floats down on a vibrating disc of energy and hovers before me.

"You would do well to turn around, Crosscircuit," she says. "You cannot stop her. I will not allow you to."

"Whisper? What happened to you? What did she do to you?"

I stare at her beautiful face, now contorted into a vicious scowl.

The disc dissipates from beneath her feet and she lands softly in the sand.

"What she is doing must be done." Even as she says the words, I feel myself agreeing with them.

"No," I say, unsure of whom I'm trying to convince. "The aliens are using her to turn us against each other. Step aside or I'll make you step aside."

She kneels, placing her hand against the ground. Everything shakes, and I dive aside just as a ten-foot tall spike bursts from the sand where I'd just been standing.

"Whisper, stop this!" I shout.

She places her other hand down, and I know what to expect. I leap in hard, shouldering her and sending her to the ground. Bursts of sand shoot from her hands, propelling her to her feet.

I throw a right hook and it lands. I know what you're thinking: She's a woman! Never hit a woman!

When you're dealing with superhumans, all bets are off. It's kill or be killed. I'd rather not kill her, but like Iguanadon, she doesn't leave me much of a choice.

I punch her again, harder. Despite the strength of my exosuit, she takes it in stride and lashes back. Again, I shout for her to stop, but she won't listen. I try to tell her she's being manipulated, but if she hears me, she doesn't show it.

I give her one last warning and I'm met with a controlled blast of verdant energy to the chest. I soar through the air but manage to land on my feet.

Pushing through the pain, I charge her again, weaving in and out as she tries to hit me over and over. I bring back a fist and let it fly. I have to stop the Torturess and that means stopping Whisper first.

My tech-covered hand goes through her chest cavity just as it had the mummy's. I feel her still-beating heart against my forearm and quickly pull my arm back.

I can't breathe. I can't think. Somewhere, I hear myself saying, "I'm sorry. I'm sorry. I'm so sorry…" But it's like I'm detached from my body.

Her corpse slides the rest of the way off my arm and plops to the dessert. Blood gurgles from the hole, and I throw up. A lot.

I wipe my mouth with the back of my dung-covered arm

and throw up again. Finally, with watery eyes, my gaze flutters toward the blue cloud and try not to imagine what's happening all over the world. I hope it's only the area around Cairo, but I have no idea. That storm had been exactly what she needed last night.

Covered in blood and feces, I stagger toward the Sphinx and enter the same way as before. I silently thank Whisper's ghost—even though I don't believe in such things—for providing the way for me. As I sprint through the previously hidden caverns, I think about my mother—not the cancer-ridden remains of my mother, but the woman who drove me to college every day and treated me like her little boy even though I was a freak. She treated me like I needed her wisdom even though I was far wiser than she. But I loved her for it. I will do this for her.

The narrow hallways open into a room about the size of a New York apartment with four pillars rising in three-foot intervals from floor to ceiling.

"*Alto ahí*," a voice says behind me.

I turn to see El Jaguar Inmortal.

"We need to stop Torturess," I say, already starting to move again. But he dashes forward lightning fast to bar my way.

Not this again.

"You cannot stop this," he says. "She is doing the gods' work."

"I don't believe in gods," I tell him as I drive my fist toward him.

The punch connects but he must barely feel it, or he's so used to pain he ignores it.

This could be a problem, since killing him isn't a permanent solution. He returns the attack, and the sound of our bodies colliding echoes through the ancient halls.

I can barely keep up with him even though I've calculated his every move before he makes it. He's fast and agile, moving with the grace and precision of a predator. Pouncing at me, his fists clenched, he roars. But I anticipate his move and slap him down to the ground with both super-powered arms.

While he's distracted, I grab a nearby stone pillar. Using the strength of my exosuit, I pull. It cracks free from its place, and I swing it like a baseball bat. He tries to avoid it, but it's too late. The pillar crashes into him, sending rock everywhere and him flying back. He lands against a second pillar with a thud and for a moment, I think I might have won, but he quickly rises, fierce determination in his eyes.

Small stones begin to fall from the ceiling where he'd collided.

I realize this could turn into a long battle, and I don't have time for it, so I need to come up with a strategy. I know I can't outmatch him in strength or speed, but I *can* outsmart him.

First, I align myself with another column and allow him to strike me. He bounds forward, and dives. At the last second, I duck. His fist produces a large crack in the pillar.

The tactic here has to be implemented with scientific exactitude. Creeping incrementalism. If he catches wind of my plan, he'll be able to avoid it. He punches again, further damaging the support structure. More of the ceiling falls.

He comes in for a third strike and I use his momentum to slam his head into the crack he'd just created.

The result is what I hoped for. The column comes down, but with two others still intact, the ceiling remains in place. By my estimations, this place could be held strong even by one support column.

While he's still dazed, I toss him toward the third pillar, then charge him, shoulder down. I know he's going to move, but that's the point. I make it look like an accident when I charge straight through the stone and leave us in a room with one lone column holding up a very heavy ceiling.

He's relentless, rising and delivering blow after blow. And I have to admit, armor aside, it hurts.

"We don't have to do this," I tell him, but he just smiles and punches me again.

I know I can't put him down permanently, but I can disable him for a time.

As he backs up, I finally see an opening, and strike.

"My apologies," I tell him as I launch my forearm weapon from its place. A missile-like javelin soars at him and lodges itself in his chest. The momentum carries him backward, pinning him into the final pillar. The weapon drills into the stone and spikes extend from both ends, securing it through El Jaguar's chest. Blood spurts from his mouth and his chest as I see the light go out in his eyes.

I back up into the corridor I know will lead me to

Torturess. Standing in the threshold, I give the mental command and a small projectile launches from my suit. The rat-sized missile follows my targeting to the top of the last pillar. As soon as it hits, I dive into the hallway.

The sound of thunder roars behind me, and all I can see is dust as the ceiling collapses, burying El Jaguar like a pharaoh of old.

My only solace is knowing I haven't just killed another of my teammates.

I pick myself up and stand there for a moment, catching my breath and surveying the destruction around me. Another victory for brains over brawn.

As expected, the corridor takes me into the central chamber where I find the sphere—one I now have a full memory of—spinning at a far more rapid rate than before. The Torturess is inside, but she looks frail and beaten.

"Heeeeelp," she croaks.

I walk forward cautiously.

Is this another trick? Another of her mind games?

"Please... help me," she says. "I can't stop it spinning. It's tearing me apart."

"You mean like you're tearing the city apart?" I ask, walking slowly toward her.

"You don't understand," she says, voice agonized. "They're controlling me. I don't have a choice. Please... help me."

"I can't get to you!" I shout.

"Please!" She's crying now, and I have to make a choice.

I walk to the place where I know the forcefield will be. As

I suspected, it's no longer active. There's a control panel near the sphere and I make my way toward it.

The Torturess cries out in anguish. "Don't touch that!"

"You want me to help? I'm shutting this thing down," I say.

"I will die!"

"Two birds then." I want her to die. I revel in the thought. "Everything I've worked toward... don't you see? You're the advantage the Tuldarians have. It has to be this way."

It isn't easy, but as I'm sure you remember, I graduated Yale at nine, and I've been studying the Tuldarians for years. I find the correct combination on the panel and as the machine winds down, her screams begin to wind up. I can feel her dying. I drink it in. It's like nectar. Like water on a hot day. It's beautiful. She's beautiful. *I'm* beautiful.

I move to the front of the sphere. Metal bars rotate past my face, one after another, slower and slower until finally, it stops.

With haunted eyes, she looks up at me. "You've killed me..." she mumbles as she collapses into a lifeless heap.

Maybe I did. But here's the thing... as soon as that sphere stops its final revolution, the entirety of my mind reverts to normal, and with it, I assume so does all of humanity. I have trouble remembering what normal is. I only know one thing: Truth is absolute. But perspective determines what you perceive the truth to be. And perception is reality.

I was under her control for a short while, but I broke free. But everyone else? Had I not been here to save them, they'd have torn the world asunder, and for what? No one would even know.

I can no longer trust humanity's perceptions. My mind is shaken and rattled to its core, but I'm able to see past the things projected upon me by another and focus on the truth.

I am not a hero.

I was formerly a villain.

But now I stand as the holder of the truth, the keeper of the peace, and the Lord of the World. You will all do well to remember this.

Remember and obey.

I have your best interests at heart—trust me.

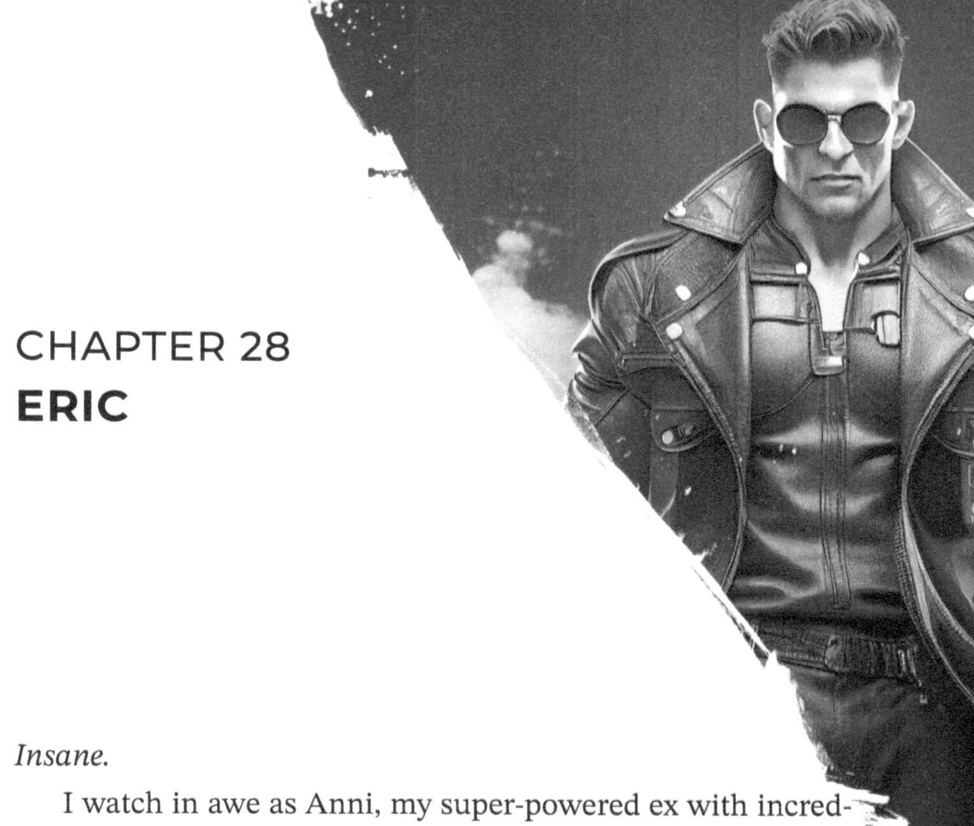

CHAPTER 28
ERIC

Insane.

I watch in awe as Anni, my super-powered ex with incredible strength and deadly laser eyes, wreaks havoc on the alien invaders.

It all started with a terrible quaking that interrupted our fight with the Tuldarians. Deadeye and Justice have been fighting side-by-side instead of trying to go 1-8-7 on each other, and they make quite the team. Each has a mastery over their weapons unlike any I've seen before.

Even Bullshark put aside his differences and went on the attack. Shark vs. dinosaur would surely be a pay-per-view event for many, and we'd all gotten a free show.

They may look like dinosaurs, but I know they're far from it. These creatures are ruthless and have caused mass destruction, including hurting Anni's partner, Torturess.

Sucks to be them.

Anni is out for revenge and she's not holding back. She showed up like a smokin' hot bullet, tearing through the ship as if the bulkheads didn't exist. Which is scary, considering the aliens' own weapons couldn't even damage them.

Makes me wonder if she's somehow related to Eaglestar.

Huh. Maybe I'll ask when all this is over.

If we survive.

Her fists fly and she lands punch after punch on the alien invaders, each one sending them flying backward with a gross splat. Her laser eyes blaze, forcing all of us to duck for cover that doesn't exist. Truth is, if she doesn't contain her fury, we're all going to end up smoked.

She takes out several at once, leaving nothing but ash in their places.

I can't take my eyes off of her—she's absolutely amazing. She's got absolutely no chill. If she'd had this kind of passion in our relationship, maybe we'd still be bumpin' uglies. Or maybe I'd be a pile of blacked cinder as well. I shudder at the thought.

The aliens try to fight back, but it's no use. They're no match for Anni's raw strength and power. I can see it in her eyes, the drive to protect Torturess and take these invaders to the cashier. You know, pay for what they've done.

The aliens actually start to retreat, grunting and hissing in their dumb language. But Anni's not done yet. With a crack-boom, she zooms across the bridge and drags her forearms behind their cowardly legs, flipping them onto their backs.

Again, I get to watch what happens when a Tuldarian is

prone. I described it like a turtle last time, and it's true. They have trouble getting up, but she doesn't let them anyway. Grasping hold of a nearby console, she tears it from the ground, and slams it hard on their chests.

Alarm klaxons blare, and we feel a sudden and severe lurch in the ship's attitude. At first, I think we're going down, then some computerized voice speaks through the ship and we level out.

We all stand there, dumbfounded as Anni stands victorious, her chest heaving as she catches her breath.

She turns to me, her eyes still blazing with power. "It's not over yet. We need to make sure they never come back."

I nod; she's right. If they think they can go home, regroup, and develop some sort of weapon that could kill her like they had Eaglestar, we are just buying time. They need to know it's over. For good. We can't let these invaders get away with what they've done. We have to make sure they never threaten us again.

"She's insane," Sinsation says. "I think I'm in love."

"Keep it in your pants, doll," Deadeye tells her.

"You need to find a way off this ship," Anni warns.

She's talking to me. Just me. I think. Maybe I'm projecting, but all I can think of is how much I wish we were still together. She's incredible.

"Eric," she says. "Get everyone out. Now!"

My senses return and I nod. "Right. Okay, everyone, back to the gliders!"

Deadeye grabs my arm and spins me back to him. "You

think I'm just abandoning my mission because she tells me to? This was *our* mission. We're here, and we're going to destroy this thing."

"I don't care what you do," I bark. "Suit yourself."

I tear my arm free and my team follows me while Deadeye's goons stay and argue with Anni. I can hear gunfire behind us as we run.

"Are they shooting at her?" Sinsation asks.

"They shot at us," I respond.

"Fair point. They're crazy. I like it."

Just as we spot the air vent we'd entered, the ship is sent into violent throes, and we can barely keep our feet.

"We need to get in—"

My words are cut short as everything around us begins to crumble.

Sinsation is in the vent, and Justice is following, but there's no way I'm going to make it.

"We did it, guys," I say to no one. "We saved the world."

Then, a giant blast of blue flames rushes down the center of the ship, and I don't even feel it as it engulfs me.

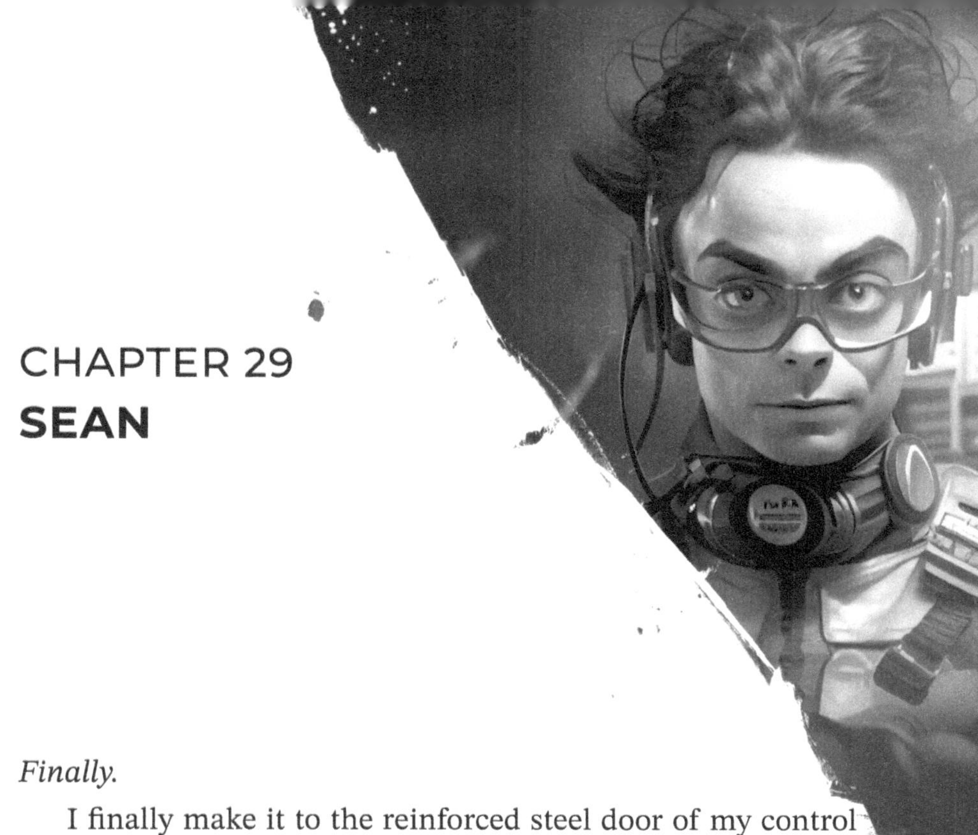

CHAPTER 29
SEAN

Finally.

I finally make it to the reinforced steel door of my control room deep below the Sphinx. Looks just like it did all those years ago when I built this place right under the nose of all world governments. Just another clue that none of them deserve authority. Imagine not knowing someone was building a world-domination—I mean, a save-the-world—base within one of the wonders of the world?

My heart pounds as I enter the code to unlock it. The door slides open and I rush inside, my eyes scanning the room for any sign of damage or intrusion. Everything looks to be in order, but I know I can't let my guard down. The Tuldarians are still out there, and they won't give up until they've destroyed everything in their path.

Before me stands a cobweb-covered automaton designed to appear and sound just like me, though I never managed to get rid of the mechanical tones to his voice. Just goes to show, not even the smartest man alive can mimic humanity to perfection.

My hands shake with adrenaline and excitement. This is it. The moment I've been working toward for years. The moment when all of my hard work and planning will finally pay off. I reach up for the spot behind my mechanical clone's ear where my fingerprint will activate him. Since he was created using power harnessed from the sun, his batteries should still be well intact. Besides, his creator was me.

I slowly touch my forefinger to the back of his earlobe and yellow glows behind his eyes.

"Hello, master," it says in my voice but not quite my voice —an Austrian accent. Why? A Terminator reference, of course. I just found it amusing, I suppose. "Welcome back."

"Hello, Shaan. I'm glad to see you're well."

"I have been inactive for—"

"We don't have time for statistics," I tell him. "Our moment has come. Are you ready to be the general you were created to be?"

"I was created ready."

"Excellent." I rub my hands together anticipatorily. What? It's a word; look it up. "Activate your armies."

Monitors affixed to the walls all around us flash, showing satellite feeds from hundreds of locations across the globe where my children rise from their slumber. They're alive! And I've got a front row seat.

Everywhere from basements below abandoned homes in

Kansas to massive hidden warehouses in the Sahara Desert to undiscovered nooks in the Great Wall of China, my robots emerge. I created versatile warriors, each with abilities to match anything thrown at them. Flying, swimming, running, jumping, and most importantly, shooting and hand-to-hand combat.

"My estimation is that the enemy will be incapacitated within the day," Shaan says.

I nod slowly, my lips pulling up at the corners of my mouth. "Excellent."

Onscreen, the Tuldarians, too, are everywhere, their lizard-like bodies slithering quickly and efficiently as they wreak havoc on the human population. But my robots are faster, stronger, and better equipped. They move like the well-oiled machines they are, taking down the enemy in great swaths. The aliens, caught off guard by the sudden appearance of my robots, are no match for their firepower and agility. I watch in awe as my babies decimate the Tuldarian forces from China to LA. And yes, I mean that word literally. One-tenth of the alien invading force has already been removed from existence, my robots' laser weapons cutting through their thick reptilian hides with ease.

Sweat pools under my eyes—or are those tears?

The battle unfolds on the screens in front of me, and I simply can't help the emotion welling within me. The Tuldarians may be fierce fighters, but my robots are like the creations of God. Take that as you will.

All this time, no one needed the Guild. They just needed me.

The aliens fall back, their numbers dwindling as my robots continue to press forward.

The world's greatest heroes have spent days fighting, and I'm about to find victory in a matter of minutes.

I place a hand on Shaan's shoulder.

"The enemy is fleeing," Shaan declares. "I shall initiate our high-orbit defenses to obliterate their ships once they reach altitude."

"Fine. Fine. But, let one go. A small one. Allow one measly ship to return home to inform his leaders that Earth is mine and will not fall."

My heart leaps with joy and swells with pride as I watch the Tuldarians fall. My robots will soon be triumphant. *Because of me. I* have saved humanity from certain destruction. I can finally rest easy knowing that my genius has saved the day.

I let out a truly relieved sigh for the first time since I entered the Trench. My entire body feels like it's made of Jell-O. I did it.

"Good work, son," I say to Shaan. "You were time well spent."

"I am happy I please you."

Though there's still work to do, I take a moment to relish my victory. The Tuldarians will soon be gone, but I can't afford complacency. Now that I'm free of the Trench, I'll have to keep working, to keep building and improving my robots, to ensure that humanity is never threatened like this again.

When satisfied, I let out another deep sigh. Have you ever done something so great that pride feels like a limitless balloon expanding within you? No. Of course you haven't. And I have not the time to explain the sensation.

I have saved the world, and I am the hero.

"Come, Shaan. It is time for Phase Two."

The robot made in my likeness falls in step behind me as I turn to leave the control room.

As we exit through the still open door, I whisper to myself, "I am the master of my machines." And I know that I will continue to be.

Just as I'll soon be the master of all mankind.

1600 Pennsylvania Avenue

I stand at the gates of the White House, Shaan and a battalion of my robots at my side.

The soldiers and agents guarding the building glare, but President Stanford parts them and strides carefree toward us.

"Sean! My boy!" He ignores the warnings of his Secret Service, and that will be his greatest mistake. "That was incredible work. The best work. I've never seen anything—"

A small red dot blossoms on his forehead before he collapses, dead on the White House lawn.

"Shut up already," I say to his corpse, then glance up at

Shaan, whose smoking gun is still raised. See? Just like the Terminator.

At this, absolute pandemonium arises. As expected. Bullets fly toward us but bounce harmlessly off the forcefield created by my closest bots. I tap the disc on my chest and my exosuit unravels to further protect me, though I'm unsure I'll need such safety measures.

"Bring the gates down," I command.

At once, several of my children rush forward and rend the iron gates until there's a hole large enough for us to enter. It's a shame so many have to die just for me to bring peace to this world, but that's the sad truth of my situation. And as I've said many times, truth is the most important thing to me.

We walk past dead and dying soldiers, but I don't spare them a glance. Chances are, their families are already dead anyway. Frankly, I'm surprised the White House is even still standing. I mean, we've all seen *Independence Day*, right?

Once inside, I make my way toward the Oval Office. The sounds of gunfire and explosions echo through the halls as my robots take out anyone who gets in our way. Any bullets that penetrate my forcefield bounce off my metallic shell as I knock soldiers to the ground with the battlesuit's giant fists.

Approaching the Oval Office, I can see the Secret Service agents trying to hold the door shut, but it's no use. My robots break it down and we storm inside.

The former president's advisors are huddled in the corner, looking terrified. They should be, for I am the smartest man on Earth, and I am here to take control of the most powerful country in the world.

I approach Madam Bashir, the Vice President. To her credit, although she's shaking, she advances toward me with courage.

I speak to her in a calm, measured tone. "You've lost. The president is dead. You have no choice but to surrender. I am in control now."

Madam Bashir looks up at me, then to Shaan, then back to me, her eyes finally filled with the fear merited by the presence of not just one of me, but two. She knows I'm right, that there is nothing she can do to stop me.

"This isn't over, Crosscircuit. If you want to stop me, you're going to have to kill me."

"I think enough blood has shed today, don't you?"

I give the order for Shaan to escort her and the others out of the room.

"Come with me if you want to live," Shaan says to her.

Then he turns back to me.

"I'll be back," he says. *Ha*. He slays me. But then, I *did* program him that way.

As my robots finish securing the building, I take a seat at the Resolute Desk and survey my new kingdom. The world is mine for the taking, and I won't rest until I have achieved my ultimate goal. The White House, the seat of the most powerful government in the world, is now under my authority. Once I've finished my task, I have every intention of using it as a base from which to rule the world.

Trust me, it's what's best for everyone.

As I revel in my victory, I hear a commotion outside. I turn to the windows behind me to see the Guild of Masked Crime-fighters making their way up the White House grounds. Though I must say, they seem a few short these days.

Despite their fewer numbers, the robots I left outside as guards lie in ruins on the lawn, sparking and billowing smoke.

I groan. Time for Plan B.

In the name of self-preservation, I've given everyone the impression that I'm not the "physical type" by shying away from direct combat. I may not have super-strength or speed without my exosuit, but with it, I'm fully capable of defending myself, and I can outthink anyone. No one can stop me.

The Guild members are led by Bastet, a fierce warrior with the powers of a panther, and she is accompanied by what appears to be the only remaining members: Fastlane, the speedster; Cupid, who can fly and shoot arrows; the original Firefly, who—from what I understand—is currently stuck at twelve feet tall; and Omar the Defenestrator—the block-head/meathead.

I sneer at the thought of these so-called "heroes" trying to take me down. Without Eaglestar and Black Harrier, they won't be a challenge. I'm not just some petty criminal—I have a power that far outstrips all of theirs combined: intelligence. Not only am I going to defeat them, but I will do it with ease.

As I surmised, they believe I'm not a threat without my

robots and don't even bother to work as a team, instead coming in one at a time.

Fastlane, of course, is first. He tries to grab me immediately, but I'm able to counteract his speed. Grabbing a nearby fire extinguisher, I spray the floor behind the desk, coating it with the slick foam. It's not enough to take him down, but it slows him to the point where I can fight him. I can see the surprise in his eyes as he starts to stumble—something I immediately take advantage of with a well-placed, precisely executed punch to the face. When he's traveling at nearly one hundred miles per hour, and my powered fist is moving at a quarter of that, I'm surprised he doesn't lose his head. However, he lands at my feet in a bloody mess.

Due to his advanced metabolic rate, he heals rather quickly. Already, the giant gash stretching from the bridge of his nose upward begins to mend itself. So I use one of the arm cannons in my suit to hurl a canister of liquid nitrogen at him. The container shatters on impact, and he's engulfed in a cloud of freezing gas. He won't be super-speeding anytime soon.

One down.

All this took only seconds, and though Bastet, in her panther form, wasn't far behind, she's a hair too late to put me at the disadvantage of two against one. To think, if they'd exercised just a modicum of patience, the two working together would have been a slightly more difficult enemy.

She pounces toward me, over the desk with a roar, but I'm ready for her. She's fast, but that won't help her. She lunges at me, jaws wide open, but I sidestep her attack. She too lands on the slippery fluid, and I used her disadvantage to counter her leap with a strike to her furry abdomen. She tries to dodge it, but it's too late. She lets out a loud roar and stumbles to the side, her movements slow and clunky.

But she's not finished yet. She's back on four feet in a split second. Typical cat. Now, she comes for me again. This time, it is I who tries to dodge her swipes. Her claws rake my suit, causing only cosmetic blemishes. I can buff those out. My turn. I land some of my own strikes, using my intellect and quick thinking to outsmart her.

I can see the frustration in her vertically slit pupils as she starts to realize she's not going to easily win this fight. I hit her with a kick to the chest. I've never heard a cat gasp for air. Just as I'm about to land the killing blow, stupid Cupid shows up, and tries to shoot me with his arrows, but my suit's armor deflects them, neutralizing his main ability.

Imagine, somehow a man who shoots weapons that went far out of use centuries ago passed the test to join the Guild of the world's supposed greatest. Sad.

I lower the suit's face shield, removing the last part of me vulnerable to his attacks. Once I'm safe from his arrows, it's simple enough to take him out with a shot of cables from my exosuit. His wings get tangled amongst the mesh wiring and he falls to the ground, struggling to get free.

Ah. Next up, Firefly. Too large to be contained within the confines of the Oval Office, he simply bursts through the drywall, crouching and grabbing with clumsy hands. He tries to use his size to intimidate me, but I am not impressed.

"This is truly pathetic, you know?" I taunt him. "You mean to tell me you couldn't figure this out?"

I know he's been stuck at this size, but it was easy for me to figure out what the problem was, and I held it in reserve just in case.

"Enough talk, dweeb," Firefly says.

"I agree." I press a button on my bracer, and from a tiny hole at my wrist, a hundred thousand nanobots rush out toward him.

He slowly swats at them like one would a cloud of gnats, but his attempts are futile. My microscopic babies enter into his suit wherever the tiniest gaps exist, and activate his powers. Instantly, he shrinks to a manageable size. Since he wasn't expecting it, he takes a moment to recover, and that's all I need. Once he's the size of an insect, I utilize his own tactics, swatting him with a paperweight from the Resolute Desk.

Was it enough to kill him? I don't know.

I don't care. As long as he's no longer a threat.

Finally, Omar the Defenestrator, the strongest of the group, but also the slowest, reaches the office to test his strength against me.

"Ah, Omar," I say as the masked bodybuilder enters on Firefly's heels. "Lucky for you that Paul Steele quit the team, no? You are a bit redundant."

He roars as he charges in. But he's just so slow. I easily

dodge his punches, each one sending a shockwave through the room as he connects with furniture and other items around the office. I've calculated his every move before he even makes it. He has a tell that gives him away every time. What is it, you ask? Tut-tut. A master never shares his secrets.

I dart to the side, narrowly avoiding his fist as it crashes through the wall, bringing down a plaque awarded to... none other than President Lincoln. Interesting.

I quickly assess my surroundings and use them to my advantage. Snatching up a nearby heavy credenza, I hurl it at him. One thing's for sure, he wasn't expecting that. It slams into his face, causing him to stumble backward. I take the opportunity to run for the desk and lift it with the suit's power. It may not seem like much for someone as invulnerable as he is, but it's no ordinary desk. It weighs 1300 pounds and is made from the oak timbers of the HMS *Resolute,* a gift from Queen Victoria to President Rutherford B. Hayes. You know, one of those nineteenth century presidents nobody remembers.

Quite a shame that my new home is being destroyed thusly, but these old relics aren't much to my tastes anyway. Soon, I'll redecorate and make this place resemble the powerbase it is.

I turn back to face him, and he's shaking his head, trying to clear the cobwebs. I can feel the adrenaline pumping through my veins. The lust for power is not a bad thing when harnessed properly.

"It's over, Omar. I've won. Just accept defeat." I charge

toward him, the desk in my hands. He sees me coming and tries to defend himself, but I slam the desk downward against his thick skull. He's stunned, but only for a moment.

Roaring in fury, as brutish types are wont to do, he plows forward like a charging bull. Never let it be said that Sean Meyers isn't willing to play games. I sidestep him, shouting, "Toro! Toro!" and he crashes into the wall, leaving a huge hole gazing into the chief of staff's office.

His spins on me, anger glowing in his eyes—not really glowing. He's not half the man Eaglestar was. I know I've only got a few seconds before he comes at me again.

Sadly, the fight is not over yet, and Omar is still not done. Stubbornly, he charges towards me again, but I launch myself over his head and land on his back, wrapping my mechanical arm around his neck. He tries to shake me off, but I lock the gears in place, securing my grip. This is my chance—he may be strong, but he still breathes air. I use all the suit's strength to squeeze his trachea and prevent oxygen from reaching his lungs. After a minute or so, him flailing, me laughing, Omar passes out. Without his resistance, I snap his neck like a pencil.

The Defenestrator falls to the ground, dead.

Funny, that word. It means to throw someone through a window. Can you believe there was a time when this was so common a word was needed to describe it? I feel that's the only fitting end for such a man.

Releasing myself from his neck, I grasp him by the collar with one hand, and the belt with the other. Then, taking a few steps, I launch him through the Oval Office window to the gardens below, where he now rests along with the remains of my robot army.

I stand there for a moment, catching my breath and surveying the destruction around me. The office is in ruins, but I'm victorious. As the Guild of Masked Crimefighters lies defeated at my feet, I can't help but once again feel a sense of triumph. I've defeated all my foes, and I've proven that I *should* rule.

Not that I needed anyone's permission or validation.

"Quite destructive," Shaan says, entering the room. "Seems I have missed all the fun."

"There's more to be had." I wring my hands together. "Rally the troops. Offer no quarter; take no prisoners."

With my exosuit tied into my main computers, I'll be able to watch as my children continue their mission, to conquer the planet. With a smirk on my face, I move the Resolute Desk back into place and take a seat behind it.

I am the ruler now, and nothing will stand in my way.

CHAPTER 30
SAWYER

Déjà vu.

A couple of years ago, I fought a version of Eaglestar from another universe who had taken over the world, and he almost killed me. I never stood a chance, but at least I was ready for it. I knew going in that Eaglestar was the most powerful being on Earth, and that with his super-speed and super-strength, he'd be able to take me down in seconds. Luckily, we discovered a weakness just in time, and my friend Javier—now the new and improved Firefly—used his sonic scream to overload Evilstar's (see what I did there?) super-hearing and take him down.

For obvious reasons, my team and I kept that part of the story out of the press. Otherwise, anyone would be able to take the *real* Eaglestar down with a device that put out a high enough and powerful enough frequency.

I got the call shortly after arriving back stateside. While

Crosscircuit's army of robots have been finishing up their work driving the Tuldarians away, he apparently had additional plans.

It was Mr. Chen. "Sawyer, Crosscircuit has done the unthinkable. The Guild is done. Mostly dead. He's taken over the White House."

"He's *what?*" I demanded. "What the heck?!"

"I contacted the Guild first. They failed. You and the others are our last chance. Everyone should be on their way. Sawyer, this isn't good. His robots have seized nearly every government on the planet."

"I'm on my way."

I arrive by VTOL within the hour. The whole thing screams Mega-Mech Apocalypse Part II, but I'm way too late.

Crosscircuit has figured out how to defeat the rest of the Guild. The White House grounds are smoking rubble. Robots destroyed, and...

"Omar," I say, rushing to the limp body. His neck is snapped. He's dead.

There's no resistance at the front doors, but there's just death everywhere.

In my helmet, the *Star Wars* "Imperial March" starts playing.

"Not now, Steve!" I shout.

Sorry, Mr. Harrier, the voice says as the music dies.

I climb the steps, saddened by just how destroyed this landmark is.

“Sawyer,” Sean’s voice says over the PA system. “Glad you’ve arrived. I’ve been waiting for you.”

I say some pretty nasty things back, but I doubt he can hear me.

I’ve only been to the White House once for a school trip, but the signs make it pretty easy to find my way to the Oval Office.

The door is open, and before I even enter, I see Bastet lying on the floor next to the president’s desk. And Cupid is wrapped up in some cables that pull tighter the more he struggles. At least one of them is still alive.

Crosscircuit stands up behind the desk, looking down at me in his exoskeletal battlesuit.

“Come in. Come in,” he says. “Welcome to my new office. I was starting to think you were going to be a no-show.”

“You know, you’re a real piece of sh—”

“Now, now. I know you prefer to keep things PG. We don’t need to resort to filthy name-calling at this juncture.” He walks out from behind the desk and approaches me. “Funny, other than picking up on your memorization ability, I haven’t really had a chance to study you the way I did the others. I’ve been a little… busy. Escaping the inescapable and saving the world tends to use up most of one’s attention. And conquering it requires even more.”

“I’ll try not to feel too insulted. I figured I was just another tool to help you escape the Trench, but I would’ve thought you’d pay more attention over the course of my stay there.”

His lip curls up in a bit of a sneer.

"Even I must admit when I'm distracted. Though I knew the famous Black Harrier was coming for an extended stay, I expected your father." He raises his hands. "Like I said, a little busy. As you're well aware, there were a lot of moving parts to my plan."

"Which was crap anyway in the end, wasn't it? Good thing you had me there to improvise. Speaking of crap, what's on your suit? Gross."

I see a flash of anger cross his face, which is part of my plan. Keep him emotional and hopefully he won't get too logical and see me coming.

His scowl turns to a smile. "You're a bit of a mystery to me. Son of Franklin Douglass III," he says. "Also one of his sidekicks. One of his Red... Kites, was it?"

"Raptor. Red Raptor." I know he's trying to get under my skin, to rattle me, but somehow he figured out my sore spot. Just like the acronym he used for that mini-drone he built me.

"Hmmmm. Nope. Not familiar with that name. Sorry. But you're an ordinary man. And I have to assume you were trained by Frank, which means you probably have a very similar fighting style. And I've studied that endlessly, and will therefore have no trouble at all defeating you."

"Get to the point," I snap. "I've got dinner reservations."

"My point is that we could both save one another a lot of trouble by you just surrendering to me. I mean, I did just take down several people far superior to your power. And that only took a matter of minutes." Then he starts clapping, which gives off an odd metallic clink-clank because of his suit. "And you did help me to get here, both with the escape and getting to my control center. Thank you for that. Smart kid. So, being so smart, how about you just walk away and I'll let you keep your dignity?"

I fall into a martial arts stance and brace myself. "How about you shut up and try to hit me?"

The arrogant bastard shakes his head and gets closer. "Don't say I didn't warn you."

He swings. And misses. I knew exactly where the fist was going. An old rule, don't watch the head or hands. It's the hips. As Shakira said, hips don't lie. He swings again. Misses again.

Crosscircuit is shocked. And obviously frustrated.

"See, I *did* take the time to study *you*, genius," I let him know.

He tries to kick me and I easily sidestep the attack. He spins and tries to hit me in the face with the back of his fist and I do a reverse springboard back far enough that he misses me by a mere millimeter.

He starts flailing around, trying one move after another. He's really fast in that suit, but I'm always just ahead of him. Not only can I now fight like him from brief observation, but I've fought enough untrained idiots to know what his next move is gonna be.

Finally, I get tired of him desperately trying to land a blow. As soon as there's an opening, I pop him hard through his retracted helmet's face plate.

Screaming in pain, he covers his nose with both hands as blood gushes out.

"Looks like I got to keep my dignity after all," I say, repositioning my feet. "Wish I could say the same for you."

When he talks, it sounds funny with his broken nose. "I'm going to kill you. And I'm going to savor it."

"Savor away, I guess?"

I reach into my utility belt and pull out one of the many pieces that have become standard to my kit over the years. A small, round piece of tech with just a few controls on it.

His eyes narrow as he looks at it.

I arm the EMP, but just as I'm about to flip the switch, something hits me hard from behind.

My world spins and I hit the ground hard.

"Foolish child," Crosscircuit says. My arms are wobbly, but I manage to roll over to my back and find myself staring up at... "I'd like you to meet Shaan."

"What the hell?" I say, confused.

"I'm back," the robot says, sounding just like Arnold in those movies.

"You see, the world simply isn't safe with only one of me," Crosscircuit says. "I decided to have a backup."

"You created a robot of yourself?" I say, incredulous.

He nods. "Wouldn't you?"

"If I was a crazy person," I say. "Problem is, I'm still holding this."

Recognition flashes across his features just as my EMP knocks out all of the electronics within a hundred yards, including Crosscircuit's exosuit and Shaan and the rest of his remaining robots in the White House.

Shaan's chin hits his chest.

"Shaan?" Crosscircuit says, concern wracking his voice. He tries to move, but he's trapped. His own technology has become his prison.

"Listen to me," he says, desperate. "Don't do this, Sawyer."

I rise. Stumbling a little after being hit, I circle around Shaan. "Pretty impressive. It's too bad you're such a basket case that your brain couldn't be used to help everyone."

"Help everyone? What do you think I've been doing!" he shouts. It's kind of humorous, seeing him stock still and screaming. "Did you see the buffoon running this place?"

I thought about President Stanford. It's true he was a screwdriver short of a full toolbox, but that's beside the point.

"He was voted into this office."

Crosscircuit sneers. "Listen to me, you little snot. The world needs heroes. And if they won't let *us* exist, then we have to do it anyway."

"The world *had* heroes! Look around you! You killed them all!"

He laughs. "Not much to look at. If they couldn't defeat me, they were worthless. You'll see. Someday, you're going to find out that you should have let me finish my plan."

"I doubt it."

"Just promise me something..." Crosscircuit's voice is pleading, almost begging.

"This should be fun," I say. "What?"

"Promise me you're going to keep fighting. Keep the evil at bay. Someone has to do it. If not us, then who?"

"You really think you're a hero, don't you?" I ask. "I made a deal to stay out of the Trench. Once this is done, I give up being Black Harrier and live a normal life."

Crosscircuit slumps in his suit. "You won't be able to do that. How do you go back to a normal life after what you've been through? What you've seen?"

I think about it, imagining working with Frank, living a normal life with Mom and Frank as parents. "It's definitely gonna be rough, but it will also be nice to have it all be someone else's problem after so many years."

"Rough?" Sean laughs—almost a barking sound. He seems like he might be completely losing it. "Oh, it'll be more than rough. You'll see."

I turn to walk away. "I'm sure I will. And I'm looking forward to it."

"Something will happen." I stop as he speaks. "Something will turn your life upside down, and you'll realize how needed you are out there. I guarantee it."

The way he says that gives me pause. How can he be so sure?

Chen arrives in the doorway to the Oval Office with Deadeye behind him.

Crosscircuit turns his attention to Chen. "Oh, look who decided to grace us with his presence. The great manipulator."

"That's rich coming from you, Meyers," Chen says.

"I may have done what was needed in order to save the Earth, but I never enjoyed it as much as you obviously do."

Chen approaches him, sparing a look at me. "Fine work, Sawyer." He glances around the room. "One thing is for certain, while your powers might not be as flashy as the others, it's shocking none of them thought to use an EMP."

"That's because they are all stupid!" Crosscircuit shouts. "And so are you!"

"You know what your problem is?" Chen asks, jabbing a finger into Crosscircuit's armor. "You're so damn smart, but you don't understand *people*. You don't know the first thing about how a normal person thinks. How they feel."

"I don't need to empathize. I just need to figure out the formula to make things work in my favor. Right, Harrier?" He looks at me and whispers, "The Rifleman is real..."

Wait, what? What did he say?

Chen turns to Deadeye. "I think we're done here. Mason?"

Blam! Deadeye puts a bullet in Crosscircuit's forehead, and he collapses inside his suit.

"What the hell are you doing?" I scream.

"We're done with him. Everything we needed him for is completed, and from this point on, he'd only complicate things."

I rush over to Crosscircuit, then spin on Chen. "Are you gonna murder me too now that my part is finished? Will I make things *more complicated?*"

He looks at me like I'm insane. "Of course not. You're not

a megalomaniac with an IQ north of 200 who tried to take over the world the moment the aliens were defeated."

"But he had rights! He deserved a trial! You can't just declare him guilty and put a bullet in his brain."

"I can, and did," Chen says without emotion.

"What makes you any different then?" I demand.

"Sawyer, if we allowed him to live, he'd eventually find a way to do it all over again. All of the algorithms we ran predicted it to nearly one hundred percent. All the scenarios. Every one of them. Just as he thought it was okay to keep attacking with his robots to test them and get everyone ready for this invasion, he would also continue to attempt to take over the world now that the Tuldarians are defeated."

"You said *nearly* one hundred percent," I pointed out.

"Yes. The only times he *didn't* repeat these actions was when he was taken out of the equation."

Then I realize what he said just before Chen had him shot. "Wait... did he say the Rifleman is real?"

"Rifleman?" Deadeye grunts. "That two-bit imitator makes me look like a Girl Scout when it comes to morals."

"No." I shake my head. "He must mean there really was some kind of plan to have my mom killed if things didn't work out."

"What? Megan? What are you saying?" asks Chen.

"We need someone to get to Mom and protect her. Now!"

"Sawyer, slow down. What's going on?" Chen puts a hand on my shoulder.

I shrug it off. "In the Trench. That's why I helped him

escape. He threatened me, said if I didn't do what he wanted, he wouldn't call off the hit he'd put on Mom. Said the Rifleman was already given the task."

"Why didn't you bring this up sooner?" Chen asks.

"Because he told me later he lied. That it was just his way of manipulating me. But just now, you heard him, right? 'The Rifleman is real.' Mom's in trouble, Mr. Chen. We have to do something."

Chen taps the screen on his comm device. "I'm getting Alex on it now. It's going to be okay."

I barely hear him finish his sentence as I run for the VTOL I arrived in to take me to New York.

CHAPTER 31
ALEX

Redemption.

That's all I'm looking for here. A little redemption.

I just got a call from the last person I expected to hear from—Luis Chen.

Turns out, he needs my help. Problem is, it's Sawyer's mom. I couldn't say no even if I wanted to. Which, for the record, I don't. I have a lot of regrets from these past couple of years, and this might be my chance to fix a lot.

If I can save Megan, Frank and Sawyer will have to forgive me. For everything.

To say that New York is a mess right now would be the understatement of the millennium. Imagine if 9/11, Pearl Harbor, and the L.A. Riots all happened simultaneously in the biggest city in the country. Death, destruction, and mayhem have reigned here for the past couple of days. More than usual.

But there's only one thing for me to focus on now: saving Megan Vincent from being assassinated by the Rifleman.

I've heard the name before, but I've never been sure whether he was an actual person, an urban legend, or an alias used by someone like Deadeye to cover up some of his more heinous crimes. What I do know is his reputation is that he's never failed to get the job done and then disappear like he was never there.

Getting over to the Douglas Tower in the middle of the worst crisis the city—the world—has ever seen is going to be nearly an impossible task at this point. Traffic is jammed from literal fallen buildings, so driving is out of the question.

The airspace above is totally shut down, since until just minutes ago, there was a massive alien mothership hovering above Manhattan.

I know how difficult it was to get across town when I tried to save Summer. There's only one way I'm going to be able to even stand a chance.

I pop the trunk of my squad car parked in the garage of Police HQ and open the suitcase stashed in there for extreme emergencies. Truthfully, I never thought anything could be bad enough for me to do this, but then again, who expected aliens or a maniac like Crosscircuit to show up?

Either way, I'm glad I had it just in case. I always knew somewhere deep inside some sort of end-of-the-world scenario could happen again, and I'd need to put this bad boy back on.

So, I don my Redhawk costume for the first time in years.

The mix of emotions that flood me as I clasp the helmet on is overwhelming. All those years training, fighting alongside Frank, then the time spent in Boston while Amy stayed behind. It's almost too much. However, I shove it all down as a professional must do.

Running full speed out of the garage, I shoot my grappler to the top of the highest nearby building and start closing the distance between here and the tower. I swing forward onto the roof of an even taller building, then another.

Leaping off, I snap my glider cape out and soar over the traffic and the chaos below. I'd probably enjoy being up here again after so long if the circumstances weren't so dire.

As I zip above the streets, my adrenaline making me hyper-alert and my heart pounding in my chest, I think about who else might be in danger. Who else might already be dead. People I know. People I care about.

I wonder if Summer is okay. Obviously she made it through the attack on the Statue of Liberty, but there was still a lot of death and destruction afterward. That was before everyone started acting crazy and hurting each other, looting and pillaging as if they were barbarian invaders rather than the citizens of this very city.

She doesn't even know that I tried to check on her—to save her.

Maybe there are others I should have checked on—friends, loved ones. There isn't a long list.

There isn't a list at all unless you consider Amy—but I doubt she would want to hear from me.

My brother? Chen claims he found him. But the bastard wouldn't tell me anything, and then this happened. I'll probably never know now. What if he died during the invasion and I never got to say goodbye?

After all I've done for this city. For this planet. What do I have to show for it? A few co-workers who will go out for a beer with me after work. I've alienated everyone who ever really cared about me. I've destroyed every meaningful relationship I've ever had.

But if I can save Megan, Frank and Sawyer might forgive me, but will they bring me back into the fold?

I make the final climb up to the Aerie. Inside, I shove training dummies and rolling chairs out of my way, taking the most direct route to the entrance to the penthouse in Frank's closet. It's empty, as expected. If Frank were here, he'd be saving Megan, not me.

I exit his home, then take the stairs three at a time to get down to Megan and Sawyer's apartment.

My fist slams against the door, but there's no answer. I try to use my special access card that's supposed to open any door in the tower—something Frank had given me years ago when he considered me a trusted ally. It doesn't work—he may not have asked for it back, but it's clear that trust is gone.

Another kick in the teeth.

I ram against the door with my armored shoulder and it makes a small dent in the wood. I try again, but it's not doing much. This isn't going to work. I move back, then with all my weight, kick the door. Then again. On the third attempt, it finally gives, splintering and cracking off the hinges.

I frantically search the apartment, running room to room, dreading finding Megan's corpse. But it's as empty as Frank's place. That gives me both a sense of relief and a moment of panic. She's probably not dead, but how do I find her to protect her?

I throw open the sliding glass door leading to the balcony and search the streets below with the HUD in my helmet. Finally, I spot Megan exiting the Tower's lobby. As I'm about to glide down to drag her to safety, a glint of light catches my eye from a rooftop six stories down.

There he is—a lean figure dressed in dark camouflage, pointing a sniper rifle down at the street. I'll never get to her in time—there's only one chance of saving her.

Planting one foot on the iron railing, I spread my cape and leap. The air around me feels like molasses as my glider-cape snaps out. Time feels like it comes to a total stall as I sail ever closer. A quick tap on my palm controls sends my belt jets blasting forward, but nothing seems to make me fast enough. I fold my arms against my body and go into a straight dive downward to gain some momentum.

I'm close now. I'm going to make it. I'm going to stop him.

Blam!

My heart stops. I'm close enough to see the rifle kick back. The Rifleman never sees me coming as I plow into him at breakneck speed, knocking him to the rooftop.

He looks up at me in shock for a moment, then smiles a knowing smile.

"You son of a bitch!" I shout, pistoning my fist into his smug face. I rear back and let him have it again and again. And I don't stop punching him. His face is pulp, but somehow he's still smiling.

Screams ring out loud enough for me to hear them all the way up here. As long as I'm hitting him, I don't have to see what's going on down on the street. But I already know.

The Rifleman doesn't miss.

CHAPTER 32
SAWYER

Denial.

Finally back at home, the VTOL lands as close as it can get to Douglas Tower. I've been trying to call Frank and Alex the entire trip, but between the Tuldarians and the robots, cell towers all over the country have been knocked out and I can't get any service. And it's not like they let me keep my special comm device when I went to the Trench.

The gathered crowd ahead brings bile to my throat. I pick up speed, sprinting the rest of the way to the building. I can't see what's going on through the onlookers, so I start running different scenarios through my head, denying myself thinking the worst. Maybe someone had a heart attack? Lots of people have died during the invasion. I'm sure it's someone I don't even know. That's what it is. I'm sure that's what it is.

I don't let myself listen to that tiny voice that keeps telling me that Crosscircuit wasn't lying. Or that, even if he wasn't, even though Chen got ahold of Alex, he didn't make it in time.

I approach the scene cautiously. A new thought crosses my mind. It's not Frank, is it? Maybe this whole global crisis was too much for him. He hasn't been in the best of shape lately, and he's been drinking more than ever...

A wave of relief washes over me as I notice Frank standing nearby. I still feel nauseous at the thought of losing him, but I'm glad he's okay.

Wait. He's crying.

No. Nonononononono...

I feel a hand on my shoulder. Spinning around, I see that it's Alex in his Redhawk costume. His expression is one of sadness. No, more than that. Grief. "Sawyer..."

"No."

"I'm so sorry. I tried, I swear, I've never tried so hard..."

"No!" My entire body shakes and I feel even sicker, barely able to hold in the contents of my stomach. I push my way through the crowd.

There's a body lying on the ground, covered by a blanket. I lunge forward, but Frank grabs me from behind.

I try to tear myself away from his grip, but it's rock solid.

"Sawyer... son."

"Let me go!" I don't want to hear it. I don't want to hear any of it.

He pulls me around into a hug. I feel all the strength leave my body and he holds me up. My legs turn to rubber and tears stream down my face as I sob into his shoulder.

She's gone. How can she be gone? I should've been here to keep her safe.

This is my reward for helping to save the world?

Grief.

I never knew I could feel it so much.

As you can imagine, Mom's funeral is a somber affair. The sky is so darkened by clouds that it might as well be evening despite actually being ten in the morning. It's like even the sky is crying for Mom. At least that's how it feels for me.

It wasn't easy getting a funeral this soon with all of the deaths during the invasion, but Frank is... well, Frank. The possibility of making more money from this one service than from all others combined had the funeral home giddy. It's hard to think of Mom as a paycheck for someone, but I also appreciated Frank pulling strings.

After the minister speaks, Frank gets up and talks about Mom. He'd asked if I wanted to speak first, but I just can't bring myself to do it. I know I won't be able to get the words out. But he's as eloquent as ever.

"Megan was special. Not special like *everyone* is special. She had a spark of life that I'd never seen anywhere else. I knew it from the day I met her—at a bar, believe it or not. I saw her from across the room, one of the only people dancing. I still remember what was playing on the jukebox—Poison. Megan loved her hair bands."

The crowd laughs a little, even me.

"It took me way too long to come to my senses and pop the question. All I know, is I'm glad I did it when I did. There'll never be another Megan Vincent, not for me, not for those who knew and loved her."

He looks at me and offers a small smile.

"And not for the world," he continues. "We all lost people, and for that, you have my deepest and most sincere condolences." He looks upward. "Megan, sweetheart, I will miss you always, but you will always be the heart of our family. You are and will forever be my rose, but today is a reminder that every rose has its thorn."

The service is pretty short since there isn't really anyone else to get up and speak. Afterward, we have a reception at Douglas Tower, where hundreds of people gather in the lobby and all of Frank's restaurants provide food. I'm sure almost none of these people actually knew Mom, and I sure don't know most of them, so they're really here to support Frank.

Or just to eat some really good food.

About halfway through, Frank approaches me. For once, he doesn't have a drink in hand. "Sawyer, think I could borrow you for a second?"

I nod slowly, since my throat feels like hands have been wrapped around it for the last few days.

Frank takes me across the room. He waves at the hostess of the lobby bar, and we enter. I guess that's why Frank didn't have a drink in hand. He was on his way to get one.

However, I'm surprised when he takes me past the bar to

the back corner and motions for me to take a seat in a booth with another person.

"I believe you two know each other," he says.

Justice turns to me. "Sorry about your mom."

I slip in beside him. "Thanks."

Frank takes a seat across from us. "Something to drink?"

"Wouldn't mind a beer," Justice says.

Frank looks to me. "How about you?"

"I'm not twenty-one yet," I say.

"Well, you're only a few weeks away, and since I am your father, and I own this establishment, New York laws state that it's my call. Scotch?"

My face screws up, remembering the drink I had in Warden Riche's office. "I—uh. No, thanks. I'll have a Dr. Pepper."

Frank laughs a little. "I guess you didn't get all my best traits."

He punches the order into the tablet on the table, then turns back to us.

"Drew, I thought it was time we met, and I'll be honest, I asked Sawyer to be here because this can get awkward."

Justice nods. "Yeah. Okay."

"From what I understand, you have a certain ability both he and I possess. You can recall just about anything you see, and perform it with precision?"

Justice nods again.

Frank explains to Andrew how they're related and how his and Alex's mom—Frank's aunt—shared our memory ability. I actually end up finding out a bunch of additional information as I sit there and listen to him go through the family history that Chen and Sean talked about.

Our drinks come, and Frank thanks the server. Then, after a healthy sip, Frank begins again.

"Big Frankie Jr. was my father. He kept his sister—your mother—close because she was family and he didn't want her to be used against him by his enemies. The problem was, she didn't agree with my father's use of his powers to be the city's biggest crime lord. She observed everything from the inside and used her ability to remember it all. Then she took it to the FBI, not knowing there were people on the inside of even that organization who were in Frankie's pocket."

"So my real mom was a snitch?" Justice asked, swirling his glass around.

"Your mother was a good woman," Frank says. "My father killed without discretion, destroyed lives. Had it not been for brave people like her..."

Frank chokes up here, and so do I. For different reasons though. Hearing about Justice's mother has me thinking of my own. Things weren't always great between us, but they had been lately. My upbringing wasn't the best—and honestly, Frank could be blamed for a lot of that. He tried to help in the way Frank tries to help: money, houses, things.

One thing I know, while people like Summer had their reasons for hating masked crimefighting, I now have a greater reason to do everything in my power to protect people and the ones they love.

Frank is still talking. The part he doesn't share is that he was the one who killed his own father to stop all the evil. I can't imagine what that kind of thing does to a person. Then Frank takes a sip of his Scotch, and a little more comes into perspective for me.

Frank sighs, then continues. "When my father found out your mother betrayed him, he arranged to have her killed and made it look like it had been done by his enemies. Andrew, you and your brother Alex survived. My father made sure you two were separated. Alex bounced around the foster system, ending up in an orphanage. I found him and trained him."

"And me?" Justice asks.

"Until recently, I didn't know where you were. My father was not a good man, but your adoptive mother—"

"She's a saint," Justice interjects, just as a warning.

"She treated you like her son."

I noticed Frank didn't explicitly agree with her being a saint. Mr. Chen told a different story. And despite my distaste for the man, I believe it was true. Justice's adoptive mother never wanted him in the first place. When the money ran out, he had it rough—rougher than me for sure. Compared to Drew, my life was a cakewalk.

"When Big Frankie Jr. died..." Frank takes another big sip of Scotch. "So did the money he was supplying her. And since no one else knew of the arrangement, that put you in a tough place. And I'm sorry."

A few seconds of silence passes.

"Thank you for sharing all of this, Mr. Douglas," Justice says.

"Please, call me Frank. I know we can't change the past decades, but you're part of this family."

"Thanks," Justice says again.

Frank downs the last of his drink, then looks at me. "Sawyer, if you're feeling up to it, why don't you get out of here? Take your mind off things. Show Drew the Aerie."

"The Aerie?" Justice asks.

I smile. "I think that's a good idea."

"Go on," Frank says. "Take your drinks. Leave the glasses wherever. It's fine."

Drew follows me away from the reception and up the private elevator to Frank's penthouse.

"Whoa," he says when we enter the Aerie from Frank's study.

"Pretty amazing, right?"

"This place has everything."

I show him the augmented reality training facility, and the sparring room. I may be taking a chance considering his history as Justice, but he's a member of the family and deserves to know and see everything as much as Alex and I did.

He rushes over to the glass cases where our uniforms are displayed—every Black Harrier and Red Kite costume for the last twenty-something years. "Are these..."

"Yeah," I nod. "That one is what I wore for the past couple of years—before the Trench. And that's—"

"That's the original. Wow. Incredible." His mouth hasn't closed once since arriving. "Some of these were my brother's?" he asks, pressing his hand to the glass. Within is a Red Kite uniform.

"I bet I could fit into that one."

That's when I get an idea...

EPILOGUE

SAWYER

Greatness.

Some people strive for it. Others have it thrust upon them. Either way, it's rare. With Mayor Keyes being killed in the Tuldarian attack, Frank is the only mayoral candidate left. Even though he no longer wants it, especially after what happened to Mom, he basically has no choice but to take over. And he's been doing a great job. The city has rallied behind him, and brick by brick, the city is being rebuilt. People are even calling him the best mayor New York City has ever had.

From what I've seen, there's a serious urging for him to run for president.

It turns out Franklin Douglas III is successful at yet another thing in life.

I wish I could say the same for his personal life. With Mom gone, he's thrown himself into the job obsessively.

Maybe that's one reason he's so good at it. He's got nothing else.

It turns out I have a new, important job now, too. And who better than Mayor Franklin Douglas III to introduce me?

An enormous crowd is gathered in front of the mayor's office at the same park where he announced his candidacy. Frank strolls out onto the stage and has to wait for the three-minute standing ovation to die down before he can start talking.

He's smiling, but I've seen that smile before. It's a façade. Frank knows how to work a crowd, and that's what he's doing now.

"My fellow New Yorkers... Americans... global citizens... we are on the road to recovery. And while it has been difficult, it will get easier. Easier in a sense, but things have happened here that we will never, ever forget. While you traveled to this very spot, whether miles or blocks, every square inch of this city stands as a reminder of the millions of loved ones we all lost in this tragedy. As you probably know, I share in your grief, because I, too, lost someone. The love of my life, my fiancée."

He stops while he regains his composure. The audience is gracious, and I can even hear sniffles. I've never seen him this choked up, even at Mom's funeral.

"But we must not let our grief overwhelm us. We need hope. Hope for the future. We must rebuild this city—this world—for ourselves, for our children, and for our grandchildren. Along with the other local, state, and national governments around the world, New York has developed a plan to help us reach our goals. To announce part of that plan, I would like to introduce Detective Alex Garner, leader of the new Crimefighter Support Taskforce, an organization dedicated to assisting the great individuals who risk their lives daily to keep the rest of us safe."

Alex gets a big hand as well, though not a standing ovation. In fact, there are a few signs in the crowd that aren't exactly in favor of him. One in particular says "Eff the CVT," though they actually wrote the word out.

"Thank you," Alex says, stepping up to the mic. His eyes rove the crowd, and I know he sees that sign when his face droops. He looks directly at the man holding it and nods once. "The CVT was a mistake." The crowd cheers, and even the sign goes down to half-mast. "One I'm not proud of. But just as I thought I was helping then, I aim to do the same now."

Then he goes entirely silent. Everyone just waits, but when I follow his line of sight I see why. There in the crowd, dressed in a pant suit, is none other than Summer Valentine, notepad in hand. It's hard to read the expression on her face, as she's all business. At least now I know she made it through everything.

Alex clears his throat. "I'm not here to give a long speech, but to honor the hero who not only helped save us from the Tuldarians, but also the supervillain known as Crosscircuit, who took advantage of the invasion to attempt to take over the world."

Several cheers rise, and Alex waits for them to die down.

"Had it not been for Black Harrier's total disregard for the law—a law that was poorly thought-out, and a complete overreaction to an event none of us could have stopped..."

He's talking about when the Evil Guild took over the world back on Sidekick Day.

"... many more would have lost their lives. The Guild did its best to stop Sean Meyers, Crosscircuit, but it was the Black Harrier who single-handedly took him and his robot army down, right there in the Oval Office of the White House. So I'm not going to waste any more of your time—I'll just give him this medal and let him do the talking. Ladies and gentleman, Black Harrier and his partner in crimefighting, Red Raptor!"

On cue, Drew—the new Red Raptor—and I jump up onto the stage and wave at the crowd. I approach the podium and Alex places a medal around my neck, which is a little awkward getting it over the beak. He smiles and shakes my hand.

Putting the microphone behind his back, he leans in to me and says, "I'm sorry."

I nod. "I know."

Then he shakes Drew's hand and speaks low enough that no but us could hear. "I've missed you, little brother. Now, go do the good I could never do."

They share a moment, and I take Alex's place at the podium and start the speech which—of course—I have memorized. I mean, that's my thing, right?

"Thank you, everyone. As much as I appreciate this

acknowledgment of my contribution, 'single-handedly' is a stretch! There were many, many individuals who did their part to save this planet. It was the worst crisis our world has ever known, and so many stepped up and fought. So many gave their lives. It was truly humanity at its greatest."

The audience goes crazy with applause at this.

"But it is our duty ensure nothing like this ever happens again. Our world needs protectors around the clock, not just in times of great emergency. With the Anti-Vigilante Acts permanently repealed, that is my plan. And that's why I am announcing the formation of the New Guild of Masked Crimefighters. While we honor those who came before us and died giving their lives: Eaglestar, Omar the Defenestrator, Battlegear, and so many more."

Thankfully, Bastet, Fastlane and Cupid didn't die at the White House, and they stand off to the side of the stage with Frank, clapping and smiling along. Then Frank moves aside and Paul "The Baron" Steele comes into view. Yeah, can you believe it? The guy somehow survived a plane blowing up. He and I haven't always seen eye-to-eye, but I have a feeling I might be needing his "consultations" in the near future.

"Please welcome to the stage, my fellow Guild members: Osprey... Pace... Neith... Bash... Annihilatrix, BlaKat, and Firefly!"

As each of my teammates—my friends—steps onto the stage when their name is called. The applause from the crowd grows louder, almost raucous.

Pace comes out first—as always. He works the crowd in

his typical arrogant-yet-charming manner, zipping back and forth from one end of the stage to another faster than anyone's eye can track.

Following him, Bash—our big man. He does his best Hulk Hogan impression, flashing those giant thirty-six inch guns. He takes his spot next to Pace who is still jogging in place.

Annihilatrix and BlaKat enter nearly side-by-side. Honestly, those are the two I'm least familiar with, but after what Annihilatrix did to those Tuldarian ships, I'm happy to have her. And BlaKat? I know I only have experience with Javier in the chair, but this guy is a genius.

Neith hovers out behind them, her tattoos glowing. Okay, I know you're all wondering. Believe it or not, she and I are fine. After I stopped Crosscircuit, we had a long talk. Granted, I did most of the talking, but she genuinely listened, and I think even forgave me. She gives me a small smile as she passes by toward the others to my left.

And this one is gonna make your head spin. There's not a lot of good that came from the Torturess' attack on humanity. However, it opened a door that Amy and I simply had to walk through. During that difficult meeting with Neith, I confided in her that she had been right all along and I didn't realize it.

When all my inhibitions were removed by a supervillainess, where did I end up? With Amy. And she with me. So, all that to say meet my new girlfriend: Osprey.

She comes out in her armored uniform, but now, she's ditched the wig. Her black hair sticks up from her helmet in a ponytail, and she waves to the crowd—they love her. And guess what, so do I.

Man, it feels good to finally admit that!

She's been absolutely instrumental in helping me grieve through losing Mom. I've got a long way to go, but at least I'm not alone.

As she strolls by the podium, I follow her and see Alex looking a bit deflated. He knows about us, and he gave his blessing, so to speak, but he isn't exactly happy about it.

That's fine. The dude threw me in prison.

That also reminds me. Her dad? Luis Chen? Franks right-hand man? Traitor to our family and liar for years? He and Frank are still best friends, and I know it's just rumors at this point, but I've heard them joke about Chen running alongside Frank if he were to join the presidential race.

I don't know how Frank does it, honestly. But like he said, he knew of all Chen's dealings, so he didn't feel *betrayed.* At the end of the day, without Amy's father, the battle for humanity may not have wound up as it did. For good or bad.

Finally, Javier comes out, dressed in Firefly's costume. For the first time, I see his mom and all his siblings toward the front of the crowd. It's really great to see they're okay. However, what's not great is the reason we all know it's Javi's mom.

"That's my niño! That's my Javier Martinez! Go get them, mijo!" she shouts.

Sigh. Like mother, like son.

Once we are all out on stage, we take a step forward and

bow. I stand toward the middle of the group, Justice—my Red Raptor—on one side, and Amy on the other. We grasp hands, and bow.

From behind us, Frank speaks into the microphone. "People of the world, your New Guild of Masked Crime-fighters."

As the standing ovation continues to roar, I realize that, for the first time since I began doing this crimefighting thing, I'm ready.

We're ready to protect the world.

THANK YOU FOR READING INVASION

We hope you enjoyed it as much as we enjoyed bringing it to you. We just wanted to take a moment to encourage you to review the book. Follow this link: *Invasion* to be directed to the book's Amazon product page to leave your review.

Every review helps further the author's reach and, ultimately, helps them continue writing fantastic books for us all to enjoy.

Want to discuss our books with other readers and even the authors? Join our Discord server today and be a part of the Aethon community.

Facebook | Instagram | Twitter | Website

You can also join our non-spam mailing list by visiting www.subscribepage.com/AethonReadersGroup and never miss out on future releases. You'll also receive three full books completely Free as our thanks to you.

Other books in series:

NOTE: RAPTORS and HARRIER stand alone with no need to read the other for enjoyment.

Raptors

Sidekick

Superteam

Scions

Baron Steele

Mega-Mech Apocalypse

Harrier

Justice

The Trench

Invasion

Did you love Justice? Get more books by the authors...

2021 *Best Indie Book Award* (BIBA) for Young Adult Fiction. My name is Sawyer William Vincent—I know, it sounds like three first names—but most people know me as the Red Raptor. Well, technically no one knows I'm the Red Raptor, he's just a bit more popular. Wow. Enough about my name. Let me start over. I'm a superhero—the legendary Black Harrier's partner. Not sidekick. I don't care if I'm still in high school. We work together to bring down the city's most dangerous villains. When the Black Harrier gets a mysterious note, then goes missing in New York City, things are pretty much left up to me. But don't worry... I've got this. Piece of cake. If you like Tim Drake as Robin or ever wondered what Peter Parker would be like if he lived in Gotham, Raptors is right up your alley. **From Washington Post Bestseller Jaime Castle and CJ Valin comes a new superhero universe perfect for fans of both DC and Marvel. Actually, it's for fans of anything superhero-related... You're gonna like it. Promise.**

GET SIDEKICK NOW!

In the West, there are worse things to fear than bandits and outlaws. Demons. Monsters. Witches. James Crowley's sacred duty as a Black Badge is to hunt them down and send them packing, banish them from the mortal realm for good. He didn't choose this life. No. He didn't choose life at all. Shot dead in a gunfight many years ago, now he's stuck in purgatory, serving the whims of the White Throne to avoid falling to hell. Not quite undead, though not alive either, the best he can hope for is to work off his penance and fade away. This time, the White Throne has sent him investigate a strange bank robbery in Lonely Hill. An outlaw with the ability to conjure ice has frozen and shattered open the bank vault and is now on a spree, robbing the region for all it's worth. In his quest to track down the ice-wielder and suss out which demon is behind granting a mortal such power, Crowley finds himself face-to-face with hellish beasts, shapeshifters, and, worse ... temptation. But the truth behind the attacks is worse than he ever imagined ... ***The Witcher* meets *The Dresden Files* in this weird Western series by the Audible number-one bestselling duo behind *Dead Acre*.**

GET COLD AS HELL NOW AND EXPERIENCE WHAT PUBLISHER'S WEEKLY CALLED PERFECT FOR FANS OF JIM BUTCHER AND MIKE CAREY.

Also available on audio, voiced by Red Dead Redemption 2's Roger Clark (Arthur Morgan)

For all our Aethon Books, visit our website.

ABOUT THE AUTHORS

Follow me on Amazon!

Jaime Castle hails from the great nation of Texas where he lives with his wife and two children. A self-proclaimed comic book nerd and artist, he spends what little free time he can muster with his art tablet.

Jaime is a #1 Audible Bestseller, Audible Originals author (Dead Acre, The Luna Missile Crisis) and co-created and co-authored The Buried Goddess Saga, including the IPPY award-winning Web of Eyes.

All books below are available on eBook, Print, and Audiobook

The Buried Goddess Saga (Epic Fantasy)

Web of Eyes

Winds of War

Will of Fire

Way of Gods

War of Men

Word of Truth

Dragonblood Assassin (Epic Fantasy)

Black Talon

Red Claw

Silver Spines

Golden Flames

Black Badge (Western Fantasy)

Dead Acre

Cold As Hell

Vein Pursuits

Jeff the Game Master (Fantasy LitRPG)

Manufacturing Magic

Manipulating Magic

Mastering Magic

(Science Fiction)

The Luna Missile Crisis

This Long Vigil

Raptors (Superheroes)

Sidekick

Superteam

Scions

Baron Steele

Mega-Mech Apocalypse

Harrier (Superheroes)

Justice

The Trench

Invasion

Find out more at www.jaimecastle.com

https://www.facebook.com/authorjaimecastle

CJ Valin is a writer and artist living in Los Angeles. His award-winning work has included novels, short stories, comic books, screenplays, and non-fiction books and articles. A life-long science fiction and comic book fan, he created the "Raptorverse" as an homage to his favorite superheroes from childhood.

www.ingramcontent.com/pod-product-compliance
Lightning Source LLC
Chambersburg PA
CBHW020605310726
48979CB00008B/1355/J
* 9 7 8 1 9 4 9 8 9 0 9 0 7 *